MOST BEAUTIFUL
THE PERSUASION PARK SERIES
BOOK I

JM BLAKE

JM Blake Publishing

ISBN (E-Book): 979-8-9904049-0-8

ISBN: (Print Book): 979-8-9904049-1-5

Cover: Sarah Hansen, Okay Creations

MOST BEAUTIFUL

JM BLAKE

PERSUASION PARK SERIES

Every year, *Persuasion Park Magazine* publishes its "Most In The City"
List of New York's most (and least) eligible bachelors. Untamable,
unapologetic, and unforgettable, these are the men riding for the most
brutal fall of them all...

BLURB

Malcolm Bancroft Clare has it all: an ancient American name, a family dynasty, a future as clear as glass-- and a face no one can forget. Unfortunately, his upcoming engagement to the perfect Park Avenue princess has all of New York on pins and needles, so he leaves suddenly, hoping to escape the pressure from society and his demanding parents.

But a night filled with anonymity, lots of beer, a baseball game, and a wild head of red hair changes his life forever. Decisions have to be made, and time is not on his side. Does he want a marriage of obligations and tradition? Or what all his friends have found--a forever and lasting love.

PLAYLIST

Playlist on Spotify——>https://geni.us/hFU3g

Cruisin'— D'Angelo
Die With A Smile—Lady Gaga, Bruno Mars
Getting Late—Floetry
We Can't Be Friends— Deborah Cox, R.L
New York Girls— Morningwood
Spirals—Nik Leng
If You Were Mine—Miranda Lambert, Leon Bridges
Face The Music—Conjure One, Rhys Fulber
Moonlight—ALIA LARA, 1Timothy
Far Behind—CandleBox
Like I'm Gonna Lose You—Meghan Trainor, John Legend
If Love Is A Skill—LP Gionni, Sofi Tukker
The Goodness—TobyMac, Blessing Offor
If You Let Me—Sinead Harnett, GRADES
Will I See You Again?—Thee Sacred Souls
Officially Missing You—Tamia

NOTE FROM JM

Hello Friend!

I'm so happy that you are reading Malcolm's story—how can you not fall in love with a man who is voted "The Most Beautiful Man In New York?"
So, where are we in the timeline? Well, this book takes place after Malcolm meets Cassidy and Ayden in "His To Belong To." Remember when he tells Ayden that his wedding is off? Well, this is right after that. You are about to meet a whole bunch of new folks (and some old ones, too), and wouldn't you know it, but somehow, they all tie in...
Anyhow, this book is a standalone, but for all of my faithful, you will, of course, recognize some stuff.
So kick back, put on your playlist, and dive in. I can smell the street meat from here...
Love and Jordans,
JM

P.S.—Don't forget to leave a review! They mean more than you know.
P.P.S— If you want to be one of the first to learn of my upcoming

releases, surprises, sales and stuff I only offer to my readers, make sure you sign up for The Blake Squad Newsletter. Thanks for giving this story a chance!

ALSO BY JM BLAKE

<u>The Power Series:</u> (*Nick and Kenna*)

<u>Impelled</u>

<u>Compelled</u>

<u>Inflamed</u>

Embraced

<u>Entwined</u>

Masen (Coming 2025)

<u>The Possession Series</u>

<u>His To Belong To</u>

<u>Hers To Belong To</u>

Free

Theirs To Fight For

Stande (Coming Soon)

<u>The Persuasion Park Series</u>

Most Beautiful

Most Reckless (Coming Soon)

<u>The Poison Series</u>

Black Cherry (Coming Late 2025)

To all the girls who love baseball—may your future be as sweet as a 101-mile-per-hour fastball, straight down the middle.

BOSTON, BEANTOWN, THE HUB, ETC, ETC

Dev "Strike Three! Yourrrrrrrre OUT!"

The boos echo off of the wooden rafters, sprays of thrown peanut shells pelting the room and the crash of a few glasses hitting the floor. The bartender, sick walrus mustache and all, joins in, throwing his wet towel at the flat-screen TV, cursing a blue streak, and pounding his fist on the scarred oak bar top. I chuckle quietly, though it's for nothing. No one can hear me over the passionate/crazy Boston fans. The smell of spilled beer and burgers drifts through the crowd.

"Best, keep that laughter down, city boy. I don't want to have to save your pretty ass because you forgot what town you are in," Summerlin, my father's old college roommate, tells me. I came up to close a business deal near the Old South, and when he heard I was haunting around our Beacon Hill house, he showed up to drag me to a bar he likes to go to when he feels like "slumming"— a Yankees fans way of saying watching games around Red Sox nation. I'm much more used to being ensconced in a private box with full service, and I laughingly tell him so.

"Spoiled. It'll do you good to mix it up everyone in a while. That rarefied air you Clares' breathe has got to be stifling." He takes a long sip of his beer, peering at me over the edge as I roll my eyes.

"So this isn't a social call then? My father put you up to this?" I drum my fingers on the tabletop, an irritation scratching my stomach. I just wanted to watch the game and relax, not be interrogated, and I told him so.

"Son, I'm on your side, here. All I want to do is spend some time with you. We don't have to talk about anything if you don't want to."

"Good, because I don't. I fucking thirty-five years old, Summ. I don't need my 'daddy' interfering in my life. When I have something to say, then I'll say it." I signal the bartender for another round, adding a whiskey to my beer order. I got home from London several weeks ago, and instead of heading back to my penthouse in Manhattan, I came to Boston to open up the family's Pickney Street mansion (okay —maybe I was hiding.) I was halfway expecting my mother to show up, but I guess they sent Summerlin instead. She would have definitely been knocking on my door if I'd gone straight to New York.

"How was London? I hear you got in early on some top-secret project," he throws back the rest of his beer, turning the glass upside down, a weird quirk he's been doing since I was a kid.

"Remember Nick Grant from Harvard? His friend owns a sustainable energy company, and they are doing some amazing stuff." I leave out my brief infatuation, which led me to solidify that my recent decisions were the right ones.

"Well, let me know if they are open to more investors. I've got a few bucks I can throw down," he taps his pocket where his slim wallet is. For all his talk about me being spoiled, Summ is just as wealthy as my family is—his is just newer. He started a boat business years ago, and it grew into a fleet of cargo and merchant ships that sail internationally. He's loaded but has never lost his down-to-earth roots. His wallet has one credit card and exactly one hundred dollars. That's it.

"I will. After their presentation, I'm sure they will be looking for more capital soon." The crowd starts yelling again as a Red Sox player slides into second base on a steal. The score is tied, and most of the guys in the bar are on their feet. I crane my neck and see that the next batter has hit a single, and the runner is speeding around the bases, trying to make it home. I stand up, screaming for the fielder to throw faster, and the ball hits the catcher's mitt mere seconds before the runner slides into home, tagging him out. I clap my hands and cheer, though once again, it's drowned out by the screaming bargoers. I faintly hear happy yelling and peer around the crowd into a dark corner. I see a woman jumping up and down and pause to admire how great her ass looks in her skintight jeans. She's got a backward Yankees cap on, and I see the long length of her ponytail snaking down her back.

"You gonna stay and watch the rest of the game?" Summerlin asks, standing up. His wife is probably looking for him to come home, and he is just as anxious to get there. They've been married forever with a ton of kids, but they still act like newlyweds. I sneak another peek at the girl in the corner and nod. "I'll have one more and then head home." I hold out my hand for him to shake, and he uses it to pull me into a tight hug.

"Call me when you want to come over for dinner. Steph will make your favorite." I squeeze him back and wait until I see his broad back leave before snatching up my glass and weaving toward the back. I close in on her, my lips twitching when I see her little Timberland-booted feet propped up on the table, her glass balanced on her stomach. Her ponytail, which I can now see is a deep auburn, touches the seat, and her navy blue Yankees t-shirt has the number "2" on it. Her table is facing a small TV, which is covered with plates of small appetizers. I look for a second person, but she's alone.

"Excuse me. Is this space open for refugees from enemy territory?" Her head snaps up, and lightning strikes. Her grey eyes, a mysterious platinum silver flecked with black and amber, plush, deep pink lips, and thick slashed eyebrows all quirked with annoyance but morphed quickly to interest and then blankness.

"Depends..." she smiles, her face lighting up, mile-long lashes batting at me playfully. Jesus.

"On what? I promise I am a dyed-in-the-wool Yankees fan—my dad raised me right. I can even pull up pictures of me in a Babe Ruth onesie if you want." I wave my phone at her, and she laughs, a deep, husky one, head thrown back and effortless.

"I definitely want to see that picture. How old were you? And please don't say in your twenties." She waves her hand, and I pull out the chair across from her and grin.

"I was two if that helps." I take in her features full-on, pinching myself under the table. How does she walk through life safely? This girl is unreal. "I'm..." I hold out my hand, pausing. "I'm Dev. What are you drinking?" I lift my hand to summon the barkeep, but she shakes her head.

"I've reached my limit. And I'm Joan, by the way." Mine dwarfs her tiny hand, but I can feel her strength and, surprisingly, a few calluses. My thumb rubs the inside of her wrist, and her pupils dilate. I keep my grip on her for a moment before reluctantly releasing it. We chat about the game, lamenting some of the new rules and whether the Yanks are making the World Series this year. She matches me stat for stat, and I feel even more intrigued. She tells me about a time she went to a game at Fenway and talked so much shit to her neighbors that it made the local news. The game seesaws the lead and the patrons are at a fever pitch of aggression, yelling colorful curses at the players on the screen. Joan's eyebrows shoot up at some of the language, her full lips twitching in silent hilarity. I laugh as she mimics some of the broad Boston "aaaaaa" and shake my head when she tries to get me to copy it. She's funny as well as gorgeous and I've never been so glad to be in a Red Sox bar.

"I don't hear a New England accent at all. Are you even from Boston?"

Her head tilts and those white teeth flash at me. She stares for a full moment before leaning forward, the deep vee of her t-shirt gaping, showing me the full swell of a pair of spectacular breasts. I don't even pretend not to look, and now I can't seem to stop.

"Dev? Did you really come over here to talk about the origin of my accent and the home run leader's BA, or are you looking to take me to bed?" Her directness takes me back, but then I smile. "Was I that obvious?"

"Yes, you were," she laughs. "But I saw you when you walked in. I only have one night and don't want to waste it with small talk. How about you?"

One thing my annoying parents didn't raise was a fool. "I only have one night too. Where shall we go?" I think about the staff at the Beacon Hill house and grimace. We have four live-ins, and they will snitch to my mother in a minute.

"Judging by the look on your face, your place is off the table. There's not a wife and kids lurking around, is there?" I shudder, which makes that laugh appear again. "Absolutely not."

"Girlfriend? Fiancee?"

Christ. "Nope, not those either."

She stands up, her height less than I expected, but her curves even more pronounced. "Then let's go." I throw a stack of bills on the table, hurrying to follow her small form as she weaves in and out of the crowd. She gets a few boos when people spot her shirt, but she doesn't break stride, tossing up a few middle fingers and jeering back. I'd worry about her, but that face stops most men in their tracks. She waves her hand at a taxi, and it screeches to a halt. I climb behind her, snatching the hat off her head, leaning down, and capturing her mouth. Her lips mold under mine, her sweet tongue twisting itself around mine. The driver makes an amused sound, but neither one of us stops. I pull her closer, the feel of her hard nipples pushing against my chest, making my cock throb. The scent of her hair—a sweet, familiar smell —envelops us, and I grab a handful and pull.

"I may not make it to your place; I want you desperately," I tell her, and she chuckles, her hands drifting under my shirt. "We are almost there. I walked earlier, and it was just far enough that I thought a taxi would be faster." I rub my lips against hers, tongue fluttering out to tease. She moans, and the sound makes my hardness leak. The taxi slows down and then stops, and I fling the door open, pulling her behind me. She murmurs directions up a flight of stairs, handing me a set of keys when we reach the top landing. The lights are out, but neither of us cares, hands frantically pulling at each other's clothes. I feel a frenzy, a desperation that is foreign to me. She leads me down a shadowed hallway, the moonlight showing me a large bed filled with pillows and a thick duvet. I lift her small frame onto the mattress, pulling off her work boots and socks and running my fingers across the soles of her feet. I lean down and kiss each toe, biting the tip of one, before running my hands up and down her jean-clad legs.

"Tell me, Joan, what's off the table?"

❧

*J*OAN

What's off the table???

Not. A. Damn. Thing.

I'd let this man do whatever he wanted to me, and that's no lie. I can't tell him that, though, because I watch the news, and there are some freaky ass people out there. I almost never bring guys home when I'm on the road, but, um, mama didn't raise no fool.

"Ummmm. What did you have in mind?" I shudder as he plucks at the button of my jeans, the zipper pushing itself down with my heaving breaths. I thank the heavens above that I have decent underwear because I am way behind on laundry, and the only panties I had left were these sexy red lace ones and a pair that said "Sunday," even though it's Wednesday. The lace ones kept crawling up my butt, but they look hot, so that's a plus.

"Well, first, I'd like to peel these pants off of you and then lick my way from those toes all the way up to that pussy and see how many times I can make you come with just my mouth. Then I'd like to see those nipples that are teasing me behind that t-shirt and make them harder with my teeth. Then I want to fuck you until you see colors. How does that sound?"

It sounds like a fucking "yes, please."

I just nod frantically because his fingers are dancing around my belly button before sliding down further, the tip of his thumb teasing my clit before retreating and starting over. A glamorous smile sweeps across his face. This guy is unbelievable. I was mid-bite on a hot wing when he walked into the bar, and no lie, I dropped it on the floor. And nothing comes between me and my food. It was like a slow-motion movie, his longish hair falling onto his face with a gust of wind, while he pushed back with one hand, propping the door open with the other He was wearing a fitted white button down, sleeves rolled up, top button undone, and a pair of dark jeans that hugged his ass like a kid with a carnival stuffed animal. His blue eyes were electric from across the room, and the rest of his face just filled in—a cosmic joke that a gorgeous, perfect man would also have an athlete's body. I had a brief fantasy of him in a pair of baseball pants, holding a bat, and then shook it off. Men like that are so far out of my league—no pun intended—that it's not funny. I took one last look at him and then went back to shoving fries into my mouth. I was so busy making fun of all the Red Sox fans around me that I didn't even see him approach. I don't know how I kept my cool, but I was a hair away from jumping on him, shocked at the plain attraction on his face. For little ole me.

So I went for it (you would too, don't judge.) And now he's pulling my jeans down and licking the outside of my underwear with a ridiculously hot tongue, promising me dirty things that I want him to do immediately.

"Jesus, look at you. I don't even know where to begin." I almost tell him that I can give him some ideas, but he beats me to it, leaning forward and nipping at my thighs, circling the throbbing wetness until I want to scream. "You smell like dessert," he says, his mouth hovering teasingly until my body involuntarily surges up to his mouth. He chuckles as I moan in frustration, but it's cut short when his tongue burrows deep, tapping my clit with ferocity. I feel a tide coming; part of me craves it, and the other wants to revel in it. I push/pull on his hair, the thick softness sliding through my fingers, and he laughs lightly. "Can't decide if you want to come or not, hmm?" I shake my head, and he takes the decision out of my hands, sucking my clit into his mouth; the roughness of the lace, combined with the wetness of his mouth, sends me over the edge. My breath halts in my chest. Are those angels singing? I've surely died.

"I'll give you a minute before I go in again." I'm sprawled out like a starfish, giving him a halfhearted wave. He chuckles, and hearing the rustling of clothes, I lift my head to see him unbuttoning his shirt down to his waist before shrugging it off his broad shoulders. I gulp at the sight of a large—very large—bulge creeping down his pant leg. I'm praying it's an illusion because there is no way...

"You keep staring at my cock like that, and I'm going to forego my original plans and just fuck you."

Do I listen? Nope.

He pulls his jeans down, the dark grey of his boxer briefs sliding down his muscular thighs seconds later.

Holy. Shit. I close my eyes and open them again, convinced his perfection is going to be replaced, but no. He really has a body like that.

"You don't listen well, do you, Joan?" He picks up his pants, fishing a condom out of his wallet. I watch in avid greed as he slides it down his thick length, expertly popping the end to make room. What size are those?

"Magnums. Now give me that." He plucks at the red lace, and they snap off on one side. He yanks the scraps off, tossing them over his shoulder, turning me roughly onto my side. He slides behind me, lifting my top leg high up over his arm and placing the head of his cock at the entrance of my pussy.

"You feel like fucking heaven," he breathes into my ear, rocking back and forth, coating himself in my wetness. "Are you ready?" I nod through my moans, and he slowly pushes himself inside of me, his thickness stretching me with a sweet sting. "Fuuuuuck. This pussy is going to kill me." He pulls out an inch before pushing into two. I bury my face into the covers, biting the fabric to stop my impending screams. He continues his easy motions until his full length sits inside of me. I take a short breath, almost afraid that a deep inhale will push him further. He's nearly too big, a centimeter more, and I would cry foul. The hand that is grasping my hip for leverage slides down, pinching my clit with the rhythm of his thrusts. My blood heats; the wave that had washed away earlier is coming back, a storm in the distance.

"Ah, ah, ah, Miss Joan. Not yet. You think I can't feel how hard you are pulsing?" He does some sort of ninja maneuver, and I'm suddenly on my knees with him still buried inside of me. He pushes my head down, pulling my hips even higher, thrusting into me with a relentless force. I scream out his name as the tide starts rushing over me, my eyesight going black in pleasure.

"I told you not yet, Joan." He smacks my ass cheek twice before pulling out of me and flipping me over once more.

"Please, please, please," I chant, begging him to continue, stop, and never let me go. My legs are draped over his arms, knees pushed back to my chest. His strikes are deep—I can feel him in my soul. He leans down, never stopping his thrusts, his tongue flicking against my lips, and I hiss when the twist of his hips hits a particular spot inside of me that sends light flashing behind my eyes. He lets one leg go and slides his hand under my head to deepen the kiss. Sexy grunts come from his mouth, drifting down into mine. The muscles in his broad back tighten as he slams into me with desperation.

"Fuck, this pussy is hot. Just a little bit more, sweetheart." I nod frantically, my eyes practically rolling back into my head. He taps my cheek, and I focus on his face. That. Face. His eyes bore into mine, a half smile on his full lips that morphs back and forth into a snarl. I smile back, a weird tug in my chest. For a brief moment, I feel like we are the best of friends. A sudden sizzle marches up my legs, and I can't take anymore. It flames into an explosion, and my back arches off the bed as the pleasure burns me inside out. He pumps impossibly harder until his shout echoes through the room, his thrusts wild and desperate until he finally collapses on me, his breath marathon-choppy. My head is a blur of emotion and pleasure, with absolutely zero regret. I wrap my arms around him a squeeze, squealing when he flips us over again, with his arms twined around me in a tight hug, mine now trapped under his back. We stay that way until I drift off to the soothing feel of his hands rubbing my back.

DEV

I can feel from her boneless relaxation that she is asleep. I'm debating whether I need to make the trek back to Beacon Hill or if I want to let her nap and then have her again. Sex with this woman was a revelation—between her hilarious stream of conscious babbling, her uninhibited responses, and her genuine affection, she rocked my foundation. I've had plenty of one-night stands in my life, tons of throwaway affairs, yet I've never felt the connection, the umbilical of emotion I've felt with Joan. A slight sadness that I refuse to let bloom flutters in my heart. It's been years since I'd felt anything like this, if ever. And it can go absolutely nowhere.

"What are you thinking about so hard? Your brain woke me up," her husky voice is hoarse. I bury my face in her shoulder, her hair a mass of silk in my face.

"I'm wondering if I should go or if I could convince you to let me have another round." I smile at her snort, her head lifting to look at me, a saucy grin stretching her face. "Ask me nicely."

"Joan, may I please have your pussy again?" I can barely get the words out for my laughing.

"Yes, you may."

I shout out at her prim response and tug my arm from under her head, leaning down to her mouth, those lips a beacon. She kisses with her whole body; her head slowly moving in tune to my tongue, her arms twining around my neck, one supple leg pretzeling with mine. Every so often she scratches her nails against my scalp and I moan with the sensation— I could live here, kissing her, for hours.

"I feel like I've been depriving you, poor thing," I pull back teasing. She cocks one of those thick eyebrows, a perfect slash of deep red, and smirks. "Oh?" I nod solemnly.

"Yes, here I've been, selfishly doing all of this work, and not letting you have your share of control. Up, up, now baby. Let me see how you ride my dick." I pat her hip and she sits up, a devilish smile on her beautiful face. Even in the low light of the room, I can see the blush on her creamy skin, the warm color spreading down to her full delicious breasts. They tempt with her movements, and I follow like a hypnotic with a swinging gold watch. She crawls to the edge of the bed, her ass facing me, and I tilt my head to get a better look. She peeks over her shoulder, and I grin at being busted. She rolls her eyes and pops up with another condom, tearing it open and sliding it down my dick which is pointed straight up and at her. She slides it down, staring for a minute, an adorably contemplative look on her face.

"It's already fit three times. You can do it." Her eyes narrow and she climbs on top, knees high, positioning herself before sinking down slowly, her head dropping back, thick hair tickling my thighs. My hands automatically grip her hips, trying to guide her movements but to no avail. She's lost in her pleasure, eyes closed and mouth open. I stare at her, fighting to keep myself from losing it. "Joan..." I snarl as she does a twisting motion with her hips that has my spine bowing off the bed. She laughs lightly, and as I slick my thumb across her clit, her laughter morphs into a moan, her sweet, sweet pussy throbbing quickly and her shout making me smile. I grunt out my release, tamping my lips tightly, not wanting to embarrass myself with the depth of my own pleasure. She collapses onto my chest, limp arms coming up to hug me, the soft puffs of her breath dancing across my skin. I hug her back, and she tightens her embrace with a little squeal. We lay like that for a while, before I crane my neck at the illuminated clock and sigh.

"Time to go?" She asks sleepily, sliding off me and burrowing her head into her pillow.

I nod regretfully. "Yeah. I've got an early morning." It's not a lie, though I wish it was. I stand up and walk to the adjoining bathroom, flushing the condom and washing up quickly. Joan is up and wrapped in a robe when I return, straightening up my clothes and finding my wayward shoes, one of which landed on the windowsill. "How in the hell..." she whispers, and I chuckle. "You can't blame a man for being in a rush." I grab the boxers and pants she hands me, leaning down to kiss her lips again. I click on the night table light and tap the button on the music speaker under the lamp. A slow, sweet song comes on, and I hold out my hand. "Dance with me." Her face lights up, and she floats into my arms, letting me sway her to the sexy beat. "I know this song. It's an update, yeah?"

She nods, her head resting against my bare chest. "Cruisin' by D'Angelo. I like it better than the original, but don't tell anyone that." I step away, grasping her hand and giving her a spin before pulling her back tightly to my body. The feel of her curves resting against me, the scent of her skin, is starting to fuck with my head. I run my hand through her hair, feeling the thick silk slide across my palm. My eyes close and I force myself to ignore the sigh that she breathes. Our bodies are like two lost puzzle pieces, finally finding their perfect fit. My grip tightens, before reality, that sick bitch, kicks in. The song ends, and I dip her, a giggle popping out of that mouth. I bow and continue getting dressed while she sits crosslegged on the bed.

I take a look around the room surprised to see how impersonal it is. There are no hints of her personality at all, no warmth. I slide on my shirt, each button a step toward our parting, toward never seeing her again. She says nothing, twitching around, fluffing pillows and blankets. Her hair is loose and wild, like deep fire, and I marvel again at her stupendous beauty. I sit next to her and tap on the bedpost.

"You don't live here, do you?" I ask as she tilts her head with a frown. "In this apartment. It's not yours, right?" She smiles slightly, shaking her head. "No, this is a friend's place. I'm headed home in a few hours." I open my mouth to ask her where home is, the impulse to connect, to see her again, overwhelming. But I don't. She seems to see through my dilemma, smiling sadly and reaching up to run her hand through my hair, scratching rhythmically. "It's okay, Dev. I've had a wonderful time, too." I grab one of her hands, kissing her fingertips, biting gently at a callous. A million words rush up my throat, but I settle on just one.

"Good."

I slip on my shoes, and feel my pockets for my keys, and wallet, pulling out my phone and calling an Uber. "Two minutes," I tell her, tugging her along with me to the door. I pull her into my arms, holding her tightly, every atom of my being, every strand of my DNA, screaming to not let her go. "Thank you," is all that can get past my throat and she leans back, her eyes pinned to mine.

"The Yanks are gonna win it all this year."

I burst out laughing as my phone chimes that my ride has arrived. "You bet your sweet as they are." I slap her on said ass, and she squeaks, rubbing it. I open the door and hold up a finger to the driver, propping it with my foot. I sweep her into my arms, our lips locking for a long moment. She pulls away first, a big grin on her face. "See ya around, Dev." I chuck her chin and head down the steps, turning at the bottom.

"See ya, Joan." I wink at her as I climb in the backseat, forcing myself not to turn around. Which is just as well because I sure as hell didn't need to see the look of devastation on her face.

❧   2   ❦

AN APPLE THAT CAN TAKE A BITE OUT OF YA

ix Months Later

"Saige, am I late? Fuck, I'm late, right? Shit, are they already here?" I rush into my office, passing my assistant in a flurry, dropping tubes and papers as I go. I bump into the corner of my desk, yelping at the sharp pain and dumping everything onto the top, taking a few deep breaths. I feel sweaty, nauseous, and hungry, with a side of annoyed. I hate being late. When I was a kid, my mother taught me the importance of always being on time and never letting people wait for you, ever. We were early for everything, and my dad used to joke that I was even born a week ahead of my due date. I was always the first kid at my desk, at a birthday party, on the school bus. It was an annoying impulse growing up, but now it's an invaluable trait for someone who lives on deadlines.

I was supposed to meet with a super important client, but this morning was a huge struggle. I barely managed to put an outfit together and couldn't find my keys, phone, or laptop—all three of which were in my briefcase. I broke three hair ties trying to tame my hair into a ponytail, and I spilled my perfume— which is a hundred fucking bucks— on my Tabriz carpet. I missed the train by one minute and decided to take an Uber, which was a huge mistake because the occupant before me had some kind of onion something for breakfast, so I wound up hanging my head out the window like a dog. I kept tripping with every step, looking down at my shoes and grimacing. I doubt they will be impressed by a pair of old Yankees flip-flops. My intern/assistant/best friend saunters into the room behind me, holding a steaming mug of ginger-lime tea and a giant apple fritter.

"Girl, calm down. You're an hour early." She hands me her goodies, studying me closely. "You look a mess, though. Rough morning?" I roll my eyes and take a sip slowly, letting it roll down my throat, settling my turbulent stomach. I wait a few seconds before taking another drink and a massive bite of the fritter. "Understatement. This sucks." I look around my office, which usually gives me a ton of pride and peace, but this morning, all I see is that the framed plans of my first project are hanging crooked on the wall and that there's a cobweb in the corner of one of the large windows. I sigh deeply.

She clucks in sympathy, reaching into a desk drawer and pulling out a brush, moving behind me and running it through my wild, heavy hair before deftly braiding it. I sigh in relief as it takes about ten degrees off my temperature, and she hands me a stick of deodorant, which I grunt at. I polish off my breakfast before falling into my chair, and the chaos I now live with is finally calm. She drops two pairs of shoes at my feet, and I nudge off my flip-flops, letting my feet go bare until the last minute. She straightens my desk, unfurling the plans from the tube and spreading them on the drafting desk by the window. She's got me all set up, and I pop open an eye to grin at her. "Have I told you lately that I love you?"

She snorts, propping a hand on her perfect hip. "Yeah, you did. Yesterday. When I ran down and got you those hotdogs at ten am." I laugh and stand up, padding over and triple-checking the schematics. Saige peers over my shoulder, and I flip through the sheets. "It looks good, Rory." I nod proudly.

"It looks damn good." I had to fight hard to win this account—the clients wanted much more experience than I had. I was up against two of the most prestigious firms in the city—Clare Design and Architecture and Patronage Studio. I didn't think I had a snowball's chance in hell, but I met with Chandler Schillings and his team, and he almost fell over when I walked in, expecting a man. I gave him my pitch, probably sounding desperate in my passion, but ultimately, he chose me. It helped that my last two projects garnered A+ awards, and I was also an architectural engineer on top of a designer, which meant dollars saved. My studio has been heating up the past few years, and this project will help us float up even higher. The Schillings are high-end restauranteurs, and their newest flagship, *Discovery*, is already the talk of Manhattan. Today, I show them the final plans, and then the fun begins.

"Do we have any interviews today?" Once it was announced that the studio was designing for the Schillings, our phones started ringing off the hook. I have three associates and as many interns, but with the influx of business, I'm going to have to hire more. I'm not in a big hurry, so Saige has been slowly setting up face-to-face interviews.

"Yup, you've got three today. Your whole day is packed, so make sure you let me know when it gets to be too much. You know I have no problem telling anyone to piss off." The phone rings, and Saige leans over, pushing buttons and answering it. She thanks the caller sweetly and hangs up, pulling me with her.

"They're here. Get your shoes on, girl. It's showtime."

৩৵৲

"Sweet God of Cupcakes and Chinese food, please help me." I'm lying on the couch in my office, eleven hours after my first meeting, everything on my body hurting. My feet are killing me, my back is on fire, and my neck feels like an ironing board. Even my hair hurts. Saige is sprawled in my vintage Herman Miller office chair, her four-inch heels long abandoned, tight bun unfurled. "I can't move. You'll have to call Port Authority to come and get me." I push a fist into my lower back and moan. "At least the Schillings loved my plans." My one big idea was to have the booths in the restaurant be built on sliding rails, which could change the space layout in minutes. I spent weeks coming up with the seventeen different combinations, which would give diners a fresh view every time they visited—' discovering' something new each time. I even commissioned artwork and draperies that would be easy to switch. It could be a different restaurant every night. This would drive people wild, which would mean more reservations — and dollars.

"You don't have to stay with me, you know. I know you have a date tonight." She makes a dismissive noise, and I peer over at her. "First of all, I would never leave you here, barely conscious and immobile—hoes before bros. Second of all, I canceled on him this morning after he sent me a dick pic." She shudders, and I laugh. "Was it too small?" She snorts as she pulls out her phone and holds it up to me. I gasp. "What the hell is that?"

"I don't know, and I am in no hurry to find out. I'm so glad I didn't try and sleep with him last week. I would have screamed the paint off the walls." I giggle uncontrollably, and she chimes in. Saige is one of the most beautiful women I have ever seen, stopping men in their tracks wherever she goes. She has dates almost every week, but they never blossom into a relationship. Because for all of her glamorous looks, she's a true nerd at heart. She'd rather go to a comic book convention than a five-star restaurant, but no one has gotten past her beauty to see that yet.

"I'm going to get your butt over to the Westside, and then I've got a bunch of hotties waiting at home for me." She does a little chair dance, and I laugh.

"Sons of Anarchy again?" Saige is obsessed with that show, watching it over and over again. Last Christmas, I got her custom Jax Teller pajamas, and she ugly-snot cried. There has never been a time I have called her and it wasn't playing in the background.

"Nope. The new *Persuasion Park Most* issue just came out—you know the big Spring edition— and I'm about to find my future husband. I'm going to curl up in bed and drool until I fall asleep. It'll be like shopping—except for permanent dick."

"What's the Most Issue?" I ask, rocking from side to side, trying to build the momentum to sit up. Saige takes pity on me, grabbing both hands and pulling me to my feet. I stumble a bit, shuffling over to my flip-flops and pushing them on. Saige grabs my bag while I hold my back and walk out of my office, shutting off the lights behind me. She stops at her desk, quickly gathering her things as I waddle to the elevator and push the button. I can hear the creak and hum as the ancient car makes its way to us.

"Here, look." She waves a thick magazine in my face, and I glance at it before tilting my head back and yawning. "Girl. It's the bachelor issue, the one where they vote all of them by reputation, looks, etc. Look at this one. Yummmmy. Malcolm Deveraux Bancroft Clare, Most Beautiful. Jesus, this man would have me speaking in Martian. He's been voted five times in a row— if I ever saw him in person, I'd climb him like a mountain goat." I laugh at her and peek at the picture.

What.

The.

Fuck.

A garbled sound comes out of my mouth, and I collapse against the wall. The room spins, and I swear I'm going to pass out. My heart is racing, and not in a good way. I try to dig my nails into the wall for balance, breaking two in the process.

"Rory!? What's wrong? Oh my god, should I call an ambulance?" Saige is in my face, running her hands down my cheeks frantically. I shake my head and point.

"Saige, that's him." Her pretty face creases in confusion and concern before it morphs into horror. It takes her all of ten seconds to realize every single problem.

"Wait. This is Dev?" She picks up the discarded magazine, flipping it quickly. She shoves the picture in my face as if I don't know it by heart. I study his features, my heart twisting, though the arrogant expression he's sporting is new.

"Yeah. That's him." I swallow hard because I'm trying not to puke and cry.

"Malcolm Deveraux Bancroft Clare is the man you slept with in Boston?" She clarifies slowly. "The five-time Most Beautiful Man in New York City?"

"Yup."

She points at my round belly. "He's your baby daddy?"

"Yup."
"He's about to be married. Didn't Dev say he was single?"
"Yup."
"Well fuck."
Indeed.

❧ 3 ❧

THE LAIR—OTHERWISE KNOWN AS MALCOLM'S OFFICE

"It's here!"

I look up as my younger brother, Montgomery, comes running into my office, unannounced, mind you, waving a thick booklet in the air. He's still wearing his scrubs under his coat, and judging by the shit-eating grin on his face; I have a pretty good guess about why this asshole is looking so pleased. I grimace hard, sitting back in my chair. I'd rather have my wisdom teeth pulled out rather than go through this shit again.

"Malcolm Deveraux Bancroft Clare is once again our Most Beautiful Man in New York, and can you blame us? Not only is our Beautiful man a stunner—six-foot-three inches of dark hair, blue-eyed American royalty, but he is brilliant; driving his storied family business to new heights. This past year, he acquired not one, not two, but three new companies, all while breaking hearts up and down the eastern seaboard. While we eagerly await his upcoming nuptials (while also dying inside), at least we will have that face for years to come..." Montgomery reads all this in a stringy falsetto voice, swooning and dancing around my office, batting his eyelashes at me. I throw a series of pens and paper clips at him, and he dodges them all while cackling. He stands a good ten feet away, holding up the pages and pages of pictures they included, almost all of them paparazzi-candid; me in a

tux, shirtless on a boat, even sweaty while running in Central Park. He kept up a running commentary of each picture, in different accents, until I finally had enough, standing up to beat the snot out of him, regardless of his identical size. He cracks up as he dashes behind one of the gold leather sofas congregated in the corner of my office. I sigh, sitting back down, rubbing my eyes, and shaking my head. You'd never know my brother was a doctor and a baby one at that.

"If it makes you feel better, Rix made the list, too." I snort as he holds up a photo spread of our absentee older brother, except his is professional, all staged and posed. That fool probably loves this crap. "What's his, Most Idiotic?" I scan the pictures, his man-bun and dangerously low pants probably about to send our uber-conservative society mother into the mesosphere. I can imagine her blowing up his phone and him cackling as he presses 'ignore' a hundred times in a row.

"Nope. Most Reckless. Fits him, no?" I snort again. Rix is our half-brother from our mother's short-lived first marriage. She was pregnant with him when his father, River, went hang gliding, only to perish in a freak accident, leaving his new wife alone—and his unborn son, heir to the biggest fortune in North America. Our mom remarried when Rix was one, and shortly after, he began spending half of the year (eventually the whole year) with his other family—all of them wild and madcap. He came into his full inheritance at eighteen and has been a crazy mess ever since—marching to his own drum while getting richer by the day.

"Mom is probably chewing her arm off right now. You can see his dick in this one," Monty points and I make a face.

"No thanks. Don't you have some babies to deliver? Some vaginas to dive into?" He laughs as he drops into one of the Eames chairs before my desk, whistling. I sigh in irritation and sit back, staring at him. "What do you want, Mont? Other than to interrupt my very busy day?" His face sobers, and he leans forward, his elbows on his knees.

"I just wanted to check on you. See how you were handling everything? These past few months have been hard, I know." My annoyance drops to almost zero. I stare at him for a moment before giving him a short nod. I've always been envious of Montgomery, jealous of the freedom his birth order has given him. He's always been able to squirm his way into his own choices: attending medical school instead of joining Clare Enterprises International Inc, at a college three thousand miles away instead of the Clare tradition of attending Harvard. Loving who he wanted to love.

"It is what it is, right? It's never been a secret that I have obligations to the family." I don't make eye contact with him but hear his sympathetic cluck.

"Obligations to the company, yeah, I get it. You're the only one with the education and experience. But you shouldn't have to marry someone you don't love to satisfy some weird old tradition. That's bullshit." I tap my fingers in the arm of my chair, twisting around to face the window.

"I do love Rachel." Even to my ears, the lie sounds hollow and sour. Monty picks up on it because he snorts loud enough to rattle the artwork on the wall.

"No, the hell you don't. Mom loves her. Dad loves her. Manhattan loves her. But you don't. You never have. I mean, I don't blame you, she's awful. You could build an ice castle on her ass. You deserve better, brother." He chatters on, listing out all of my fiancee's faults, of which, admittedly, there are many. Rachel Van Pyke of the Park Avenue Van Pykes is (on paper) perfect. She's beautiful, a dark-eyed brunette with a slim modelesque build, phenomenal manners, and an Ivy League education. Everything on her glistens: her teeth, her skin, her hair. Our younger sister, Val, always asks snarkily if she is oily, and Monty laughs like a jackal.

When I was fifteen, my parents sat me down and told me they had a wife picked out for me, per family tradition. For eight generations, the oldest Clare son has had his future wife decided for him whether he liked it or not. It was always based on the shallowest criteria: bloodlines, wealth, and proximity to more money. My grandparents had picked out my mom, but the Le Lauriers, Rix's family, got to her first. As soon as they found out she was a widow, they snatched her up despite her undesirable first marriage and extra child. My dad did as he was told, and they've been married for over thirty years. They never seemed unhappy—but nor did they seem blissfully in love. Right after that declaration, Rachel and her family started showing up everywhere we were, and she began slowly digging her claws in. At first, I was intrigued by her, this gorgeous girl who would one day be mine. But after a few years (and many women), I realized I didn't like one thing about her. Not one. I tried to talk to my father about it, but he wouldn't hear it. And my mother was a definite no-go. She took unapproachable to an extreme. As far as she was concerned, my marriage was a future fact, and nothing would sway her.

At twenty-six, right after law school, my father handed over the CEO position of Clare Inc., effectively retiring but still running Clare Design and Architecture— his passion project. Everyone expected Rachel and I to get married shortly after— but I jumped into my new role with both feet and ignored her nagging. We went everywhere socially together and had been sleeping with each other on and off for years. I was content to let this continue, but she was not, and she told me so every chance she got. I let the years slip past until one day, my parents sat me down to tell me they were sending out my wedding invitations and would need me to clear my calendar.

It wasn't my finest hour.

I finally told them that I didn't want to marry Rachel and could barely stand her, let alone spend the rest of my life with her. I got so lost in my immature freak out that I didn't notice they weren't listening. They let me finish and then calmly told me in short words to get the fuck over it. I stormed out, called Rachel, and told her the marriage was off. Then, I jumped on my plane and flew to Mexico for two weeks, then ran off to Europe. When I returned, there would be hell to pay, but I didn't care. I finally felt free. That lasted a New York minute before reality and obligations came crashing in. Now, everyone is getting what they want.

Except for me.

I had my one moment of pure happiness months ago. It would have to last me for the rest of my life.

"...all I'm saying is that you shouldn't have to be locked up with that wench forever just because some old fart a million years ago said this is how it's got to be. It's bullshit." Montgomery is still ranting, and

I smile lightly. My calendar reminder goes off, and Eve, my assistant, buzzes to let me know I have an appointment in fifteen minutes.

"Time to go kid. Make sure you tell Cam I said hi." I stand up and grab him into a hug, pounding his back a little harder than usual for bringing in that stupid magazine. "Will I see you two for Sunday brunch?" He shrugs without a hint of remorse.

"Maybe. Babies don't follow a schedule, you know. Plus, Cam might want to do something else. I don't think I'll be in the mood to listen to Dad yell about losing that restaurant project or Mom and Rachel planning your funeral-- I mean wedding. I'll let you know." He hugs me again before his pager goes off, and he smiles.

"Got a baby coming. Call me." He hurries out of the office, calling something out to Eve as she yells back. The hospital is only three blocks away, and I know from some past conversations that he sometimes doesn't make it in time, even with it being that close. One time, he had to deliver the baby in the parking garage.

I look at the edge of my desk and see that Montgomery has left that damn magazine. I pick it up, frowning at my face on the cover. The first issue that I was featured in was flattering. Even my mother, who could have been cast as a Puritan in the Scarlett Letter, found it amusing. The pictures inside were a little over the top and the public attention was annoying, but I enjoyed it. But then it happened year after year, and the paparazzi interference was too much. I could barely leave my house without being jumped, and I'm sure this year will be no different. I sigh, throwing it into the trash.

Most Beautiful? It's more like Most Miserable.

THE LION'S DEN

I wish teleportation was real. I could push a button on my watch, and I would evaporate in front of everyone. Except instead of specific coordinates, it would just drop me onto a mountain in the middle of nowhere. Or maybe even another planet.

Sunday brunch at the Clare compound is almost a mandatory thing. Sure, my parents make it sound like you have a choice—calling and saying that they 'hope to see you' but meaning 'get your ass here or else.' There are always acceptable exceptions, of course, and over the years, Montgomery and Valentina have managed to cry off more often than not, only getting away with it because I make as many as I can. They are content to let their younger children run amok as long as The Heir is present. AKA me.

Just as Montgomery predicted, my father is griping about a project he missed out on, a restaurant concept from a group he's worked with in the past. He was horrified when they told him they wanted to go in a more modern direction, and he has been like a wounded animal ever since. I don't know what is biting his ass more—the modern part or the press that the restaurant is getting before a shovel has even hit the ground. I tuned him out, even as he waved his phone around, trying to get someone to feel sorry for him.

My mom, Rachel, and Rachel's mom, Ingrid, are neck-deep into wedding planning, and I hear snatches of their conversation: flowers, china, and music. There is a wedding planner I have seen once, and though she is supposed to be the best in the city, they are steamrolling over her, too. I think they asked my opinion a few times, but I pretended to be on the phone, knowing they would have ignored anything I had to say anyway. One time—one—I suggested a courthouse wedding like Montgomery and Cam had, and their furious silence made the hair on the back of my neck wiggle. I plowed forward, trying to make a case for privacy, and Rachel turned on the waterworks, crying that I was ashamed of her blah blah blah. My mother laid into me while comforting her, though Valentina glared at Rachel and rolled her eyes. I never made a single suggestion after that, though Rachel likes to lie and tell people how excited I am and how involved I am in all the planning.

"Dahling, don't you agree that our colors should be gold and silver with a hint of cream? So rich, yes?" I barely refrain from snarling, instead just raising a brow at Rachel, the one move telling her my thoughts. I could give a chicken-fried fuck about colors, and she knows it. There is a hint of arrogance, of triumph in her eyes. She's never forgiven me for publically calling off our engagement and embarrassing her in front of her friends. The 'rich' remark is moot—Rachels's family is old-money rich but nowhere near mine. She is taking several steps up the social ladder, the new Queen Bee. It's all she really wants.

"Oh, my dear, he just wants you to be happy, right Malcolm? You shall have whatever you want." My mother waves her thin hand around, and I shiver at the blue veins so visible through her fragile skin. I give a weak nod and zone out again.

"...You watching any of the preseason?" I startle as I realize my father is speaking to me and shake my head. "Yeah. The Yanks look good so far."

He nods, spending a few minutes complaining about our rookie shortstop, who dropped the ball in a crucial play that caused us to miss the last playoff spot last year. I make the appropriate noises, my mind wandering to that sweet voice telling me, "The Yanks are gonna win it all this year." I pinch my eyes tight, shaking my head to clear it, squashing the feelings, down, down, down.

"You alright, Malcolm?" My dad's voice is mildly concerned, and I realize that I probably look crazy with my face all screwed up and muttering under my breath.

"Yes, of course. I'm just thinking about something I forgot to tell Eve," I tell him with the fakest of smiles. He stares at me for a moment, his mouth opening to say something, before he is interrupted by our housekeeper, Elena, announcing Montgomery and his husband, Cameron. I sigh in relief and stand to give them both tight hugs.

"Thank God," I whisper in Cam's ear, and he laughs lightly. "We knew you needed us," he whispers back, patting my shoulder as he politely greets my mom and the other ladies. Dad has already launched into his old tirade, and Montgomery is listening with a smirk. I have no doubt he is goading him about being too old to design anything and judging by the red creeping up Dad's neck; he is succeeding.

"Malcolm, come outside with me for a moment. I need your advice about something." Cameron nods at me, and I sprint so fast, his face contorts, lips tucked behind his teeth.

In 1888, Carl Pfeiffer re-designed this brownstone for my great-great somebody, and it is one of the few in New York with a full English garden in the back. It's been in the family forever, and when my dad decided to gut it, my mom's only request was not to touch one inch of the green space. Cameron walks to the back, where the wrought iron chairs and tables are gathered around a custom water and fire feature, currently lit for the nip in the early spring air. I sit down heavily, rubbing my face in both hands.

"That bad?" Cam asks, sitting beside me, crossing a foot over his leg. He drapes his arm across the back, peering at me in concern. Cam and Montgomery met when Cameron was bringing one of his third-grade students in with a broken arm. Montgomery was walking by and took one look at Cam's bright green eyes, and that was it. They had a huge uphill battle with the family; my mother was content to ignore Montgomery being gay as long as he didn't date anyone in her face. He brought Cam to Sunday brunch one day, announced they were getting married—with no prenup—and that we were welcome to come or not; it was still happening. Valentina jumped up, squealing, and started posting to her social media, effectively forcing our parents to support it or look like jerks. We all showed up at their emotional courthouse ceremony, even Rachel, though I don't think she was actually invited. They've been married for three years now, and he's the best thing Montgomery has ever done. I speak to him more than my siblings—and he knows all my secrets, good and bad.

"I just feel like I can't breathe when I'm here. Like, does no one notice that we are not a family? It's just a bunch of people in a room—there's nothing, no feelings, no warmth. It's driving me crazy." I tug on my hair, and he sighs.

"That is about five different issues in one breath. You don't have to go through with this wedding, Malcolm. I know, I know, you want your mother to be happy, but to what end? Is it fair to you, to what you want? And even though I think she is the spawn of Satan, it's not fair to Rachel, either." He makes a face, and I laugh. "I don't think anyone in that room realizes what they are missing. It's just not part of the DNA of the Clares—maybe it's the money, the power. It took your brother a long time to relax around my family, and now he and my dad are best friends—they tell each other they love each other daily. I want that for you, Malcolm." He squeezes my shoulder, and I take a deep breath.

"If things were different, I would want that too. But they aren't. I've accepted my fate. All I can do is ensure I don't repeat it with my children." I give him a half smile, sitting back with the weak fall sun touching my face. I ask him about his work with at-risk children, and he tells me some funny stories, his handsome face lighting up. We speak on it for a few minutes and I make a mental note to have Eve look into a larger donation to the school. The last time I did it, Cam gave me the scolding of my life before crying and hugging me.

"God save me from the corpses in that house!" Montgomery shouts, popping up from behind the hedges, his arms raised dramatically in the air. Cameron snickers, and I roll my eyes.

"Dad is never going to get over not getting to design that restaurant. Do you know he thought about buying that other design firm just so that he could save face? I guess the company, Miller Jones something told him to take a hike. He's livid. I'm toying with the idea of having them design our house to watch him whine some more." Cam snickers as I shake my head. The funny thing is he would totally do it, and my dad would freak. It might be worth it.

"And did you know that Rachel has gone off of her birth control? She's in there telling our moms that she is on some special diet that guarantees boy babies. And of course, Mama Clare is all about it and made Elena tell Cook to change the whole menu for today, though the food is already made." His voice matches his disgust, and Cameron stands up to hug him, calming him down instantly. She told me the same thing a few nights ago, and though we don't live together yet, she made my kitchen staff throw out everything in my pantry and replace it with a bunch of bullshit. I didn't find out till later that she wouldn't even let them donate or take any of it for themselves. Good times. "Have you heard from Val?"

Monty answers from the inside of his husband's neck. "She's in India. She should be back in a few weeks. Rix found out where she was and sent over some security and a private plane. She's pissed as shit, but he told her to suck it up or he would show up himself. We think she's got a boyfriend over there or something." I raise my brows. My mom has been after Valentina for years to get married, parading a bunch of assholes in front of her, pushing her to decide. And every time she does, Valentina traipses off to another country, doing volunteer work, each trip being longer and longer, until Mom realized that Val would stay gone forever if she didn't stop. The only one who can get through to her stubborn ass is Rix, and ninety percent of the time, he takes Val's side, which drives Mom even crazier. "I don't suppose he's coming to brunch?" Cam snorts, and Montgomery cracks up. The last time Rix came over on a Sunday, he brought two, um, women he had been with the night before. The three of them reeked of booze, and one of them had a nip slip over coffee. He was never invited back, which I'm sure was his intention.

Elena shows up to tell us it is time to eat, and the three of us follow behind her little, efficient form, taking our same weekly seats. Mom,

Ingrid, and Rachel are in their own gilded world while Dad tries to make small talk with Cameron and Monty, his discomfort masked by his manners. I listen with half an ear, smiling when appropriate and nodding when told, never letting the scream lodged in my throat loose, fearing I would never stop.

❅ 5 ❅

THIS PLACE SUCKS

My phone goes off for the twentieth time in the last ten minutes, and I grimace. Saige is panicked beyond belief that I wanted to do this by myself, and though I would have loved the backup, I know she would have acted like a damn fool the whole time- going between screaming at Dev, I mean Malcolm, and drooling all over him. She came over this morning, helping me pick out an outfit and making me torture myself with "fuck him" heels; though she snarked, it was too late, and I already did. I wanted to wear elastic waist pants; she insisted on this emerald green deep-vee dress. I wanted a simple braid or ponytail; she blew my hair out to this mass of curls and waves. I wanted a bare face, terrified any makeup would melt off, and she scoffed, using a ton of something called 'setting spray.' I insisted on taking the subway, and she arranged a fancy limo instead. She shot me down at every turn, and I'll never admit it; I was grateful not to look like the sweaty lump I would've pulled off on my own. Saige called last week and made an appointment under my real name as the CEO of Miller-Jones Design Associates. I was able to snag a lunchtime appointment, and now here I am, shooting up to the fiftieth floor of Clare Inc., trying not to panic, sweat, or pee involuntarily. The elevator stops, and the doors open to a spacious cold space, all metal and light wood, with sharp edges and cool colors. The carpet is thick, and I recognize the dense Berber construction, my heels sinking into its luxurious thickness. I mentally break down what I would change to give this place some life. It's like a damn mausoleum in here. I shake my head, smiling at the pretty blonde sitting behind a sterile desk, her mouth open, staring at me. I tilt my head at her, and she snaps to, her spine straightening. "May I help you?"

"Yes, I have an appointment with Mr. Clare. I'm Rory Miller-Jones?" Her blue eyes get even wider before she looks down at her laptop, nodding. "Yes, Miss Jones, I'm Eve. Please have a seat. Mr. Clare is in with family, and you are a bit early. Can I offer you anything?"

I would kill for a pretzel with mustard, but I don't tell her that. "No, thank you. Perhaps you can point me to the restroom?" She looks at my belly and gulps. "Yes, of course, follow me." She stands, and even with my heels, she towers over me, her long legs eating up the floor while I struggle to keep up. She looks over her shoulder, slowing when she sees that I am huffing about ten feet back.

"Sorry," she says sheepishly. "I always walk fast. Native New Yorker." She waves at a door, and I push through, not shocked that the decor matches the meat locker foyer. I snap a few pictures before peeing, my bladder giving me a high five, and the baby kicking out too. I sigh and pull out my phone, looking at all of the nine-one-one texts from Saige.

> Did you make it okay?
>
> Check your hair before you get on that elevator. Don't get off looking like Darth Vader!
>
> Don't drink anything, or you'll pee!
>
> Wait, go pee if you can!
>
> Ewww, is that the bathroom? It looks like Straight Outta Jail.
>
> The mirror is nice, though.

I roll my eyes and finish, admiring the quiet flush system. I wash my hands and dry them with an actual towel, pleased that my makeup and hair are somewhat okay. I take a few deep breaths, steeling up my courage and nodding at my reflection. I snatch up my briefcase and coat and head back to Eve, who is typing furiously while fielding the non-stop phone calls. I sit, pulling my silk dress over my knees, fidgeting and twitching. My phone vibrates, and I see it's five minutes before my appointment. Eve must have the same alarm because she picks up the phone and murmurs into it before placing it down and smiling at me. "He will be ready shortly." Before the words leave her mouth, I hear a scuffle from behind the door, and it flings open, a younger version of Malcolm grinning and speeding toward me. I slide back, and he grabs my hand and squeezes while pulling me to my feet. "Miss Jones? You have no idea how happy I am to meet you. I'm Dr. Montgomery Clare, the younger brother." He looks at my belly and grins wider. "About eight months?" I grimace and shake my head. "No just over six. The baby is big, my doctor says." I think about what Saige told me about the Clare family and realize Montgomery is an OB. "And it's actually Miller-Jones. But you can call me Rory."

"Gotcha. You look beautiful either way. Did Eve offer you anything to eat or drink?" His fingers are resting on my wrist, and I wonder if he realizes he is taking my pressure. "She did. But I'm fine, thank you."

"Honey, let the woman breathe," an amused voice says from behind him, and I peek around him at an extremely handsome man blocking the doorway to the office. He winks at me before coming forward and reaching out to shake my hand. His eyes are kind, and I feel myself relaxing. He stares at me like Eve did, though there is something else in his gaze, and I gulp, wondering if he knows something. "Forgive my husband. He's a fan of your work. I'm Cameron." He elbows Montgomery, who is still grinning like a jackal.

"Yup. I look forward to seeing your designs on the Schillings restaurant." I open my mouth to answer when Malcom's exasperated voice filters over me.

"Monty, leave my guest alone, please. Miss Jones, please come in." I swallow hard and glance at Cameron, who is watching me closely. They move out of the way, and suddenly there he is— immaculately dressed in a navy suit, his sculpted face and stance so familiar yet foreign.

Waves of longing and joy wash over me, and I wait for the heartbeat of time it takes him to recognize me. His face flushes, and his mouth drops open. "Joan?" I nod jerkily and try to smile.

"Joan? Her name is Rory. Rory Miller-Jones. Why are you looking at her like that? Cameron, get off of me. Why are you dragging me..." His voice fades as his husband pushes him around the corner, leaving Malcolm and me staring at each other. Even Eve has disappeared.

"How are you here?" He steps toward me, his Chagall-blue eyes focused on my face. I open my mouth to answer before a look of utter horror strains across his. His eyes are now pinned on my stomach, and that tiny sliver of hope, the beat of the fairy wings of longing, dies. I mentally sweep the remnants aside for later, stepping forward and swinging my arm to him. "Let's talk, Malcolm." I walk past him into the office, relieved it's a warmer space, though it still looks like a morgue. I stop at his desk, placing my briefcase on top and withdrawing the paperwork my lawyer drew up last week. He almost keeled over when I told him what I wanted but did as I asked. Malcolm is behind me, walking slowly, a growing frown on his lips.

"I won't take up much of your time, so let's just cut to the chase. Yes, the baby is yours. I am willing to have a DNA test done if you want, which I am sure you do. I realize this is a huge complication to your life—I'm sure your *fiancee* would be mortified to know you fooled around on her a few months ago." I give him an evil look, and he tries to interject, but I cut him off and continue. "I don't want to complicate your life, nor do I want you to fuck up mine. So..." I wave the papers at his face, noticing that his hands are fists at his sides. "This is a contract asking for a few things. One- you relinquish all parental rights to my baby. You get nothing, nada. No visitation, no say in anything. Two- I waive any right to child support or monetary inheritance the baby would have. I want nothing from you—I can care for him alone. Third--the only exception would be whether, in a medical emergency, you would be willing to consider any type of donation he may need. It's not a must, but if all other options are exhausted, my lawyer may reach out. That's it. My lawyer assures me that it's ironclad, but I'm sure someone of your stature would like your attorneys to look it over. That's fine. My lawyer's contact information is at the top of every page. I'll leave this copy with you. Thanks for your time." I snap the case closed and salute him, headed toward the door.

"Joan, wait," he grabs my arm gently, and I shake him off. "It's Rory, *Dev*," I snarl at him. His face twists in annoyance before smoothing out.

"Fine, Rory. You can't just drop something like this on me and walk out. We should talk, don't you think?" I try not to fall into his eyes, pinching my leg to stop myself from flinging myself into his arms, before remembering he is a cheating hoebag. I grit my teeth and wait for him to get his thoughts together.

"Did you do this on purpose? Meet me like that?"

I blink hard, letting his idiotic question settle in, remembering that I am pregnant and cannot suplex his ass into the Giovanni Luca Ferreri table behind him. I wait for him to realize the danger he is in, and when he doesn't, I take a beat, trying to unloosen my jaw before my teeth pop out like bullets.

"You mean did I use my super-duper precognition skills, time a job site visit to Boston, post up in a random bar, wait for you to approach me, and then lure you back to my Airbnb and pray that the condoms *you* brought would be faulty? Is that what you are asking me?" I glare at him, his stupid, perfect face scrunched up before relaxing.

"You can't fault me for asking. You know who my family is. It wouldn't be the first time a woman tried to claim a Clare got them pregnant. When you are as rich as we are, people gravitate toward the power." He shrugs, that arrogant look sliding across his eyes. I count to ten in my head, absently rubbing my tummy.

"I'm going to ignore the fact that you just basically inferred that I am some golddigger who cooked up a scheme to get pregnant for a paycheck. That your family is so *desirable*, that you are such a *prize*, that I would throw away my pride and use my kid. I am going to let that slide because I think you are struggling with reality right now." I nod my head repeatedly. "Yeah, you couldn't possibly accuse me of that. Because out of the two of us, you are the fucking liar. Not me."

"I did not lie to you. I told you the truth," he yells. His hand comes up and rubs his face, scrubbing at his scruffy, dimpled chin. He sighs deeply, his mouth opening to say something before snapping shut, his shoulders slumping. "I don't appreciate you calling me a liar." Well, too fucking bad. "Is this about Clare Design? Because we are your competition, because you are trying to establish yourself?"

Heaven be a meteor strike. This fool might send me into an early labor. "I don't need to make up shit to be better than your firm. In case you didn't know, I won two contracts out from under you. Stop trying to make this something I am doing to you, Malcolm. You ain't some innocent lamb in this."

He scowls, those thick black brows slashes of pure anger. "Well, I can't see how else I am supposed to take it. You show up here with that big belly, claiming the baby is mine and waving a contract around, ordering me to sign it, and accusing me of being a liar, which, by the way, I am not. If this is some kind of ploy, I can assure you it will not work in your favor."

"You're not a liar?" *Don't kill him, Rory. You don't look good in orange.*

"No, I am not."

"Question, are you engaged?" He grimaces before nodding. "Yes, I am."

"Cool, cool. And your name is not 'Dev', it's Malcolm, right?" He stares at me before nodding again slowly. "And your name is not Joan," he taunts cruelly.

I get on my tiptoes, a finger in his face. "No, but it's what my nickname used to be when I was in high school, you assface. I didn't lie —*you did.*" I stick my fingernail in his forehead before easing down and taking a deep breath. I step back and turn around, headed toward the elevator.

"And when we were in Boston, did you, or did you not tell me you had no girlfriend, fiancee, or wife lurking about?" There is a heavy silence, though I can feel his breath on my neck.

"And you are marrying Rachel Van Pyke in March next year, right? The same girl you've been with since you were a teen?" I look over my shoulder and see the answer on his face.

"Jo-Rory, listen. I was not engaged when you and I ummm, met. We were on a break..."

Oh.

My.

God.

I turn slowly, feeling wildfire shoot out of my eyes. "No. You. Didn't! Did you just try and pull the 'we were on a break' on me?" My voice escalates to a near scream, and he winces. "You asshole!" I slap him with my briefcase, and he yelps. I stab the button for the elevator, relieved when it opens right away. My breath comes in furious pants, and the baby is kicking up a storm. I pat my belly and push for the lobby level.

"My lawyer will be waiting for your call." I glare at him one last time, and the door closes on his gorgeous face, full of confusion and anger. I gasp and lean on the wall, fighting my tears. As Saige would tell me, "Don't give them the satisfaction, honey. Keep your head up." I pull out my phone and speed dial her.

"Rory? How did it go?"

"Awful. Can you meet me at my house? I don't think I can make it to the office today." I hate the tremor I can't keep out of my voice.

"Girl, I'm on the way. Don't you dare cry until you are in the limo, you hear me? That jackass doesn't get that from you." I nod, though she can't see me.

"Okay. Saige?"

"Yeah?"

"Can you bring me a pretzel?" She snorts over the phone.

"Mustard?"

"Yes, and maybe a shish-kebob too."

"You got it, babe."

❧ 6 ❧

WHIPLASH, BUT MAKE IT IN YOUR SOUL.

What.

The.

Fuck.

For some reason, I look at my Patek watch and mentally calculate the few minutes she was here—maybe ten? Six hundred seconds. That's all it took to turn my life upside down and rock my very foundation. I'm still standing near the elevator, the scent of her perfume and her voice's vibration still in the air.

"Holy shit! Malcolm, you are about to have a baby! That woman is stone-cold gorgeous, too. That hair! Those eyes! Oh my god, Mom is going to FREAK OUT. Does this mean we can finally kick ol' Rachel to the curb? Can I be there when you do it? Ohhhh, I have to call Val. She has to come home immediately. I wonder who her OB is? Well, I want to deliver my nephew. You heard her, right? It's a boy—that kid will be unstoppable. A real headturner..." Monty's rambling is non-stop, and I can't process a word of it. I'm still in the same position. I feel a firm hand on my arm, guiding me into my office. Monty is still on a tear behind me, and I hear him interrupt himself long enough to tell Eve to cancel my afternoon before he starts up again.

"Mal? Drink this." Cam hands me a rock glass, filled to the brim. I gulp half of it in one swallow, the cool burn of the whiskey making me cough and putting my feet back under me.

A baby. With Joan. No, no, not Joan.

Rory. A strong name, unique in a way. It suits her.

I take another swallow and look up at Cameron, who is looking at me worriedly. "Boston?"

I nod, draining my glass. "Yeah." Shortly after I left Rory and everything fell apart, I confided in Cameron about my time with her. I left nothing out (well, some things), especially my regret for not getting her contact information, though it wouldn't have mattered. My life was signed and sealed one week after I left her.

"Wait, you knew about this, Cameron? How could you not tell me?" Montgomery is outraged, but his husband rolls his eyes and shushes him. "Can you hush it long enough to see that your brother is in shock? Get over here and check him out." Monty huffs but comes over, pulling his stethoscope out of his shirt. He takes my pulse and checks my breathing and pupils. He sits back and pats me on the head. "You are a bit shock-y, but it will pass. Now, where is that contract-thing? I want to rip it to shreds and throw it at Rachel like confetti."

"Monty..."

"I expect to be the godfather, too. You better not pick Rix—he'll have your kid juggling beer cans at two years old."

"Montgomery."

"And we need to talk to Rory about the whole name thing..."

"MONTGOMERY DAVIDSON BANCROFT CLARE!" I yell at him finally, my breath coming in hot pants. He finally shuts up, and I point at the chair, and he sits slowly. Cameron sits beside him, ready to stuff a sock in his mouth if necessary.

"Monty...I have to sign that contract. If I tell Mom that I knocked up a one-night stand, she will get sick again. I can't risk it," I tell him quietly, watching all the joy drain from his face. "The doctor said her heart is fragile, remember? She's not well enough to take a shock like that, not to mention the scandal." His sorrowful disappointment is nothing compared to my own. The thought of Rory having my baby is a heaven I never expected to find and also the worst hell of my life. I don't know if I will ever get over it.

"Well, you can't just do that, Malcolm. This is your son, the family heir that we are talking about. You can't just go about your life as if he doesn't exist. I won't let you. We can make some kind of arrangement," he argues as I shake my head.

"I can, and I will. I don't want Rory ostracized because of this—she has a business and career. And you know Rachel and her cohorts will go after her and the baby. Mom will never accept him, and what about when he gets older? This may be a modern city, but our part of it isn't. They'll make his life hell."

"He'll be a Clare," he argues, and I cut him off with a slash of my hand.

"But he won't. You know, as I do, that just having the name will mean nothing without the family behind it, and Mom and Dad will never do that. He is better off with his mom and her family, anyway."

"We can figure it out. You can use me and Cam as a go-between." His face is desperate, adding to my guilt.

"Monty, I can't do anything in life without a paparazzo following me. Just this morning, there were pictures of me getting in and out of my car and stopping for coffee. I'd never be able to pull it off and you know it."

"But Mal," his eyes well up, and I swallow hard.

"It's got to be this way. You see that, don't you, Cam?" I look at my brother-in-law, silently pleading with him to support me. His dark green eyes are sad, but he nods anyway. "Monty, this isn't our decision, and right now, Mal doesn't need us to make him feel worse, okay? Let's go now and give him some space, hmm?"

"Just don't sign anything yet, alright? Sleep on it for a couple of days. Promise?" He lets Cameron pull him to his feet and push him out of my office. I hear him admonishing his husband for keeping secrets, and a thin smile ghosts my lips. I sit down heavily, head hung between my shoulders.

A soft knock interrupts my thoughts, and I look up and see Eve standing tentatively in the doorway, her jacket and purse in hand. "Mr. Clare, I am going to go home and answer emails and calls from there.

I've turned on the messaging system for anything that slips through. All of your appointments for today and tomorrow have been shifted. Is there anything else I can do for you?" Her pretty face is professional but looks sad, like my brother and Cam. For me.

"No, thank you, Eve. You've been amazing today. I can trust in your discretion, I assume?" It's a dumb question because Eve is as loyal as the day is long, but the lawyer in me asks anyway. She would never say anything for many reasons, especially to Rachel, who she cannot stand. She nods, her lips opening and closing several times before blurting. "Miss Miller-Jones is very beautiful. I read that she is designing the newest Schillings restaurant. The paper said she is one of history's youngest *Pritzker Award* winners." Her voice fades, and she smiles before slipping off. I waited until I heard her board the elevator before calling and telling security I was still there but not to be disturbed for any reason. Then I locked the elevator and grabbed a bottle of *Balvenie 40 Yr*, no glass. I uncork it, not even appreciating the spicy scent, just hoovering down a huge gulp. I place the bottle on the table, shrugging off my suit jacket, ripping off my tie, and untucking my shirt, the ghost of old claustrophobia easing somewhat.

I let my mind wander, and it jumps right into today's memory of Rory's face. Her beauty is even more vivid and more awe-inspiring than I remembered. Were her eyes really that stormy gray, her lips really that plump, her hair that deep fire? Pregnancy agreed with her—she was radiant despite the scowls and evil eyes she was throwing at me. I absently rub my hip where she belted me with her briefcase. I chuckle out loud at her spunk. She'll be an outstanding mother—fierce, loyal, and loving. I think back to our one night, how she hugged me and let her affection spill over without reservation. Yes. My son will be loved.

It will be more than I ever had.

❧   7   ❧

IF I IGNORE IT, IT DIDN'T
HAPPEN

„He's awful, Saige. He's nothing like the man I met in Boston, nothing. He was mean and arrogant." I sniffle for the thousandth time, a soggy tissue plugging up my right nostril. I spent the whole limo ride back to the Westside, alternately sobbing uncontrollably and spitting truck driver curses. The poor chauffeur didn't know what to do, so he just nodded sympathetically, letting me keep the air conditioner on Alaska and not once complaining about the frostbite I was about to leave him with.

"Maybe he was just in shock, Rory. I mean, I would be if some girl I hooked up with one night showed up at my office with a belly as big as a beachball, telling me that she was pregnant, and 'oh, hey, I don't want you involved in the kid's life.'" Saige is lying on my living room floor with a pillow under her head and her sleek blonde hair in a long braid. She was waiting for me when I got home, mustardy pretzel ready, three shish-kebobs warming, and two boxes of tissues. I had already eaten the pretzel and used up one whole box of Kleenex before I even put my purse down. Now I'm in my favorite loose sweatpants and men's XL t-shirt and nibbling leisurely on a shish-kebob while crying my eyes out.

"Stop defending him. He accused me of getting pregnant on

purpose! Me of all people! I should've kicked him one while I had the chance." Saige cackles before sobering.

"Rory, he has no idea about your past—one-night stand, remember? From what you told me, you two didn't do much talking?" She looks at me pointedly, and I scoff, shifting my weight to prop myself onto my side. The baby rolls with me, giving me gentle kicks and nudges. "It doesn't matter that he doesn't know. He still shouldn't have said it. And to top it all off, his brother asked me if I was eight months pregnant! You don't ask a woman that, doctor or not!" I huff, and the baby kicks in solidarity. "And then Malcolm had the nerve to ask if this was some ploy to undermine Clare Architecture and Design—like what? Their last few designs were lame—why would I need to do anything to be better than them?" I snark, taking a vicious bite of street meat. Saige makes a revolted sound before continuing.

"You should have done a better job explaining to him, Rory. I told you doing it this way was a bad idea." She had. I was all for barging into his office, dropping the contract, and then hightailing it out of there. Saige thought I should have been more understanding and tried a softer approach. Maybe I would have. Perhaps I should have. But once he accused me of orchestrating our meeting, all common sense went out of the window. I grunt, a sour taste in my throat.

Up until I was in high school, I thought my parents had a perfect marriage. My dad, Roark, was a landscape engineer—he worked on big, elaborate gardens and spaces for museums, corporate offices, and public parks. He was a larger-than-life man—tall with dark auburn hair and snapping green eyes. Everyone who met him loved him—he was always the life of the party, the dad every girl wanted, a friend to all. He was the guy who shoveled your driveway after a snowstorm, who helped you bring in your groceries, would jump your car battery, and volunteered for my little league team. He was my biggest champion and told me I could do anything in life I wanted. He bought me my first Erector set and stayed up all night to help me assemble it. He was my everything. One season, we went to Yankee games almost every Saturday, and one time he caught a Derek Jeter home run ball. I still have it. And right next to him, for all his wild ways, was my Mom, Laura. She was much more reserved than my dad; organized, methodical, and shy. Dad was always so loving toward her, affectionate and attentive. One of Dad's favorite things to do was to loudly proclaim his love for her in public and watch her face turn red. My dad and I would laugh, and she would swat at us, embarrassed but pleased. Everyone wanted a marriage like my parents had.

That's why I didn't notice the cracks at first.

My dad's schedule was always erratic. He traveled a lot, and when he was at home, he had meetings at all hours. It was normal for my Mom and I to have dinner, just the two of us, leaving my dad a plate to be warmed later. We spent a lot of weekends alone, going to museums or buildings I wanted to emulate one day. So I thought nothing of it when the days between my dad being home and not started to stretch longer and longer. I was tied up in all of my teenage nonsense—boys, parties, and sleepovers. I'd joined an exclusive architecture program for high school students, so my time at home was even more brief. It wasn't until a few weeks before Christmas that I noticed I hadn't seen my dad in a while, only exchanging texts and pictures. I asked my Mom where he was working, and I will never forget the look on her face. She went utterly still, her face pale, the new dark circles under her eyes more pronounced. Her chin went hard, her head lifted, and she told me flat out that he wasn't working anywhere. He was splitting his time between us and his new apartment in town. Dad had things he needed to work out, and they both thought it was the best way to deal with it. They had planned on telling me that weekend together.

I immediately jumped on my phone to call my dad, and for the first time in my life, he didn't answer. I tried him a dozen more times, getting sent to voicemail each time. I remember staring at my phone, my brain eating up possibilities. I waited until early morning, then tracked my father to an upscale townhouse complex using our family location-sharing app. I spotted his car in the driveway and, without a thought, banged on the door. It wasn't even seven am, but I knew my father would be awake. It took a while for the door to open, and when it did, it wasn't my dad. I stared at the woman who had the smarts to look somewhat embarrassed before pushing past her and screaming my dad's name. He came bounding down the stairs, hair sticking up and wearing no shirt. To his credit, he looked devastated to see me there and made no contest when I told him in no uncertain terms to get dressed and meet me outside within two minutes. I shoved past the woman and stood right outside the door, and when he came out a few minutes later, I laid into him.

I called him every name in the book, called her even worse, and told him I never wanted to see him again. Dad said nothing, taking my anger with quiet shame, his leonine head falling back, not meeting my eyes. I don't remember much; I barely remember driving home, where my Mom was waiting for me, tears on her face. She sat me down and explained that my dad was caught in a terrible place. He had a brief affair with the woman, Mandy, and when he tried to call it off, she begged him for one more night. He gave in, and she got pregnant. My Mom and dad were convinced she did it intentionally, and Mandy never denied it. She called my Mom herself, boasting that she had won, and Mom kicked Dad out that night. Dad begged her, but Mom stayed firm despite her shattered heart. Mandy, at the same time, was threatening to terminate her pregnancy, horrifying my Irish Catholic father. He didn't know what to do and felt that he could work things out in a way for all of us, but he never got the chance.

One night, he and Mandy got into a wicked fight; he wanted to attend an award ceremony I was honored in, hoping to find his way back to our relationship, while Mandy wanted to go shopping in the city. They were on their way home when they hit some loose gravel, and their car flipped three times into a ditch. Both were killed on impact. Ironically, it was found that Mandy was never pregnant, and my Mom shut down after that. Two days after my high school graduation, she died of sudden heart failure. At her wake, all of her friends were whispering that it was really a broken heart—she'd never never gotten over losing my dad. I don't know what would have happened, but I would like to believe they would have found a way back to each other.

Maybe I should have told Malcolm all of this, but you know what? Fuck. That. He made me The OW— The Other Woman, the Mandy of my own story. I don't owe him shit.

"All I need is for him to sign the contract and let me and little

Amadeus here live our lives. I ain't gonna be no sidepiece." Saige squints at me, her head cocked to the side.

"And if he doesn't agree? And wants to be part of Wolfgang's life?" I grin at her slightly.

"He won't. You see all of that stuff about their family, Saigey. These people are like olllld money, old money. I read that both of his parent's families came over on the *Seaflower*— the Mayflower sister ship. They intermarry with other old families like shoelaces—consolidating money and power. Almost no scandals are attached to the Clare name —and he won't want to start with us. His mama is like this upper-crust boogeyman, and his daddy is ruthless. He'll want to keep this as invisible as I do, especially with his big old wedding coming up in the spring." I try to keep my voice even but fail. Saige's mouth twists in sympathy, and she clucks her tongue.

"Rory? I'm here for you, alright? I know you are hiding a whole bunch of feelings, and that's okay. When you are ready to let them out, I'll be ready. And you, me, and Theophilus will be okay, too." I crack up before dissolving into another sob. I hold my hand out, and Saige squeezes my fingers, pressing a fresh tissue into it.

❦   *8*   ❦

I KNOW WHY CAIN
KILLED ABEL

Do you know what expression I hate?

'Life goes on.'

I hate its stupid, simplistic, unburdened rudeness. I hate that it's a three-syllable shrug, a sarcastic pat on the head, a *nudge nudge* push in the back. Because unless there are terrible circumstances, of course, life goes on. It may suck, it may be challenging, it might crack your heart in two, but you will still wake up, still brush your teeth, still face the world, still live.

The days following Rory's shock drop (still having a hard time thinking of her as not Joan) are a distorted blur. I spent the night in my office, a drunken, messy shadow of myself. My phone buzzed and rang, and I thanked god for Eve, who answered everything for me, letting me stew in my misery until I could pull myself together and head back to my penthouse. I half-heartedly responded to a few emails and gave Rachel excuses and promises about some events she expected me to attend. I had no desire to mix and mingle with anyone, but I knew if I didn't throw her a bone occasionally, she would complain to my mother, and then I'd be in for the guilt fest. I managed to text Rix and ask if he could recommend a discreet lawyer, and he sent his personal, on-call, twenty-four-hours-a-day attorney, Wicker, to my house. I didn't want to use anyone associated with Clare Inc., not trusting them to leak anything to my parents or have anyone wonder why I was meeting with one to begin with. Wicker was terribly efficient, almost silent in his service. I had read the contract but needed a clearer, less emotional eye. He poured over it and declared it ironclad, holding out a pen for me to sign it, his calm brown eyes giving me no room to refuse. I can only imagine the calamities he's had to extricate my brother from, and with a lump the size of a baseball in my throat, I signed it. He whisked it away, nodding at me and disappearing like a wisp of smoke.

Over the next few days, I took several mental beats, avoiding Monty and my thoughts. I made it through several important meetings, two dinner parties, and a charity ball, smiling for the paps and giving into Rachel's demands for more public affection and devotion. It was all going well; *life went on* before it became too much, and I had Eve maneuver a few days off again. I decided to office from home, though this huge penthouse, its luxurious bones rattling in emptiness, wasn't helping. Nick Grant, my old college friend, had another proposal he wanted me to look over, and there were some lower Manhattan opportunities that I'd gotten a heads-up about. Clare Inc.'s main focus is real estate— owning, developing, and designing it. When I took over as CEO, I branched us into the future: sustainable energy, materials, and technologies. My dad was against all of it at first, but once he saw the accolades I was getting, he backed down. Now Nick has another goldmine he is inviting me into, and as I read over the prospectus, my mind drifts to Nick and his wife MacKenna— a whole spitfire of a woman with a spine of steel but the heart of an angel. They had gone through hell and back to be together and are now parents to three beautiful little boys. It's rare that I speak to him, and one of them isn't present, or his wife—who he barely lets out of his sight.

My house manager, Boone, interrupts my thoughts, his usual smirk in place. Boone never takes anything seriously, which is why he is in my employ and not my parents. Boone's family has worked for mine for years, and when he graduated from college a few years before me, my dad offered him a place at our Connecticut compound. He took it—

but anyone could see it was a bad fit. When I got my first apartment, I snatched him right up, and he's been with me ever since. His irreverence masks a keen mind and fierce loyalty. I'm not looking forward to Rachel moving in—their fights are legendary. The latest is about the staff uniforms—Rachel wants everyone in all-black fitted suits and skirts, with Boone flatly refusing to change from the jeans and polos everyone is currently sporting.

"What is it, Boone?" I roll my eyes as his smirk gets deeper.

"Your brother is here." He jabs a thumb over his shoulder, and I frown. The last thing I need is Monty here, making my guilt and sadness multiply like mold. I open my mouth to ask him to make up an excuse when an amused snort comes from behind him.

"He's probably trying to think of a way to avoid me. Forget it, kiddo." Rix's deep voice is riddled with sarcasm, and I put down my paperwork and stand up to give him a hard hug. I haven't seen him in months, our paths never crossing, though we live directly across the street from each other. He slaps me on the back a few times before folding his long body into the leather chair across from mine. "What are you doing here?"

"What, I can't check on my little brother?" He smiles, that bandit smile that has dropped a thousand panties and broken a million hearts. Rix looks exactly like his long-dead father, tall with shoulder-length honey-blonde hair that he continuously keeps in some elaborate hairstyle, wicked hazel-green eyes, and tattoos that stretch from thumb to neck. He looks like a filthy rich pirate, an escaped billionaire bad boy, which I guess is exactly what he is. Our mother has given herself a lifetime of heartburn trying to correct his behavior, giving up after he turned eighteen and came into the billions of dollars in his trust fund. I know she still tries to interfere in his life, especially since his exploits are in the tabloids every day, but Rix laughs at her—and then does worse. Today, he is wearing a snug white t-shirt- custom, I'm sure- and black slim pants and boots. His hair is parted and in two buns on top of his head-- a style that would look crazy on any other man but somehow suits him.

"You never just check on me, fool. What gives?" He gives me a crooked eye before reading the prospectus upside down, tapping it with an inked-up finger. "I want in on this. Hook me up." I nod as Boone brings a tray with an elaborate crystal bottle and a pair of antique Waterford glasses. "I just bought this distillery; tell me what you think." I take a sip and hum at the warm honey flavor. "I like it."

"Good. I'll send you a few casks," he drains his portion before setting it down and pouring another full glass. He leans back, tilting his head at me, booted foot crossed over a thick thigh, before throwing down a file I didn't see him come in with. A few pictures spill out, and I only need one glance to see the deep flame of a braid before I quickly look away. "Monty called you?" I can feel the air starting to thin.

"Of course he did. That kid hasn't been able to hold water since he was born. He hadn't left your office for two minutes before he had Val and me on a three-way. He was distraught at the thought that you would sign that contract, and Cam couldn't calm him down. Val was almost on a plane back here, you know. I had to talk them both down from the cliff. Then Wicker told me that your business was successfully concluded, so I knew you had agreed to it. You want to talk about it?" I shake my head slowly.

"What's there left to say? You know I had to go through with it. I can't think of a single way this could work out in anyone's favor—least of all, Rory and the baby. I've spun this over in my head a million times, Rix, and the only outcomes have them hurt over and over again. Not to mention Mom—this might literally send her to her grave. She's a pain in the ass, but she's still our mother. I would never get over it if I caused her to get sick again." I give him a look, and he scoffs.

"If my lifestyle hasn't killed her yet, nothing will. Malcolm, at some point, you have to live your life for yourself, not your family. I can't believe there isn't a way you can have your son if you wanted to." His handsome face is severe, a look I haven't seen for years.

"Do you remember Dorinda Pillings? Maybe not, because she is a few years younger than us. Cute little thing, really brainy. Anyway, she fell in love with a guy she met on her gap year trip to Europe. She brought him home, hearts in her eyes, all hopeful. They were broken up within a week. Dorinda's mom, our mom, and some others got together and ran that guy out of town. Devastated that poor girl. She was up and married to another man within six months. I still see her out sometimes. They've got kids and everything, but she always looks lost, like her real life is just a wish peeking over her shoulder. I will not do that to Rory. She's got the right to ask me to do what's right for the baby, and I'm going to do it."

Rix is silent, running his fingers over the rim of his glass. He pulls out one of the photos and stares at it. "She's ridiculously beautiful. Jesus. Even pregnant, she is perfection. Your son will be a killer." He flips it over and shows it to me—an action shot. She's looking down the street, about to cross it, her long hair blowing in the early spring wind. She's wearing a belted trench that hides her round belly, and I unconsciously smile at the Yankees hat perched on her head. I wonder if she is wearing Timberlands.

"You know, Mal," Rix drawls. "I might have a solution to all of this." I raise a skeptical eyebrow, knowing Rix's solutions sometimes can get a person arrested.

"How about I marry Rory— claim the baby as mine. No one will bat an eyelash at me; they're too scared of what I might do. She would have the protection of the Le Laurier family at her back, and you could visit the baby whenever you wanted— no one would think twice at you visiting your nephew. It's a win-win."

I blink slowly, a deep, black feeling welling up in my chest. "What do you know about being a husband— your zipper has its own area code, Rix. You'd want Rory to have an unfaithful spouse? She already called me every name in the book because she thinks I used her to cheat on Rachel. You would subject her to ridicule like that? She would skin you alive." I glare at him, wondering what piece of land we own that I could bury him on, one where birds could eat his remains.

He picks up another photo, this one older. Rory is in a short black dress, her hair a wild nimbus around her head. She's at some party, and even in the picture, you could see all the men enraptured by her. "You think I couldn't be faithful to a woman like this? She would have to kick me out of her bed—I'd chain myself to it if she let me. Shit, we'd probably wind up with a barn full of kids. That's what is called a lifetime fuck, little brother." He grins at me, and it takes everything in me not to take the chain around his neck and strangle him with it.

"Get out. Now." I stand up, my fists two bricks at my sides. Rix still has that stupid smile on his face, not even flinching at the anger that is radiating off of me. Boone comes out of nowhere, snatching up the glasses and bottle, quickly whisking them away, probably worried about a mismatched set once I throw them at Hendrix. He comes back and waits— his face a mix of worry and excitement.

"Just think about it, Mal. I'd be happy to take one for the team." He strolls out of the room, saluting Boone, and I can barely stop myself from running and tackling him from behind. I stand there for a long minute, letting my breath come down from its frantic pace. Boone is still standing there, and I open my eyes to see him biting back laughter.

"I don't want him back in here, understand?"

"He has a key," Boone shoots back, and I growl. All of my siblings and I share keys, just not our parents, if that tells you anything.

"Get it deactivated. Immediately."

THE NEXT DAY, I PICK UP THE PAPER AND SEE RIX ON THE FRONT page—a salacious photo of him at a private club with his arm around a young blonde, wearing only a pair of panties on her voluptuous body. The panties have some writing on the ass, and I can barely hold back my laugh as I read them.

"Daddy's Dinner."

❧ 9 ❦

WHEN YOU HATE THIS SONG,
AND IT'S ON REPEAT

You know when you start dating someone new and suddenly see their car everywhere? Like, how many times in your life did you pass a red Ford Focus and never notice, and then poof! There's one at the grocery store, at the doctor's office, at the airport, on the TV show you are currently binging. It gives you a secret squishy feeling, like your connection to this lovebug is surrounding you. Until you break up and then slowly stop noticing. Once in a while, you come upon one and roll your eyes at the thought of an old flame.

I've lived in New York, hell, the United States, my whole life. While Clare Design & A has always been in my consciousness, and later, as a known competitor, I never once saw pictures of Malcolm or his family. I've never liked gossip, especially with my family's drama, so Page Whatever and the Whomever Blog were never on my radar.

Now I see these fools everywhere.

The day after my lawyer called me (and I had a breakdown ten minutes before a client meeting, which I blamed on the baby,) I had a doctor's appointment, and there was a newspaper in the waiting room and wouldn't you know it? Malcom and his fiancee were on the front page at a charity ball for—get this—orphaned children. The angel on my shoulder, the one that helps keep me from acting like a hormonal mess in public, urged me to put it down and not read any of the drivel in the article. But the other half, the little demon perched in my ear, told me to have myself a good ol' hate read. So I did. It was only about three paragraphs, but one hundred percent gushing bullshit about how long they've been in love, the guest list for their upcoming wedding, and what designers they were wearing. There were two smaller pictures beneath it, and both were shots of them kissing and slobbering on each other. I threw it down, jumping up when the nurse called my name.

On the walk home, I passed a newsstand and thought about grabbing a trade magazine, except the whole thing was covered in that damn Most In The City issue, including a full-size poster of just Malcolm's face. I screech and stomp the rest of the way home, not even paying attention to my favorite hotdog man, Joe, who greets me, nor the poké place I sometimes visit late at night. I grumble until I get to my building and see a new scaffold on the corner. Wouldn't you know it? The damn construction company is Clare Construction and Demolition. I scream out loud, rushing past the doorman and throwing myself (sideways) on my bed.

It doesn't stop any time soon.

This damn family surrounds me. I'm sure it's probably just that pesky phenomenon creeping up to get me, but now that I know—it's relentless. The Schillings invited me to a press event for the new restaurant, and though people were congratulating me, almost all of them brought up Malcolm's family firm. I left the party annoyed as all got out and passed a billboard with Malcolm's face on it again. Saige told me to get used to it—I'd probably spend the rest of my life with them over my shoulder. I threw a cup against the wall and grumbled the whole time I was cleaning it up. She said nothing, handing me the dustpan and rubbing my back when I cried. When I thought that 'Dev' was the baby's father, I went through a million emotions—most of them tied up in fear about raising a baby by myself, fear of knowing nothing about his father or his family history, and sadness and longing for a man I knew a few short hours. Now the feeling is jumbled, anger being the top one— at myself for believing a man who looked like he did wouldn't be taken and at him for lying to me. I forced myself not to do too much googling, but the little I caved into showed me I made the right decision. Though they were a successful, powerful family, they didn't seem to be...right. Sure, Montgomery seemed nice, and his husband was cool, but there was something off about the whole clan. There was apparently a younger sister who spent all of her time overseas, and the few pictures of them all together looked like one of those Victorian daguerreotypes where no one was smiling, and it kinda looks like a funeral.

I show them to Saige one morning, who shudders while reminding me about the nanny interviews I have later in the afternoon. I groan and spin in my chair, facing the Escher lithograph on the wall. The nanny interviews have not been going well at all.

"Girl, you are due in two months; we need to make some decisions here," Saige scolds me, plopping down a thick stack of CVs with photos and resumes attached. One of my clients recommended an agency; while they have been great, the prospects were not. Almost all of them were either too old or too young, too experienced and judgy as fuck, or no experience at all but excellent educations. I had one that I liked, and she turned me down for another opportunity. Apparently, even the nanny world had social climbers, and I didn't fit the bill.

"I just want a nice lady who isn't going to give me the stink eye for being a single mom and who will be good to my baby. I didn't think it would be this hard." I sigh deeply, missing my Mom for the thousandth time.

"We will find someone, don't worry. Now, there are some rumblings going on that Chanteuse Cosmetics is looking to move its world headquarters to NYC and will be accepting design bids. Let's throw our hat in the ring." She stands up, proud as punch as I squeal and do a dance in my seat. "How the hell did you hear about that?"

Chanteuse Cosmetics is just one of the many arms of *Chanteuse FTA—Fashion, Technology, and Automotive*. They are the biggest and best at everything, with their global headquarters a stunning Brutalist-style campus in the heart of Paris. They have a few satellite offices in the States, but a whole building? My design senses are tingling, big time.

"Well, remember that date I had the other night? The Moaner?" I snort and crack up, nodding. Saige called me from the bathroom of an expensive wine bar, whispering that the guy, Pierre, was doing this weird hum/moan thing with every sip he took. It was driving her up the wall, and even the people around them were starting to notice. She kept me on speaker when she returned to their table, and sure enough, I could hear him making an odd noise that came from his chest and ended with a little gurgle. Thankfully, she put me on mute because I was howling like a stray dog. I spent the next two days making the noise at her until she threatened to cut off my hotdog supply.

"Anyway, it turns out he's a lawyer for Chanteuse and was in town to look at some real estate contracts. He went back to France but said that he would see me in the new year because he's back for the relocation." She waggles her eyebrows, and I give her a fist bump.

"Machiavelli will be born by then. I need to knuckle down on the nanny thing now." I pick up the thick stack and start sorting through them, separating the ones that look mean from the ones who are at least smiling. "Let's get to work."

ॐ

"I cannot believe this. Not one of them was good, Saigey. Not. One. How is that possible? Am I being too picky? I am, right? Tell me the truth." I'm laid out on the couch again, this time surrounded by the discarded resumes. The last applicant just left; honestly, that interview only took ten minutes. The woman was perfect on paper, and even her picture was nice. But while her face lit up when I told her I was the CEO, she was visibly disappointed in my address and my lack of a husband. She also expressed her expectation of an ensuite for herself, and I had to let her know that while she would have a small bedroom of her own, the only two bathrooms were attached to my bedroom or the nursery. She shook her head the entire time I was speaking, and Saige could see my pregnant temper spiking, cutting off the interview and escorting her out.

"You're not being too picky, honey. This is someone who will be a big part of your life, and you have every right to want to like and trust that person. For what it's worth, I didn't like any of them either." One of the women spent her whole interview asking Saige where she got her hair done, how much her shoes were, what dating apps she was on, etc. Another told us she was only interested in newborns, yet another was in school full-time during the day.

"I just..." We are interrupted by a knock on the door, and I frown at Saige, who peeks out. "Can I help you?"

"Yes, I am here about the nanny position. I'm sorry it's so late, but the agency told me if I rushed over, I could possibly catch you. My name is Julian Akira. Here is my resume." I'm practically falling off the couch to get a look at the owner of that deep voice, Saige blocking my view. I only see a clean pair of loafers tucked under dark-wash jeans. She moves out of the way, and I'm caught half-off on and half-off, my arm holding me up from the floor. The voice chuckles, and strong arms gently lift me into a sitting position. I brush my hair out of my face, and a pair of twinkling brown eyes meets mine. "Sorry about that," I smile at his handsome face, taking in the deep dimples and short messy brown hair.

"You're a nanny?" I blurt out, hoping my incredulous tone doesn't offend him. It doesn't. In fact, that broad smile gets bigger if possible. "Sorry."

"Yes, I am. And don't be sorry; I am quite used to the reaction." He sits next to me, crossing one foot over a knee. I know I am staring at him, but I can't help it. I peek at Saige, who is in the same boat, her fingers with a death grip around his resume. "And the accent? British?"

"My mum is Irish, but I was raised in Bristol. Your name, Miller-Jones—Irish as well?" I nod, smiling.

"Well," he looks at both of us. "As you can see by my CV, I have a degree in Childhood Youth Studies and Psychology. I have nannied for three families, though just one here in the States. I'm also fluent in French and German." He lowers his head slowly, as if prompting me to ask questions, and I sit up, blinking out of my trance.

"Um, why nannying? Why not teaching or something else?" I glance at Saige, who still hasn't recovered, and she gives me a thumbs up. Good question.

"I like the one-on-one aspect as opposed to the temporary. I am the oldest of eight, so I've always had little ones around. My mum has always called me the baby whisperer; I love them all. Tell me, Ms Miller-Jones, is this a live-in position? I have a flat that I love."

"Please call me Rory. Well, in the beginning, it will be days, maybe a few overnights, and maybe a weekend day. This is my first baby, and I don't know what my life will look like since it's just me. I don't know anything about babies—Saige and I are taking classes at Hunter. I only have a small bedroom, and you'd have to share a bathroom with Pendothesium, but you should have lots of time for yourself." I shrug, hoping it doesn't sound too chaotic.

"Pendothesium?" He laughs and raises a brow. I shrug and smile. "I don't have a name picked out yet, and since I am an architect, we figure little man will need something kinda dramatic." He laughs again, and I ask him more questions, Saige piping in, too. He still has a few more weeks left on his current contract which dovetails perfectly with my due date. After about an hour, I realize how late it is, and I push my self to standing, Julian leaping up to help.

"Since I'm not due for eight more weeks, that should give you plenty of time to finish up and then move some stuff over. I'd really like you to work with me, Julian." I shake his hand, and he gives me that gorgeous smile, nodding happily.

"I'd love to Miss Rory. You have my references, yes? Let me know what else you may need. I can also provide a criminal background check, credit report, and health report as well." Saige murmurs and walks him to the creaky elevator as I gather my stuff. I feel as if a twenty-ton boulder has been lifted off my back.

"Rory, I cannot believe that hottie is going to be your nanny! Oh emm geeeee! He's got to be at least six foot three. And that voice! Do you think if I dressed up as a baby, he would sing me a lullaby in French?" I throw her purse at her, laughing.

"Saige, keep your horny mitts off of my nanny," I warn her playful-ly. "Now let's go. I want to catch the last few innings of the Yankees game."

"Maybe we can play "Maid In The Scullery? Or Highwayman and Helpless Countess? Henry the Eighth? Oh wait, he was chopping off heads..."

"Saige!"

10

KILL 'EM WITH KINDNESS...OH WAIT, YOU CAN'T

"Dahling, you're not ready yet?!"

I look up from the contract I was fine-combing and see Rachel dressed to kill in the doorway. Eve was long gone, and I glanced at my antique desk clock, seeing it was past seven o'clock.

"What are you talking about, Rachel? There is nothing on my calendar for tonight." I pushed a few buttons, and sure enough, I was clear from six till morning.

"Impossible! I know I told that awful assistant of yours that there was a reception tonight I wanted us to go to." She pulls out her phone, flipping through her messages, a spiky heel tapping the floor in annoyance. She is wearing a scandalously short white dress, long-sleeved and high-necked, but totally backless. The thigh-length white ermine coat draped across her shoulders, though with spring finally here, is overkill. Her deep brown hair is straight and slick, her center part sharp, the ends perfectly aligned. I roll my eyes at the get-up, knowing she has been wearing different shades of white and cream everywhere, reminding the city that she is 'a bride to be.' She's spent a large fortune on European designer pieces, which my parents insisted I pay for as part of her trousseau. I handed her a black wedding credit card and was shocked it hadn't caught on fire yet. She has spent well into seven figures, and when I dared to bring it up—you guessed it, she complained to my mother. In revenge, she purchased herself a large ten-carat ruby ring, justifying it by saying she could pass it down to our oldest daughter. "Though I hope I only have sons," she told my parents with a smile, pissing off Valentina, who has spent a lifetime feeling like an afterthought.

"I don't know why you are looking at your messages. You know Eve won't allow you to text her," I drawl, still looking at the papers before me. Rachel tried that with Eve a few years ago, and Eve slapped a resignation letter on my desk within the hour. I had to ease her down, promised that she would never have to be subjected to my future wife's demands, and tossed a bunch of money at her. Rachel threw a fit, wanting to insinuate herself into every aspect of my life, but I drew a hard line at Clare Inc. As my wife, she will have no inroads to the company, and even my will states as such. If I die with no heirs, control goes to Montgomery and his son or, lastly, to Valentina's oldest son. If none of us have sons, it goes to the closest male cousin. Primogeniture at its finest, I guess.

"Well, I still think I should. That twit still has me make an appointment to see you and won't interrupt you when I ask her to. I'm going to be your wife, A Clare. I come first." She drapes herself haughtily into a chair, crossing her legs, her dress riding up indecently. I give her the requisite once over, knowing she expects me to drool over the display. Rachel is a stunning woman, commanding most rooms she walks into. She can have any man she wants, really, but once her parents told her she would be Rachel Van Pyke-Clare, no one else would do. She never had any other plans, and though I know she has had other lovers in the past, she has never been seen with anyone publically except me. I sometimes wonder what those men thought of her, if they enjoyed her more than I do because, for all of her hot looks, she's cooly aloof in bed. She doesn't seem to respond to much, hating the mess, the intimacy.

"You don't come first here, Rachel. We have discussed that. And maybe if you weren't such a bitch to Eve, she would be more amendable to communicating with you," I snark at her, and she scoffs with a wave of her perfectly manicured hand. "She's the help, Malcolm. If you'd stop treating her like a friend, like a confidant, then she would do what she was told." I sigh and throw down my pen, rubbing my eyes and scratching my cheeks. I need a shave.

"Speaking of help, I called Boone today and asked him when the staff at the house would be getting fit for their new uniforms. He started making noises, told me we had a bad connection and hung up on me. I'm not budging on this, Malcolm. It's important that the staff is invisible; right now, the guests would get distracted by the casual mess they are wearing. It's so low class." I hide my smile and cough lightly to mask my laughter.

"We need to set an example, Malcolm. I'm serious about this."

I think it's more about Rachel wanting to impose her will and belittle people, but I don't say that. "Rachel, Boone is busy managing a twenty-three thousand-square-foot house. I trust him to make all the personnel decisions, including attire. And you know, as I do, when we have guests, the staff wears formal outfits. I wish you would drop this." I give her a stern eye, making her slim nose touch even higher air.

"Well, I've spoken to Mother Clare about it, and she agrees. She's given me the contact for her staff's uniforms. I'll leave it to you to pass it to Boone." She flicks her nails at me, and I roll my eyes again at her use of "Mother Clare." I think my mother has been Rachel's idol since birth. She tries to ape everything my mom does, down to the toothpaste, I bet. In her mind, my mother is the perfect example of how a Clare woman should act and be treated. And, of course, Mom eats it up, treating Rachel better than she treats her own daughter. I can feel that tightening in my chest again, and I try to shake it off.

"Speaking of the house, I'm hiring an interior designer. I simply must have a bigger closest, and I think we need to knock down a few walls. If we start now, I can have the furniture shipped from Italy before the wedding." Her face is lodged into her phone, so she doesn't notice the anger creeping across mine.

"We are not knocking down any walls, Rachel. And we don't need a designer. The penthouse was completely turned out a year ago. The closet in your room is huge, four thousand square feet, if I remember correctly. That is bigger than most apartments. You will need to find a way to make it work." I stand up to pour myself a drink, knowing she would somehow make this an issue.

"But Malcolm, Mother Clare thinks it would be a good entré for my new position. I've already approached a few magazines about a feature. It's so avant-garde for married couples to have their own suites, and we would set a trend." I think it's stupid and bad for a new marriage, but what do I know.

"I don't care. New furniture is fine, but no construction, and that's final." She glares at me, those deep brown eyes promising all kinds of hell, but then her face smooths and she smiles. "Of course, dahling. I'm sure we can meet somewhere in the middle. Now, can you finish up so that we can go? All of my friends are waiting." I watch warily as she approaches me, hips swaying, a demon in angelic white. She reaches up and wraps her arms around my neck, and I stay still, hands at my sides. She leans forward, pressing her cool, glossy lips to my cheek. Her breath smells sweet with a hint of wine. She's not wearing a bra, her perky tits rubbing my chest. "We both know you are going to give me what I want. You don't want to upset your mother, now, do you?"

And there it is.

Rachel is many things (all terrible), but the one thing she isn't is stupid. She knows that my concern about my mother's health and making her happy is holding this engagement together. On the surface, she shows the world her gracious forgiveness, a clever 'what can you do' shrug when asked about my sudden departure last year, adoring glances, and sweet kisses when cameras are present. Whispers in the ears of New York's biggest gossips about how much I am spoiling her, how contrite I am. The whole city believes it, a collective sigh whenever we are out in public, the epitome of true love prevailing.

All bullshit.

Behind the scenes, in real life, Rachel could care less about what I think. She is still blindingly furious that I embarrassed her—it was bad enough that I kept pushing things off, but then to outright cancel it and leave her behind to pick up the pieces is more than she can forgive. My mother's illness couldn't have been better timed. Now, she has me where she wants me, and she will use it against me until the day I die. She will push and push, seeing how far she can force me to the edge until I give in. She only wants what I represent: money, power, and absolute privilege. Being my wife will elevate her above every other woman in the city— the only thing she has ever wanted. And once she has a son, an heir for the Clare name, she will be untouchable.

"Don't threaten me, Rachel. My appetite is big, but even I get full." I look her dead in the eye, and she pouts, unwrapping her arms from my neck and prancing to her coat.

"You're so serious, Malcolm. Maybe you need to lighten up a little —take a joke sometimes. Can we go?" She cocks her head to the side, that crocodile smile pinned to her mouth. I make a mental note to warn Boone. Rachel would think nothing of going around me and having whatever she wants done started. Boone would probably relish fighting her off.

I grab my trench, switch off my office light, and meet her at the elevator. "Where are we going?" I want nothing more than to go home and bury myself in work, maybe a drink or four, and watch the Yankees — my new nightly normal.

"There is a fab new bar that a friend just opened, and tonight is VIP only. Everyone is going to be there," she boasts, pulling out a compact and fixing imaginary smudges. I stare at her, and my mind drifts, changing her hair to a deep auburn and her brown eyes to soft silver. I shake my head and squeeze my eyes tightly. Going out may be a good thing.

"Malcolm?" I open them and see Rachel waiting, her confused expression mixing with the impatient tap of her fingernails on the button.

"Yeah," I tell her, "I'm coming."

11

THIS IS WORSE THAN I EXPECTED

"Zero out of ten, would not recommend," I spit out as another contraction rolls through me, rippling my stomach and sending the fetal monitor into overdrive. The pain makes me grit my teeth, and even though Saige is trying to coach me with breathing this and that, it isn't helping. I should have taken that fucking epidural, but one look at how big the needle was, and I changed my mind. Now I'm trying not to scream the hospital down and flying through ice chips.

"The doctor says you are doing great," Saige says, and I growl. I don't want to hear it. I want to eat, nap, push this baby out, nap, and scream-- in no particular order. Another contraction hits, and I squint, bending over at the waist and trying to pant as instructed. The pain is singular, like something I've had before but times two thousand. The agony eases down, and my breathing goes back to normal. "Has Julian texted?" My new nanny started a few days ago, moving in with three suitcases and a lavender plant for the baby's room. He quickly toured the nursery, checking that the crib was secure and taking a quick inventory, making a list of things he wanted to stock up on. The first few weeks, Horatio would be sleeping in a bassinet in my room, and he checked that, too. He also ordered groceries and got my apartment professionally cleaned. So far, he has been a godsend, and if I hadn't had him sign a two-year contract, I would be terrified I would lose him.

"Yup. He will meet us with the car seat once you are released. I can't believe he's got a car in the city, but apparently, it was a gift from one of the families he used to work for." She's reading a magazine, looking like a million bucks, in a soft blue ALO sweatsuit, thick socks, furry slides, and messy topknot. As my best friend, you'd think she'd have the decency to join me on the hellfire mess express. But noooooo. She's got to sit there, model-like and clean. Not even a bead of sweat on her face.

I'd been feeling wonky all day, kind of tired, kind of wired. I couldn't get comfortable standing up and pacing during our weekly staff meeting, wanting to walk but also wanting to lie down. I'd had an ongoing backache for two days that was making me miserable, and I tried every yoga stretch I could. I decided to go home early and managed to fall asleep before waking up to the worst pain of my life. I immediately called Saige, who suspected my discomfort, and she called Julian, who was out shopping. She told me to hold tight and got to my building within fifteen minutes, telling the rideshare driver her nephew was on the way. My contractions were a decent time apart, but as soon as we got to the maternity floor, my water broke, and they sped up. That was eight hours ago, and let me tell you, I am DONE.

"Can you pass me my ice chips?" My mouth is dry from all the panting, and Saige looks at the large cup and shows me the bottom.

"You're all out. I'll go get you some more." I nod, but a contraction rips at me, and I suck in my breath as it tightens everything I've got. I lay back when it ends, and Saig checks her watch, eyes wide. "Uhhhh, that was less than two minutes apart. I'm gonna find your doctor." She runs out of the room, and I close my eyes, knowing another wave is imminent. I counted the seconds, and sure enough, another lightning strike hit me. I suck in all the oxygen and hold it, squeezing my eyes tight, though I'm not supposed to.

Suddenly, a pair of sure hands gently turns me on my side, pressing something large and hard into my lower back. The pain eases, and I can breathe again. "Better?" My eyes fly open as I recognize the voice.

"Montgomery?" I peek over my shoulder and see his handsome face smiling at me.

"Yup. I saw your name on the board and thought I'd come in. I hope you don't mind," he says nervously. "Hold on, you're going to go again." He speaks to me soothingly and coaches my breathing, and for once, I listen. "Pretty close together, hmm? Where is Dr. Kenneth?" He looks at the tape from my monitor with a practiced eye. I stare at him, marveling over his similarities with Malcolm—they look alike but don't.

"Saige went to find him, I...oh." He quickly comes back to me, pushing his fist into my lower back. "Ummmm, I think I need to push. I feel weird." He rolls me on my back just as Saige and Dr. Kenneth come back.

"Monty! What are you doing here?" Two nurses come in as Dr. Kenneth sits on a stool, and my legs are propped up.

"Rory and I are friends. You don't mind if I stick around, do you?" He asks me, and I shake my head.

"Look at that head of hair! Rory, my girl, you are fully crowned. When I tell you to, I want you to bear down and count to ten, okay? Here we go, push!" I push with all my might, hearing Monty and Saige count out loud for me. As the doctor does some stuff, I sit back, Saige wiping my face with a cool cloth and Monty holding my leg. I briefly think about the fact that another member of the Clare family is getting a really good look at my vagina, but the pain forces the thought away.

"Excellent. This boy wants to be born. Let's do that again, alright? One two three, push!" I bear down again, feeling something moving. I continue pushing for long minutes, everyone encouraging me, but I'm tapped out.

"I don't wanna do this anymore. Can I switch with someone?" I say tiredly. Everyone chuckles, and Dr Kenneth pats my leg. "One more, my girl. He's almost here." I nod, exhausted, but bear down and feel a giant relief as a loud cry fills the room. I smile big as Dr. Kenneth lays him on my stomach, his cries stopping immediately. I put my hands on his back and shush him, crying and laughing.

"Who's cutting the cord? Miss Saige?" Saige's face turns green, and

I laugh harder. She's already looking at the goo covering the baby and trying not to gag.

"I'd like to," Montgomery says, and I see tears in his eyes. I nod, and he takes over for Dr. Kenneth. He smiles big and steps back next me.

"That's a big boy. Let's get him checked out, shall we?" One of the nurses picks him up, and he immediately starts fussing, pissed that he's being disturbed. Montgomery follows them, and Saige steps into my view, both of us ignoring whatever Dr. Kenneth is doing down there.

"You did it, girl. I'm so proud of you. You're a mama now," she kisses my forehead, rubbing my nose with hers. "You okay with the whole Dr. Clare thing?" She whispers while glancing over her shoulder. Montgomery is watching the nurses with a gigantic smile on his face.

"I mean, I guess? He seemed so sad; I couldn't exactly say no, without looking like a giant bitch. It's not like he's going to be around —this is probably the only time he's going to see him," I whisper back. I elbow her when I see Montgomery returning with a swaddled-up burrito in his arms.

"Here you go, Mama. An absolutely gorgeous boy. Prettiest baby I've ever seen." He hands me the chunk of kid, and I get my first look at his face, bursting into tears immediately. He really is beautiful. He's got a head full of dark hair with auburn highlights, chubby cheeks, and a tiny cleft in his chin. His eyes are still closed, little plump pink lips making tiny sucking movements. I pull down the blanket a little and see rolls on rolls. Later, I will unwrap him and get a good look.

"Ten pounds, eleven ounces. Perfect Apgar score, too," Dr. Clare says with pride.

"Rory, you gave birth to an eleven-pound baby? Oh god, your poor vag..." Saige blurts out, cracking me and everyone else up. "Ohhhh, he's amazing," Saige sniffles, stroking the back of her finger down his cheek. "I knew he was going to be." She cries some more, and Dr. Kenneth hands her a tissue, a besotted look on his face for her again. I roll my eyes, patting the padded booty in my arms.

"Pictures?" Montgomery holds up my phone, and I nod, adjusting the baby so his little face is visible. He snaps a few of us alone, getting some close-ups of both of us, telling Saige to join us, and even some with Dr. Kenneth and the nurses. Saige carefully takes the baby as I'm helped to my feet to get cleaned up. The nurses are quick and efficient, and I'm back in bed within a few minutes. Saige sits in the chair beside the bed, murmuring stuff and rocking the kid. Montgomery's pager goes off, and he leans over Saige's shoulder for a final look before promising to stop by later.

"Have we got a name?" The nurse is back with a clipboard, and I nod, looking at the new human I am responsible for. I feel such an overwhelming rush of love, of contentment. I smile.

"Meet Roman Stassi Miller-Jones. Roman for me and my dad, and Stassi for my mom." I tear up again, missing my parents. I hate that they are not here, that they are missing out on my son.

"Roman Miller-Jones. I love it, Rory." Saige leans in, kissing his button nose. "I'm your Auntie Saige, Ro. We are going to get into such trouble together; you just wait."

12

SHOULD'VE, COULD'VE, WOULD'VE

I'm surrounded by the scent of heather and roses mixed with Bubbalicious strawberry gum and a hint of silk.

Valentina.

I squeeze her harder, though her skinny little arms are already choking the life out of me. Monty and Cameron had invited me over for dinner, and I tried to beg off but then felt guilty. I hadn't seen Monty in weeks, unconsciously avoiding him and keeping Cam at a distance. I'd buried myself in work and late nights with Rachel, throwing myself into my future life like a man desperate for parole. I finally answered one of his many texts, feeling like shit because I realized late that he hadn't even stopped by my office like he usually did. I accepted the invite, chuckling at the admonishment to not bring Rachel with me. I had Eve deliver some wine and desserts to the office and took them with me, preparing to grovel at my brother's feet. Monty and Cam live in a fantastic building in the upper fifties, deliberating not owned by Clare Inc. My parents were livid but had no say, especially since Monty is independently wealthy, even without his trust fund. I knocked on the door, and it flew open, and I was tackled almost to the ground. The wine and dessert tumbled, and I laughed as she rained kisses all over my face.

"Squirt! When did you get in?" I lift her off her feet and take her into the apartment, closing the door behind me. I pull back and stare at her beautiful face, pinching her dimpled chin and grinning.

"Yesterday. I came here first because if I went to my apartment, Mother and Father would have known within ten minutes." She links arms with me, pulling me to the overstuffed sofa and plopping me down. Cam comes out with the wine bottles, leaning down for a hug, and Monty brings the glasses, winking at me.

"So they have no idea you are back in the States?" I take a sip of the dry Rijoa, leaning back and relaxing. Cam and Monty's place is big but feels like a small, intimate home. Everything is done in warm beiges with teal accents, lots of thick carpets, and floor pillows everywhere. The lighting is warm, and Cam's green thumb is everywhere in vases of flowers and bright green plants. I've always loved it here, though I don't visit as much as I should.

"Nope. I'll tell them in a few days, though it won't mean much. I've heard that Mom and Rachel are fully up each other's asses, so I should be able to get out of being the prodigal daughter for a little while longer." I snort, taking another sip.

"It's true. I've been fighting the two of them for weeks over the most trivial bullshit. If one doesn't get her way, then the other is calling. And god forbid they are together. It's exhausting. I just want some fucking peace, you know?" I stop realizing that all three are looking at me with different degrees of pity. I don't need it. I'm a grown man, and I've got to live with my decisions.

"You look beautiful, kid. That tan agrees with you." I tweak her nose, taking in her blue eyes—exactly like mine— and her dark hair in a loose braided crown. She's dressed comfortably in black sweatpants and a patterned homemade shirt that unbuttons to show off layers of thin gold chains. As always, she's a knockout.

"You always say that because we look so much alike," she laughs. I shrug with a smile, partly because it's true. Val and I take after our Clare grandfather, Cyrus, who died when I was a teen. Montgomery looks more like Mom's Deaveraux relatives.

"A party without me, this won't do," I hear uttered laughingly and see Rix stroll into the room, double-fisting bottles of whisky. Val squeals, jumping up to greet him, and I sit up, trying not to snarl. I still haven't forgotten our last conversation, but I can secretly admit that it's good to have all my siblings in one place. I can't remember the last time it was just us without the trappings of our parent's web and expectations. Rix sits across from me, smirking at my obvious discomfort. I laugh silently, thinking that he and Val have the same hairstyle, which makes my shoulders come down from my ears. I feel like a cat who's back is arched at an enemy.

We polished off the wine I brought and one of the bottles of Rix's whiskey. Cam had ordered pizza, and now we are all sprawled out in the living room, in different levels of drunk, except for Cam, who always plays Sober Solider. He's laughing at the four of us, listening to us fight over old arguments and pranks Rix denies playing on us.

"You totally did! I thought Mom was going to kill you! She had to have a hairdresser come out and get that green out of my hair before the dance," Val screeches. I vaguely remember the incident as I was in college, but I do remember my mother's fury that Valentina woke up with bright green streaks in her raven hair, with no idea how they got there. She went about her day with them until about an hour before her debutante debut. Mom gave Valentina hell for it, but we all knew it was Rix, who was well into his twenties by then.

"I can neither confirm nor deny those rumors," he grins. He was always doing shit like that, and it was my mother's biggest cross to bear that she never caught him. My dad never really interfered with Rix's upbringing, but even he got a kick out of his wife's frustration.

"Well, all I can say is that I can't wait until you guys have kids of your own. It'll be payback time." The room falls silent, all the goodwill and happiness swirling down the drain of unspokenness. It takes Val a minute to realize what she said, and when she does, tears immediately fill her blue eyes.

"Oh Malcolm, I'm so sorry," she sobs, her hands over her mouth. She stands up, looking for an escape like she always does when in trouble.

"It's okay, Val. I know you didn't mean anything by it." I try to soothe her, which just makes her cry harder. Cam takes her by the hand and leads her to the kitchen, where we can still hear her cries. I feel like shit, even though I didn't do anything.

The room stays silent, and I say nothing to break it, just watching the golden brown liquid swirl in my glass. I can feel Monty twitching, barely able to keep himself still. I sigh and look at Rix who is watching me.

"She had the baby, you know," Monty blurts out. His eyes widen, and I put down the glass, dropping my head between my shoulders. My heart twists, and I take a shallow breath. "Monty..."

"No, Malcolm. I'm going to talk about it. I was on duty that night and saw her name on the board. I went in just before the baby came, and I was there when he took his first breath. I even cut the cord. He's so beautiful, Malcolm. Chubby with dark hair and blue eyes. It should've been you there, Mal. Not me." He holds out his phone, and I stare at him, not wanting to see the pictures but also unable to look away. I slowly take the phone and stare at the photo of the chunky monkey baby with my chin and his mama's lips. I flip through a few of the others, all different angles, one of him with no blanket, showing off his pudgy arms and little toes. There are some with the baby and a very attractive blonde, and a ton of him with Rory. Her face is shiny, her hair a mess, but she is as bright as the sun, holding tight to the bundled baby, a smile as blinding as a star stretched across her face.

"His name is Roman. Roman Stassi Miller-Jones. Stassi was her mom's maiden name. Um, I don't know if you know this, but both of her parents are gone. Died back when she was in high school." I *didn't* know that, which makes the pain worse. Does she have no one? What else don't I know?

"Is that her sister?" I tilt the phone, thinking that they looked nothing alike. The blonde had a much deeper tone to her creamy skin. She's gorgeous on second glance.

"No. It's her best friend, Saige. They met in college and have been together since. Saige works for her at Miller-Jones." I nod absently. "No siblings?"

"She's an orphan, Malcolm," Rix interjects. I look at him, barely able to tear my eyes off of the photos. "You've seen these?" He nods slowly, and I frown. The last photo is of Roman, all swaddled in a navy blue Yankees blanket, a knit hat on his head. "How long ago was this?" I tap the top of the photo and see the date. Four weeks. My son is already one month old. I wonder how much he's changed, if he's healthy, and if Rory is doing okay. "He's beautiful."

"Looks just like you except for that mouth. Got that from his mama. If you look closely, hair's got some red in it." Rix leans forward and taps the screen over to another photo. He's right. I feel the tightening again, the fist of shame and longing. I yank at the collar of my shirt, though it'd been unbuttoned hours ago. I suddenly need air, and I need to be alone. My lungs feel like leaden bricks.

"I'm going to go. I'll talk to you both tomorrow," I stand up, tapping the phone for my driver.

"Malcolm, don't leave.."

"It's alright, Monty. I need to go," I grab my jacket and stride out the door. I don't bother saying goodbye to Val, knowing this would send her into a fresh round of sobs. The elevator is taking too long, so I take the stairs, not noticing that it's twenty flights. I hurry down as if ghosts are chasing me, finally breaking out of the stairwell and into the lobby. My driver is outside, and I jump in the backseat.

"Home, please." I close my eyes and rub them violently with the heel of my hands, hoping to leave the burn of tears behind.

Roman. Monty was right. It should've been me.

13

THE CONSPIRATORS—
MONTGOMERY

"Where's Malcolm?" Val and Cam come out of the kitchen, Val with her hands wrapped around a cup of tea. Chamomile, I'd bet. It's Cameron's go-to therapy. Whenever I have a bad day or am plain worn out, he will greet me at the door with a steaming mug, usually with a slice of coffee cake.

"He left. Dr. Clare here showed him the pictures, and he turned about six shades of white and ran out of here," Rix points the finger at me, and I glare at him.

"We both decided it was time, you ass. Don't try to pin this on me." I throw a pillow at his smirking face. He picks it up and smacks it against my leg, kicking me at the same time.

"What pictures?" Valentina asks, ignoring our antics. Being the only girl and the baby at that, with three boys above her, has made her immune to our usual violence. I sigh and look at Cam, who shrugs. Val has been very emotional about this whole thing, vacillating between sorrow and pure anger. She has hated Rachel forever and will never forgive our parents for forcing this marriage on Malcolm, regardless of his noble (and idiotic) motivations. I hand her the phone, which had already been opened in the photo folder. She blinks as she looks at the picture pulled up, taking only seconds to recognize who she is looking at. The tears Cameron managed to chase away come running back, automatically streaming down her pretty face. She sinks onto the chair next to Hendrix, spending time on each picture. She pauses on one of Rory holding Roman, a light-filled smile on her face.

"He might be the most perfect baby I have ever seen. Monty, you see babies every day. He's the best one, right?"

"All babies are beautiful, Val," I tell her, though some doctors will tell you that is debatable. I've had some colleagues rate the babies they deliver, but I've always thought each one is an angel. Even though my nephew is the best-looking angel of them all. Val makes a rude noise with a hand gesture.

"This kid is gorgeous. Did you get a chance to hold him?" I sit down and tell her about Roman's coming out party and how gracious Rory was, allowing me to not only cut the cord but to spend time slobbering on the baby, even changing his diaper and feeding him. She could've told me to take a hike, especially since the contract Malcolm signed stipulated that no family members should have contact. Rory never once brought it up, and for that, she has my heart forever. I tell her about Malcolm's reaction, his frozen heartbreak so plain to see.

Valentina is silent for a moment. She's idly flipping through the photos, a determined look on her face. "Guys, we have to do something. I don't think I'll be able to stay away from Roman. I already love him so much." She hands me back my phone, standing up and pacing, her hands gesturing wildly, wisps of raven hair coming loose and flying about her face.

"Start spitting out ideas. There is enough brainpower in this room to solve world peace. Let's go." She claps her hands, a deadly serious expression on her face.

"Well, I already told Mal my idea, and he didn't go for it," Rix drawls. Val stops her frantic pacing and stares at him. "What did you suggest?"

"I told him I would marry Miss Miller-Jones, claim the kid as mine, and then Mal could visit him as much as he wanted. Roman would be a Le Laurier, much better than a Clare. And unlike Mother and her fucked up society standards, my family would welcome him with open arms. It solves several problems. But as I said, he wasn't on the same page. Kicked me out, and Boone informed me that I couldn't come over without an appointment."

Valentina's mouth is on the floor, as is Cameron's. I knew there had been some rift between the two of them, but I never expected this. Malcolm has holed himself up emotionally, most of all. He's been working grueling hours, hopping on and off planes, and spending nights wrapped up in Rachel's frantic race to be Queen of Manhattan. There are endless photos of them coming in and out of exclusive clubs, five-star restaurants, and private parties. In all of them, they look glamorous, expensive and in love. That's if you dont know them. If you look closer, you'll see Rachel's tight hold on his arm in every picture, her nails curled in as if he is about to run away. Malcolm's eyes constantly look away, his teeth gleaming, but his eyes are vacant. It's an expression I've seen on my brother's face for too many years.

"How in the hell did you think he would take it?" Cameron asks, laughing.

Rix just shrugs. "I thought he would be able to see its benefits. Guess I was wrong. Everyone would have benefitted, especially the child."

"Rix, did you forget that Rory would have to agree to it? You think you were going to snatch her up like that?" Valentina snaps her fingers with an eye roll.

"Do you really think she would have said no to *me*, pet?" Rix gives her a lazy smile, and Cam chokes. Hendrix has always been an over-sexed woman-eating beast of a boy. Even when we were very young, he was surrounded by girls falling all over themselves for his attention. Mother sent him to a private all-boys school, and even that did nothing. He spent every weekend on dates with different girls, charming his way through their panties with a grin. He's a lethal combination of arrogant grace, animal energy, and stupidly good looks. I've heard stories about his father, River, and the apple barely fell off the tree.

Valentina huffs. "Maybe, maybe not. The point is that the goal is not to have Roman raised by anyone but Malcolm. Preferably with Rachel lost on a raft in the middle of the ocean." I snicker, knowing Val would love to be the one to push that raft right on through.

"May I interject? I don't think anyone in this room has the juice to change things. Rix, Malcolm will never allow you to go near Rory, so that's off the table. Val, Husband, neither of you has the social status to pull this off either. I know your last name is Clare, but you don't spend any time using it. Malcolm and your parents are the only ones who really represent that name. Not to mention, Malcolm is determined to sacrifice himself to keep your mother happy and healthy—which means we have Rachel to contend with, too." Cam ticks these off of his long fingers. Val sits dejectedly with every point, and even Rix is quiet.

"So then what can we do?" I ask my husband, marveling at his calmness and the greenness of his eyes. I'm a lucky man.

"We need to call in the big guns, guys."

"The big guns?" Val tilts her head, frowning.

"Yup, the BIG guns." His eyebrows raise, and I see the lightbulb go off for my sister. Her blue eyes widen, a devilish gleam in them.

"Oh shit. Really?"

"Yup."

"You think it'll work?"

"Yes, I do. Here's what you are going to say..."

❧ 14 ❧

NEW FRIENDS, NEW LIFE

I stare into the deep brown eyes, trying to find the strength not to give in. Except he knows I am a complete sucker and don't have a wisp of willpower. All he has to do is give me that face, and I cave in. Every. Time.

"No, Bernoulli. You already went to the park today," I scold, but he doesn't budge, just staring at me with that puppy grin and his ball at my feet. His wet nose nudges it, and it rolls to the Moses basket that Roman is busy gurgling to himself in. Dammit.

"Okay, fine. But when I say it's time to go, I don't want any sad-puppy eyes." I hold a finger up to him, and he just barks, his furry tail wagging like crazy. I sigh, leaning down and scratching his head while giving him a big smacking kiss.

About one week after I brought Roman home, seven days full of new-mama panic and little sleep, my doorman called and said I had a special delivery. My hair was big red ratsnest, and I had milk on my shirt, so Julian went downstairs to pick it up. Roman was asleep on my chest, so I didn't scream out the curse I wanted when Julian walked in with a giant fluff of fur and a blue bow around his neck. There was no card, just some adoption papers addressed to Roman, filled with medical data, bloodline provenance, and a paid subscription service for food and check-ups. My initial reaction was denial because the last thing I needed was a newborn baby and a ten-week-old puppy, but when Bernoulli— the name he came with—rolled his fat little self over to Roman's carrier and plopped his head on his feet and fell fast asleep, I caved, of course. Bernoulli is a Bernese Mountain Dog, which means they are typically low-key, but of course, my puppy loves to go to the park and run around with other dogs as often as possible. He normally grunts and howls when we have to leave, hence the warning I have to give him daily. He's got Julian and our doorman, Wallace, wrapped around his paw, and though I'm usually the disciplinarian, I'm also the biggest sucker.

I wrangle Roman into his carrier, grab a small crossbody bag, and put Bernoulli on his leash. He's already leaping and yipping, and Roman is leaning over watching him, a drooly smile on his face. We pass Wallace, who gives him a good scratch, and head out, passing the tiny Theodore Roosevelt Park straight into Central Park. I live near the Natural History Museum, so I'm used to all the extra people milling around. There is a small off-leash dog area, and Bernoulli pulls me that way, his furry feet almost running in place. Several people who pass him ohh and aww at his antics and adorable face, a few even snapping his picture. We finally make it, and I barely get his leash unsnapped before he takes off, spotting his girlfriend, Daisy, an energetic goldendoodle who loves him just as much. They jump and kiss each other before Bernie comes tearing back, and I pull out his ball, tossing it to him. He catches it and scampers back to Daisy, both chasing it at top speed. I wave at her parents, seated a few benches away, both looking at something on a tablet. I pull Roman out of his carrier, nibbling and kissing all over his chubby cheeks and neck, before settling him on my lap so he can watch the action. His arms and legs wheel, making huffy noises as he squeals. I smile and kiss the top of his head.

Being a mom has been the hardest and best thing in my life. I thank the stars daily for Saige and Julian, who help me out and talk me down from my worries. Roman is a perfect baby, sleeping through the whole night almost immediately, eating like a champ (as his many rolls show), and just being a giant lovebug. He's actually funny, even though he's only a few months old, and wants nothing more than kisses and hugs from anyone and everyone. It's rare that I don't get stopped by a stranger asking to talk to him or commenting on his cuteness. I will say I made a stupendous-looking kid, though Saige likes to snark that his father has a lot to do with it since Roman looks identical to Malcolm, though his dark curly hair has a decided auburn tint, and he has my wide smile.

"Do you mind, dear?" I look up, startled at a smartly dressed older woman hovering over the empty part of the bench beside me. I see a man behind her at a discreet distance, holding an umbrella and a cane. He is dressed super formal—a black suit, highly polished lace-up shoes, and a cap.

"No, of course not; please sit. I apologize in advance for my rowdy puppy and my noisy baby." Roman makes a slobbery squeal at that, and I laugh. She sits primly, her expensive pantsuit not even wrinkling, placing her legacy Hermés bag on her lap. She peers at me through a lightly shaded pair of sunglasses, her shallow-brimmed hat tilted saucily over one brow. I grin at her perusal, sure that my baggy sweatpants and Yankees hoodie are making her catch hives.

"It's quite alright, my dear," she smiles, and just then, Bernie comes galloping over, sniffing at the lady quickly, before barking once and running off again. "A protective little wolf, isn't he?"

"Yup. He loves everybody, though, so I'm not sure how much of a guard dog he will be. He's only a few months, so we shall see."

"And your son, how old is he?" I think she is staring at Roman, though her sunglasses make it hard to tell.

"He's four months old today. I know he looks bigger," I laugh at her light scoff. "He was almost eleven pounds at birth."

"A proper fellow, then. Let's have a look, shall we?" Roman has been watching the dogs play, so I shift him around so she can see him. He's just started chewing on his fingers, so there is a good amount of drool, but he still gives her a wide, gummy smile. The lady is silent for a moment before reaching forward and running a few gloved fingers through his thick curls. "He is a spectacular child," she whispers. "Truly an angel."

"I think so, but I'm his mama, so I may be slightly biased." I lift him and kiss him all over, going for the spot on his neck that makes him belly-laugh like a grown person. I plop him back down, bracing him with one arm while holding out a hand.

"I'm Rory. This is Roman." She takes my hand in a firm shake.

"I'm Bea. It's a pleasure, Miss Rory." Roman holds out a wet hand, and she chuckles, grasping his fingers and tugging gently. "And to you, Young Master Roman." He grins at her again, his little dimple popping from his chin. "I've never been to this part of Central Park before. I quite like it. More young families and museum-goers than typical tourists. Do you live nearby?" Roman still has hold of Bea's hand, though she seems content to let him. I point at my building, which can be seen in the distance, and she soon starts asking about my job, surprised when I tell her that I am the CEO of an architecture firm. We talk about my past projects, a few of which she'd heard of, and she shared that she has three children and many grandchildren. She normally lives overseas but has come back to the city to conduct some business. I can hear a slight Continental accent, but I can't tell if it's just her proper, old-fashioned speech or if she's got other languages under her belt. She asks about my parents and makes a sad face when I tell her they are both long gone. And not once does she ask about Roman's father, though I guess my avoidance has made the situation somewhat obvious. Roman falls asleep, and soon Bernoulli comes over, making sad noises that Daisy's parents have taken her home. I carefully put Roman back in his carrier and latch Bernie to his leash.

"It's been nice talking to you, Bea. I've got to get my babies home for dinner." Bernie's face lights up at the word, and Bea smiles, patting him on the head. "It was a pleasure for me as well, Rory. Perhaps I'll see you again soon. I'll be in town for a while, and as I said, I like this part of the Park. I'll bring a bone for Sir Bernoulli." She waves as she walks away, the now obvious chauffeur holding out his arm to steady her precise gait.

"Come on, Bernie. There is a nice pouch of puppy goodies waiting for you at home. Plus, the Yankees game is starting." I tug at his leash and wave once last time at Bea, who has stopped to watch us.

15

AND IN THIS CORNER,
WEIGHING IN AT...

The traffic is a typical Manhattan snarl, taxis, limos, buses, and cars twisting and honking, all jockeying for a few inches of space, trying like hell to get an edge over each other. Bike messengers, skateboarders, and scooters dodge in and out of tight spaces, motorcycles zooming past everyone. Our driver, one of several from the service I use, sits up, leaning over the wheel, hands tightly fisted at ten and two. He's muttered a few curses already and chuckled darkly at some of the angry honks. I smile grimly at his determination, deciding to give him an extra tip.

"Jesus," Rachel mutters as he darts across three lanes, making a left onto a quieter street.

"You were the one who demanded that he do everything he could to make our reservations. Don't complain now." She glares at me, eyes widening as the driver makes a sharp right, the wheels on the Aston Martin slightly squealing. She sends a dirty look to the back of his head, and I decide to double that tip.

"I don't know why you chose this restaurant; you know how hard it is to get here for dinner." We make another turn and stop at a light.

"Mother Clare insisted that we go somewhere new, especially since Montgomery and Cameron will be joining us. *Biloxi* is the best right now." There is a hint of something in her voice, a coldness that tinges her voice, but quickly disappears. "You know your parent's usual haunts are so stuffy. This place is hot and new but still exclusive. I heard that reservations are backed up by a year. Of course, they made an exception once I told them the Clare family was coming," she says smugly. I want to tell her she is not a Clare yet, but bite it back. The last thing I need is to start a fight with her just before we see my family.

We finally arrive, and the driver pulls us straight to the front, promising to be ready with a text. He helps Rachel out, and she pauses for a few paps as I round the car, holding my elbow out to her. There is no line outside, and I wonder why the paparazzi are here, but I give them a smile, dragging Rachel with me. The young, brunette hostess gives me a big grin, and asks us to follow her to our table. Monty, Cam, and Valentina were already there; Val finally called our parents and told them she was temporarily back in the States. She refused to stay with them at the brownstone or at her small LES apartment, instead bunking with Monty and Cam. I offered to let her stay with me, but she flatly told me that the thought of running into Rachel was nauseating, so thanks, but no thanks. She's evaded every family get-together but couldn't turn down tonight, with our mother's direct mandate.

The hostess drops us at a comfortable table with plush chairs and great lighting. I lean over and hug my siblings while Rachel passes out air kisses and a brief wave at Valentina, who ignores her. They've already ordered cocktails, and Rachel automatically starts looking around for our server.

"This place is great. I've seen some dishes go by, and I can't wait to try everything," Val says, sipping her outrageous-looking drink, complete with a cucumber slice and some greenery. Biloxi is a southern food fusion restaurant with an interior that combines old-fashioned tapestries and furnishings with jazz influences. It's luxurious, to be sure, but also fun and modern.

"Well, maybe not everything, dahling. We don't want to have the poor seamstresses working overtime to tailor your bridesmaid dress. It's bad enough that the dress you're wearing is screaming for help." There is a short silence, and I slowly turn to Rachel as Valentina takes a deep breath. "You're absolutely right, Rachel. Maybe you can text me your diet. Is it still the "Bones Rattling Underneath My Skin" regime?" She does a little shimmy, and I hear Cam cough gently into his napkin, and Monty stares at the ceiling with a massive grin on his face.

"It's called health, Valentina. And I am gifted this body through genetics and good breeding."

Val rolls her eyes. "Huh. I thought it was a steady influx of illegal stimulants, but what do I know?" She takes a sip of her drink, gulping loudly.

"I will not even dignify that with a response..." Rachel snipes.

"Uh, you just did, Raquel."

"It's Rachel. I swear you must be adopted. There is no way you are a Clare."

"Oh, I am for sure. Too bad you're not. Still just a lowly Van Pyke." Ouch. "Valentina..." I warn her, knowing that once she gets going, the whole evening will go downhill.

"It's just a formality at this point. I am a Clare, according to your mother. Maybe there's a reason she's so eager to have me as a daughter".

I know that's a hit below the belt to Val, whose fights with my mother are legendary, but she still smirks. "Even the sainted Penelope Deaveraux Clare can lapse into questionable taste, dahling." Rachel takes a deep breath, the red crawling up her bare chest a precursor to a flaming snit. "Look, you..."

"Hello, everyone. It's lovely to see you," my mother's overly cultured voice interrupts. I don't know if she heard the impending argument or if she has impeccable timing, but I stand up to greet her, grateful for a change.

"Mother." I kiss her cheek as Monty and Cam also stand up. My father is a few steps behind, having stopped to greet some business associates, catching up finally to kiss Rachel and Valentina lightly. Mother chooses the chair beside Rachel, pointedly ignoring the empty one beside Val. They immediately lapse into a bubble conversation, gossiping about a few people in the room, snickering at those angling for an invite to our wedding. Valentina discreetly gives me a sympathetic look, rolling her eyes at Dad's complaints about the lighting and decor, talking to no one and everyone. My stomach burns with the need to run, scream, and throw my glass. Cam and Monty are talking to Val, trying to include me from across the table, but I smile and shake my head at their efforts. I quietly sip my whisky, letting the noise fade out, entering a wished-for mindspace where my family is normal and I actually like my life. I peer around the room, admiring the luxurious ambiance. Despite the paparazzi, (who I'm now sure she called,) it was a good choice by Rachel.

Our food arrives hot and spicy, served on mismatched plates with gold chargers, which I find charming, though Mother makes disparaging comments. Everything is delicious, and for a brief moment, there is a blessed, peaceful silence as we enjoy our food. Of course, that doesn't last long.

"Percy, Penelope, good to see you." I come out of my haze to see Chandler Schillings and his wife, Sari, reaching out to shake my father's hand. Chandler is the biggest restaurant developer on the East Coast and has worked with my father many times. Of course, all that is probably out the window now that Chandler has chosen you-know-who for his next project. Monty's eyes are wide, and Valentina has pulled out her phone, no doubt to video my father's reaction. That burn in my stomach has turned into an inferno.

"Chandler, Sari. A pleasure as always," Dad says, a block of ice in his throat. Mother nods, and Rachel, ever the parrot, does the same. I roll my eyes and stand, giving Chandler a hearty handshake and his lovely blonde wife a kiss on the cheek. For his part, Chandler seems amused by the frosty reception, smiling with a discreetly saucy wink. "Checking out the competition, I see. What do you think?" He waves his hand to the packed restaurant, and Dad frowns. "Competition?"

A big, shark-like smile blooms on Chandler's face. "Oh, you didn't know? Miller-Jones designed this restaurant. It's the main reason I chose them for *Discovery*. Rory, do you know Rory? Well, she is just a phenom. Truly has a fresh and distinct point of view. You give her a few words, and it's like she reaches into your head and designs your dreams. It's why I'm convinced she will win the Chanteuse contract." I peek at Montgomery, whose mouth is on the floor, and Valentina, whose face is buried in her hands, shoulder shaking with laughter or tears.

"I didn't know that Miller-Jones was throwing their hat in the ring," Dad says smoothly, though if you knew him, you'd hear the anger painting every word. "I wish them luck, though I think they are punching above their weight, no? A few eateries don't give them the experience for such a project."

"Oh, I think she would be fabulous at it. My brother sits on Chanteuse's board, and I intend to have him recommend her." Every one of Chandler's teeth is on display, and his wife's calm face has a hint of smugness. I'm sure the Schillings have heard the rumblings of my father's biting displeasure he has been spreading around the city.

"How fantastic that you have a pet project, Chandler. I wish your protégé the best of luck," Mother interjects, her hazel eyes cold with dismissal. The smile never moves off Chandler's face, though the gauntlet has been thrown.

"She doesn't need it, Penelope, trust me. We'll leave you to enjoy the rest of your meal. Speak soon, Percy." Sari gives a little wave, and they walk away, greeting several people on their way out. Our table is silent for a long moment before Rachel breaks it.

"What Chanteuse contract?" Dad fills her in while Cam and Monty stare at me. I swallow the rest of my whisky, signaling the server for more. Or a bottle. Maybe a crate.

"I'll start appearing in just Chanteuse clothing from now on. Their newest collections are fabulous. I have a girl at their Madison Ave boutique," Rachel tells him, tapping on her phone despite the late hour. "It won't hurt to remind them of the influence that comes with choosing Clare Design." Val lets out a barely disguised vomiting noise, and Monty has a sneer on his lips, both of which Rachel ignores.

"An excellent idea, my dear. Perhaps I shall reach out about acquiring Miller-Jones again. I made a tender offer, and they were less than charitable about it. An additional ten percent should do it." My mother nods, as does Rachel again. I think about Rory's fiery disposition, those silver eyes flashing with contempt for me. Then I think about that chubby blue-eyed baby, his fat cheeks and dimpled chin.

"I didn't realize you were afraid of a bit of competition, Dad." Cam's face suddenly beams in pride, and Monty grins.

Dad turns to me slowly. "That's preposterous, Malcolm. It's about choices. I want Clare Design to be the only choice. Surely that's easy to understand?" He waves his hand in dismissal.

"That's not what it sounds like. Do you want it to get around that we were so afraid of a small upstart firm that we had to buy them? That smacks of insecurity. If you think they are over-matched, then go forward with that narrative. Once it gets out that you have been turned down twice—and they will turn you down— it will be embarrassing. I'm not interested in dealing with the press about it." I stare at my father, his brows creasing at my words.

"Sure sounds like you're being a chicken, Daddy. Brah, brah." Rachel makes little chirping noises, and I almost spit out my drink.

"You may have a point, son. I'll consider it." His words close the conversation as he ignores Val's clucking noises and glares in her direction. The talk turns to the wedding again, and I let out a slow breath, catching my sister's eye. She gives me a deep wink and a grin, turning back to Cam and Monty, who are whispering to each other. I smile at no one, thinking that maybe the only coward at the table is me.

16

THE BRONX— HOME OF
WINNERS AND BOMBERS

R*ory.*
"I forgot to tell you that I finally met Bea. She is as fabulous as you said." Saige passes me a napkin, as the mustard from my hotdog threatens to plop out onto the top of Roman's head.

"I told you. She's amazing. I feel bad, though, because I think her family doesn't spend time with her. Every time I see her, she has some sort of gift for Roman. I tried to turn her down a few times, and she gave me the dirtiest of looks—I was actually scared." I pluck at the solid gold bracelet on the baby's wrist, admiring the Celtic scrollwork. A couple of weeks ago, Bea appeared, as usual, clad in an expensive custom suit, with her shaded glasses and a prim hat tilted on her head —a look I've privately called the 'Bea Special'— handing me a small ornately wrapped box. The previous few times, she came with other things: a thick hand-crocheted blanket with Roman's name, an antique toy sailboat, and an adorable little silver suit, complete with a jacket and waistcoat. And never to be left out, Bernoulli got plenty of bones and a fancy red leather collar. The bracelet looked custom, and Bea told me in her imperious voice that it was a good luck charm with her family's coat of arms engraved through the pattern. The bracelet was adjustable—it would grow with Roman. I protested, embarrassed that this lovely lady was buying my son such expensive things, but held it down when I saw some hint of sadness in Bea's eyes. After that, I accepted everything with a big smile and a kiss—something I could tell made her uncomfortable.

"Yeah, she spent the whole time asking about Roman's routine, whether you were getting enough sleep, etcetera— God, number sixteen looks good in those pants. Anyway, I guess she is down with Julian too—they're besties." The ump calls a final strike, and the whole crowd booed, even Saige, who I think is only upset that a fine piece of ass is leaving the field.

We have these fantastic seats, thanks to Bea, who handed the tickets to me yesterday, a small smug smile on her face. I almost keeled over when I saw they were behind home plate, with access to the private VIP club and in-seat service. Saige has already delivered ridiculous things to us, though my favorite was the tiny noise-canceling headphones they handed to Roman. He's decked out in his first Yankees jersey with matching pants and a hat. The cute little blonde concierge has been fawning over him since we sat down, and true to his nature, he's been giving her drooly grins the whole time. "Wait, what just happened?"

"Infield fly," I tell her as the fans groan and yell some more. It's a perfect night for baseball, with the late summer sun dancing along the outfield fence and a warm light wind teasing the infield. Saige has taken about two thousand pictures of Roman at his first Yankees game, even getting a stranger to take some of the three of us. "What does that mean?" I briefly explain it to her, though it's one of my least favorite baseball rules. The giant scoreboard flashes the night's charity, and I grit my teeth to see it sponsored by the Clare Family Health Foundation. I feel like a hunted animal.

I stand up, handing her Roman, who is gumming a piece of hotdog bun to death. "I'm going to the bathroom. Try not to sell my baby while I'm gone." She snorts, nibbling on a neck roll and waving me away. I head down the steps, sidling past a pair of suits and into the private club, where more people are networking and business dealing more than watching the game. The whole club screams money, and I remember reading somewhere that the membership fee is in the middle of hundreds of thousands per year. Digital boards dot the walls, touting the amenities available to members and guests, with others tuned to rival teams' games, all jockeying to beat the Yanks for a playoff spot. Bars with top-shelf liquor frame the walls; there is even a carving station with expensive imported meat and a matching charcuterie offering. It's packed, but the layout gives the impression of space and exclusivity—the designer part of me approves. The bathrooms are in a discreet alcove, hidden by a gold leaf latticed screen, and I hurry to finish up and accept the offer of hand lotion and mouthwash from the attendant. There is a small crowd at the door, a group of women wearing tight shorts and low-cut shirts with baseball hats perched artfully on perfectly coiffed ponytails. WAGs, maybe; I eye them as I look for a crease to squeeze through. I see an opportunity and dive forward, almost busting my butt, but a strong arm catches me, and I blink up at a stupidly handsome, ponytailed bad boy who is grinning at me like I haven't got a stitch of clothes on. He's got the look of a whole devil, and I can feel the involuntary tick of an answering smile before I push it down, giving him a scolding look. His face is almost too sexy, and I can only imagine how he uses it to lure in his prey.

"Thank you," I stutter out, his sparkling hazel eyes promising stuff no sane woman would turn down.

"You have no idea how much the pleasure is all mine," he drawls, giving me a very thorough once over. My face turns ketchup red, and I realize he still has hold of my waist. I pull back gently, and his wicked smile widens.

"Uhhhh. Bye?" I wince, hurrying back to my seat, not even waiting for him to respond. Saige is sipping a cup of what I can smell is wine, and Roman is still going to town on some bread.

"Why do you look like that?" Saige asks me, and I wave my hand in the air, still trying to cool off my hot cheeks. "I almost ate floor and an absolutely gorgeous man caught me."

"Did you get his number?" She cranes her neck around, and I pinch her.

"Hell no! I am not in the market, and he was... a lot. I couldn't have handled him if I tried."

MALCOLM

"Damn, trust Rix to find a hot piece of ass at a baseball game. I'd stick her in my pocket and run away," Warran says. I crane my neck in the direction my brother went, seeing him looking down at someone, a flirty smile on his face. A couple moves out of the way, and I spot a deep flame ponytail tucked under a worn Yankees hat. My stomach plummets as the rest of her form comes into view. I'm on my feet and moving just as she pulls away and scurries through the double doors and up the stairs. Rix follows behind, and I pause at the entrance, heart pounding but sanity prevailing. I swallow a few times and make my way back to Warran, an old college friend of Hendrix, who is still on the prowl despite having two ex-wives and five kids.

"Did you get a better look at her?" Warran leers at a group of women who giggle past us, turning around to look at their asses. I shake my head, sipping on the *Torres Reserva Del Mamut,* which the club stocks just for me. Rix pulls out his chair, that stupid, infuriating smile on his face, staring at me expectantly.

"Dude, she was HOT as fuck. I could write poems about her ass alone. Did you get her number?" Rix is still staring at me, and I feel an uncontrollable burn in my hands, the fiery need to wrap them around his neck and squeeze.

"Nah. She was gorgeous, but she had a kid with her." He sips a beer that a flirty waitress dropped off without asking. "She's sitting right near our family section, so she's got to belong to someone we know." I blink and feel the burn start traveling down my sides. Belong to someone? It never occurred to me that Rory might have someone in her life who got to claim her.

And my son.

"A kid? Yuck." I glare at Warran, just barely halting the reminder that he has a passel of kids he never sees. I've never liked him, just tolerating his presence whenever he tags along behind Rix, looking to snatch up his scraps. He's not a bad-looking guy, but he's got a hunter's eye that most women run away from.

"Yeah. I'd brave it, though. A woman like that is once in a lifetime.

But I'd hire a bodyguard —I saw at least ten guys checking her out," Hendrix says, eyes pinned to my red face.

"Excuse me, I've got to make a phone call," I stand up, pushing my chair in and making my way to the exit. I take a deep breath, bracing myself against the railing, before slowly walking up the stairs. The Clare family has owned a large section of seats behind home plate since the sixties and a private box rows above. I rarely use the club seating, uninterested in being recognized and harassed, but Rix insisted. I stand in the corner, looking out and spotting her immediately, that hair a beacon. She is with her best friend, who is standing up and yelling something at the dugout, her arms full of a chunky, drooling baby. Rory is sitting down and laughing hysterically, and like Rix said, she has the eye of almost every man in the vicinity. She's wearing a tight retro Yankees t-shirt, short cutoff jean shorts, those shapely smooth legs tucked into a pair of old broken-in Timberlands, braced on the wall before her. Motherhood has been good to her. My feet move before my brain, and I have to push myself back down forcefully. I need to leave; the temptation is too great. I send a text to Rix, followed by one to my driver, who meets me at the small private VIP entrance. I sit back on the tufted seat, my eyes closing, stomach still in knots.

What were the odds she would be at the same ball game, sitting in seats near ours? It has to be some cosmic punishment, Karma sticking her foot out and tripping me, the universe having a good fucking laugh.

Is this how my life is going to be? Years of me trying to do the right thing, but doomed to be confronted again and again by the best mistake of my life? I go to loosen my collar, grimacing, and then I realize it was never buttoned in the first place. My chest is tight, throat full.

Is it possible to die of despair in the back of a four-hundred-thousand-dollar car?

17

THE CONSPIRATORS-
VALENTINA

One of the best things about New York is the coffee shops. I mean, everything about it is fantastic, but ohhhh. The. Coffee. There is every type you can imagine: Italian 'bars' (what they call them in Europe,) elegant French cafes with sumptuous pastries, Vietnamese shops serving rich *cà phê sữa nóng* coffee with sweet condensed milk, and then run in and out places with just plain old American brew. I love the smells, the warmth, the jolt of energy. I just love coffee. When I asked my brother to meet me, I expected him to suggest a fancy place with white tablecloths and delicate china cups. Instead, he texted me an address off of Lexington, and I was shocked to find an out-of-the-way teeny establishment with only three deep, tall booths and cracked red leather seats. The rounded cases were full of giant donuts and other goodies, and the workers periodically broke into opera. I freaking love it here.

"How the heck did you find this place?" I ask Malcolm as a full-bearded, smiling man places a large recyclable cup in front of me and a plastic container with a giant croissant. I can smell the complex mix of beans, vanilla, and the hint of something spicy. I pop the container and take a huge bite of the flaky pasty filled with apples and peaches. Yum.

Mal smiles at me, taking a bite of his own croissant, oblivious to the two women staring at him from behind the kitchen door. "Eve lives near here, and she stops by almost every day. The coffee is amazing, and it's kind of private. Plus, the owner is a big Yankees fan, so we commiserate." I admire his fine light wool suit, a creamy grey with subtle pinstripes. He's not wearing a tie—instead, his top button is open, the tan of his skin glowing against the white silk. The admirers are not so subtly holding up a copy of the magazine with Malcolm's face on the cover and squealing when he glances over.

"Speaking of Yankees games..." I start and wince when a strange look crosses his face. Rix told me all about his reaction to seeing Rory at the game: a sad mix of fury, despair, and resignation. He didn't even stay all nine innings, running away and sending Rix a sorry-butt text message. Rix managed to snag a few pictures, and my heart twisted seeing my nephew, whom I've never met and already adore. "I guess you don't want to talk about it?" He slowly sips his coffee, staring off into the distance. "What is there to talk about?"

I open my mouth and then close it, remembering to stick to the script. "Maybe you're right. Anyway, Mother and Father are requesting our presence at their house tomorrow. I tried to get out of it, but Mother was insistent that all of us, including Hendrix, had to be there. You know what it's about?" I violently slurp down more of the excellent coffee; lady be demand.

"Rachel and Mother want to have a pow-wow about the wedding. They are finalizing the guest list, and I guess they have some kind of media strategy they want to go over with everyone. The invitations are going out in a few days." He avoids eye contact, and I wonder if he realizes how beaten down he looks. My heart twists— so many things brimming on the tip of my tongue. I want to hug him, maybe smack him around a little, then hug him again. "I was planning on skipping it —you know as well as I do that we have no say in anything."

Uh-oh.

Stick. To. The. Script. Valentina.

"Well, Mom made it sound like it was mandatory; if I've got to go, then you have to. It's your wedding, after all." He sighs, and I feel like crap for pushing him, but I know someday he will thank me. "I guess you're right."

"What time are you getting there?" This next part is crucial.

Malcolm pulls out his phone and taps on his calendar, not knowing Eve has moved some things around. "I have a meeting at five and a conference call at six, which I will take from the car. I could be at the brownstone by seven. Why?"

"Can I ride with you? Monty and Cam are going straight from work, and I don't want to arrive alone." This is a complete lie, and I hope he can't tell by the twitching on my face. I've never been good at it, especially to Malcolm or Hendrix.

"Of course. Luckily, Rachel plans to go over early, so I don't have to separate the two of you." He gives me a pointed stare, and I grin. We lapse into other family gossip, including Rix and his exploits. There was some scuttlebutt about a yacht and some naked women, but he wasn't answering any of our phone calls. We chatted some more, and Malcolm stood up, looking at his watch, kissing me on the forehead. I turn down his offer of a ride, wanting to stay and enjoy the ambiance a little longer.

"See you tomorrow, Squirt." He waves at me with a glamorous smile, ignoring the sighs from every woman in a four-block vicinity.

"Cool. I'll be ready."

I just hope Malcolm will be. And that he doesn't hate us forever.

❧ 18 ❧

LIFE IS A BOX OF DONUTS...
CHOOSE WISELY AND OFTEN

"Bernoulli, I swear if you don't hurry up, I am going to feed you turnips for the rest of the year," I threaten the furball as he slinks around the dog run, giving me the side eye. This week has been rough, with some construction delays on the Schillings project and another potential client demanding revisions to revisions that I've revised. To top it off, Saige went on a quick vacation to visit her parents, and I think Roman might be teething. He's been up at night and running low-grade fevers while gumming and crying constantly. Even Julian, his favorite person, can do nothing to soothe him. I've tried everything except rubbing brandy on his gums, as Bea suggested. At this point, I might try it while swigging some myself.

"Bernie, dude..." I warn him again, and of course, he stops and stares at me, a giant puppy grin and a warning of badness on his face. He's already been on several walks today, and I'm hoping this one will finally wear him out.

"Is Sir Bernoulli misbehaving, Miss Rory?" I look over at Wallace, admiring his fancy new uniform. A big corporation recently bought out our building, and they immediately implemented a bunch of upgrades, like Wallace's uniform and this new puppy run in the courtyard.

"He's just restless today. I'm not sure if it's because Roman is fussy or if this is the beginning of doggie adolescence. Either way, if he doesn't hurry up, I'm going to sell him to the circus." I give Bernie a squinty eye, and he just turns and runs the other way. Wallace laughs and hurries over to a fancy Bentley pulling up the driveway. He opens the back door, and I'm shocked when Bea steps out.

"Bea!" I yell, waving, and she lifts a fragile hand in return. Her chauffeur, ever-present and still nameless, parks in the VIP spot, following behind her at a discreet pace.

"Hello, Rory dear. I was hoping to catch you." She leans over, giving me a gentle kiss, while I grab her and squeeze her, my kiss loud and obnoxious. She chuckles, patting my cheek. "Might we sit?"

I hold her arm and guide her to an ornate bench facing the small garden. Aside from the security, one of the reasons I chose this building was the little oasis just inside the entrance. The whole structure is built around a quadrangle, with tons of prewar pillars and this tiny flower bed.

"Is everything okay?" I look her over worriedly. Bea has never shown up at my house for all the weeks we have been acquainted. I've invited her a time or two, and I know Julian has as well. But each time, she just smiles and shakes her head.

"Yes, dear. I'm on my way to see my son and his family, and I wanted to see you beforehand. How is our little Roman?" We met in the park a few days ago but left almost immediately because Roman was so miserable. She fussed over him but understood. I'm also shocked because I had no idea that Bea had a son in the city.

"He's the same. I think his little gums are definitely the culprit. His pediatrician gave us some suggestions, but nothing is making him happy. Poor guy." I peek over and see my puppy rolling around, and I pray it's not in his own poop. Again.

"It'll pass, my dear. Just keep him comfortable. And how are you?" She shifts slightly, and I notice that she is not in one of her usual fancy pantsuits but a silky tea-length grey dress with ropes and ropes of different colored, glowing pearls. She looks elegant, but there is a weird glint in her eye. "I'm good," I shrug. What am I supposed to say? That I'm monstrously exhausted, overly energetic, constantly worried, and weirdly lonely? Um no.

"You know, Rory, we have never discussed Roman's father. I rather hoped you would have confided on your own, though I gave you your privacy." She stops, peering at me, and I squirm. "You are such a gorgeous girl with a bright future — I cannot imagine that any man would willingly give you up. Or your son."

Ha. If she only knew.

"Well, Roman's dad and I, uhhh, only had a short time together. And then, um, I decided that his lifestyle was not a good example, so we decided it's best if he stays away permanently." Cringe. I probably made Malcolm sound like a serial killer.

"It still must be difficult for you. Raising a child alone. I'm sure if things were different, you'd prefer his father to be heavily involved. You know, when I married my husband, it wasn't my choice. I was a young girl and did what my family expected. My husband's family was wealthy and influential, and my family had a pedigree. It wasn't a love match, and I vowed that my children would marry well, but only if they loved their spouse. My two daughters did, but when it came to my son, my husband pushed him to choose someone I'm not sure he would have without his father's influence. I think everyone, regardless of their status, should have choices, don't you agree?"

"Ummm, yes, of course. My parents chose each other, and for almost their whole marriage, they were super happy." I have no idea where she is going with this.

"Good. I'm glad you agree. I have become very fond of you, Rory. You are an amazing mother, and Roman could have no better. Whatever the future holds, always remember that." Bea leans forward, pressing her face to mine and stroking my ratty hair. "My sweet girl. Take this," she lifts one strand of pearls and places them around my neck.

"Bea, I can't take these!" The necklace hangs down to my navel, and despite my limited knowledge of jewelry, I can tell it is worth a fortune.

"Nonsense. Now promise me that whatever choices come before you, you choose with your heart, hmmm?" She clucks me under my chin before signaling to her helper. He jumps forward, both of us helping her to her feet. She smiles at me again, smoothing down her dress and patting her perfectly coiffed hair. I realize that she isn't wearing a hat, either. Her hair is a clear silver, shiny and thick, coiled into an old-fashioned chignon at her neck. "Have fun at your son's house," I tell her, and she laughs, a single tinkling bark.

"Oh, my dear Rory, I think tonight might be the most fun I've ever had. Next time I see you, I suppose we will have much to discuss. I look forward to it." She waves again before being helped back into her car and taking off. Bernoulli finally settles his furry butt down, coming over and whining as if he's been forced outside against his will. I roll my eyes, scrubbing under his chin. I check my watch and hurry to the elevator, wanting to let Julian have a little time to himself. I frown, fiddling with the smoky black pearls around my neck.

How come Bea never mentioned a son?

🍃 19 🍃

MIC DROP

"Mother is not going to be happy with that outfit, you know," I grin at my rebellious little sister, taking in her flowing patterned pants and off-the-shoulder sweater. "You know she prefers more tailored clothing for dinner." Our mother has drilled into us the importance of appearances from the cradle. We were never allowed to be in public in less than pristine clothing, no wrinkles, no dirt, and everything tucked and tied. The only exception was Rix, who would scream and make a scene, often with fake tears and even pulling off his clothes when pressed. He only had to do it a few times before Mother threw her hands in the air and let him be. After that, he would wear the most outrageous things possible, including his hair, which he started growing out at ten years old. I never heard if anyone had a problem with it, probably because he was a Le Laurier, and they are rabid about their heir.

Val shrugs, the beads hanging around her neck clinking. "These were made by a women's collective—the proceeds can educate the village kids for a year. She can take her elitist crap and stuff it." I sigh, shaking my head. If Mother wasn't such a...well, wasn't such a Clare, I'd almost feel sorry for her. For all of her strict rules and cold nature, she raised four disobedient kids. It's a miracle we are as close as we are, but we have the horror in common. In reality, we are all we have.

"I'd tell you to behave, but years of you running off has taught me to keep my mouth shut." Val laughs, tapping her fingers against her pant leg. She keeps checking her phone, jiggling and jittering in her seat.

"Is everything ok, Squirt?" Her head whips around, a small smile on her lips. The driver makes a tight turn, and I crane my neck out the window, spotting Hendrix's new custom black Ferrari SF90 XX Stradale parked in front of the brownstone. I turn back to my sister, whose face is red in the dim light. "Val?"

The driver stops, climbs out, and opens Val's door. She swings her legs to get out before reaching back and giving me a huge squeeze. "I love you, Malcolm." She sniffles before getting out and waiting for me on the curb. I hold out my arm, and she clasps it tightly. "I love you too, Squirt. If you need to talk, I'm here." I frown as she stares straight ahead, looking like a prisoner headed towards execution.

"I know, Mal." The door opens before we can ring the bell, and Elena is already waiting. She waves us in impatiently, always afraid someone will sneak in behind us. "Hurry, hurry. Everyone is in the study." She pushes us lightly, and we round the corner, bumping into Hendrix immediately. He's got a full glass of liquor and takes a healthy gulp.

"Thank God you are here. I'm about two minutes away from throwing Mother's china around the room. She and Rachel have been worse than the Stygian witches. I've never heard such bullshit in my life." Like me, he is wearing a dark suit, but while I added a snow-white shirt and discreet tie, he decided on a skintight gold t-shirt that clung to his abs. His hair is normal tonight; if you count two French braids on either side of his head, normal.

"Hendrix? Is that Malcolm with you? Do hurry in. We have a lot to cover." Hendrix takes another large swallow, and Val snorts. I drag them both behind me, and Mother watches, immediately frowning.

"Hendrix, must you drink so much while you are here? I'd like it if you chose sobriety when visiting my household. Valentina, whatever are you wearing? That outfit is horrifying. You have a closetful of beautiful clothes, and yet you constantly choose to dress like a beggar—this is not how I raised you. Perhaps Rachel can take you to her stylist— she would love the challenge. And Malcolm, you are far too late. This is your wedding, and I need you to take the time to participate in the planning. As CEO, you should be able to dictate your schedule better. Percy, you should go to the office, look at his calendar, and help him clean it up. Montgomery, where are you going? This is not the time for you to be sneaking off. I didn't hear your pager, so don't tell me you have a child to deliver. I swear the lot of you act feral—get your manners together, for goodness sake. Rachel darling, do message your stylist; I don't know how much longer I can look at those dreadful pants." Rachel, the little mini-me she is, smirked at Val and immediately started texting. Monty is still trying to edge out of the room, only freezing when caught. Cameron's face is twitching, and as usual, my father is mute.

"Penelope, for goodness sake, take a breath. Have you nothing positive to say to your children?" I whip around, a giant grin popping up on my face

"Grandmother!"

"Mother?"

"My lord, Mother Beatrice, how on earth are you here?" My mother looks horrified, and I can feel Valentina shaking and laughing behind me. If the boogeyman has a boogeyman, it's my grandmother.

"I suppose I took this modern contraption called a plane, Penelope. Have you heard of it? Malcolm, you handsome scamp, come and kiss me. Now I hear we are wedding planning? What have I missed?"

⚜

Victoria Beatrice Demelza Cavendish Clare, Lady Holland, or simply 'Bea.' I haven't seen my grandmother in years, though she writes letters to me often. When my grandfather Cyrus died, she retired to one of my aunt's estates in England. She likes to tell people it's because she missed him too much, but we all know it's because she and my mother were constantly in knockdown fights. She never got caught up in the whole Clare mystique and could barely stomach my mother's obsessive need to lord it over everyone else. She's still a strikingly beautiful woman, with an old-fashioned posture but a rebellious twinkle in her eye. I used to confide in her a lot when I was younger, but then Rachel was thrust in my face, and she left the States. I've missed her something fierce.

"When did you get into town, Mother Beatrice?" My grandmother is seated next to me, holding my hand, while my mother is in Siberia, at the furthest corner of the room.

"Oh, I've been here quite a while. I had some business to attend to and new friends to visit." I lift her dainty hand to kiss it, and she pats my fist.

"You might have told me, Mother. I would have arranged help for you. And, of course, you would have been welcome to stay with us here." My father looks put out, but Grandmother raises an arched brow.

"Percival, I am more than capable of taking care of myself—as you know, the Earl has a place here in the city. I have no desire to invade your space." He still looks annoyed, though he nods.

"It just seems silly to open such a large space up for one person. It would have been much easier just to set you up in your own wing upstairs." My mother's voice has a chiding tone, though she tries hard to hide it.

"Don't tell me you've missed me, Penelope? I shan't believe it if you do," Grandmother's voice is smooth, cutting like a knife. There is a short silence before Mother clears her throat.

"We haven't seen you in a long while, Mother Beatrice. It would have been nice to have a heads up—perhaps plan a reception or two for you. There are still many people who would like to see you."

"Oh? Like who?" There is another silence before Rachel comes to her idol's rescue. "Grandmother, those are lovely pearls around your neck. Are they family heirlooms?" I look down at the Cavendish Strands, which have been in the family for generations. Each pearl is flawless and rare, with the clasps made of diamonds and rubies. Grandmother's father, the old Earl, presented them to her at her wedding to Grandfather Cyrus.

"Why yes, they are, Rachel, though they aren't part of any entailment. Thank you for noticing."

"Mother, weren't there five strands? Are the grey ones missing?" Dad is sitting up and staring at Grandmother's neck. "Yes, how observant of you, Percy. I recently gifted them to someone, if you should know."

"You what? Those pearls are..." My mother is furious, probably because she's had her eyes on them for herself, forgetting that she is not a Cavendish, and Grandmother has two daughters of her own.

"The pearls are mine, Penelope. They are not some grand prize for being a Clare. I shall disperse them as I see fit. Now the hour is getting late, and we should be talking about the wedding, no? Hendrix, be a dear and get Elena to bring me a spot of tea. That's a good boy." Two giant red spots are on Mother's cheeks, and I sneak a peek at my siblings, who are all in similar states of hilarity, though Cameron at least looks calm. You'd have to know him to see the slight tic at the corner of his mouth.

"She'll be right out, Bea." Hendrix bows to her, and she pats him on his cheek. Elena brings out a vintage Edwardian tea set and quickly prepares Grandmother's cuppa, probably sensing the tension in the room. She hands one to my Mother and one to Cameron. Mother takes a few sips and then takes a deep breath. She goes down a list rapidly, assigning us roles and then the run of the show for the next few months: parties and showers, press events, and interviews. Rachel has a spread with a national preeminent magazine and a few local TV stations. It all sounds exhausting and terrible, and I wonder if I can defect to the Amazon jungle and live in a hut.

"I know the wedding is a ways off, but the time will pass quickly. My secretary will put all these events into your calendars, coded by mandatory attendance or just a 'need-to-know.' I will hear no excuses —this is a big deal for Rachel and your brother. Mother Beatrice, would you like to be included in the correspondence?" she asks politely, but I know she would rather pull her teeth out with gold pliers.

"Well, being included is certainly a nice thing in any family. Tell me, Penelope, where is Malcolm's son included?"

I freeze in my seat, and Montgomery makes a loud, honking cough.

Valentina's hands are covering her face, and Rix that asshole, is grinning like a jackal. God love my mother; she looks at Bea with a look of pity on her face, as if Grandmother has just gone off the rails. As always, Father looks like he is in a different country and on a beach. Like my mother, Rachel looks puzzled, her face a mask of supreme confidence.

"Beatrice, you must be confused. Malcolm doesn't have a son—he and Rachel aren't married yet. Perhaps you are just tired. I can have Elena prepare a room for you. Percy, maybe we should have Dr. Fall come and have a look at her." She stands, reaching for the servant's bell, when Grandmother lets out a rather rude snort.

"Penelope, you have always had a dreadful habit of speaking as though you are the only one in the room; it's quite rude. I assure you I am well in charge of my faculties—nor do I need to see a doctor. I have spent a lot of time with my great-grandson. I'm assuming by your reaction that Malcolm hasn't shared the happy news," she turns to me, a gleam in her eye.

"Darling, go ahead. I've got your back," she whispers. I stare at her, a ball of emotions spinning in my chest. I look at my mother, worried sick this news will send her back to the hospital, at my siblings, who all have battle-ready expressions, and lastly at my Father, who is now frowning. I take a deep breath and turn to face the room.

"It's true."

20

THAT'S WHAT YOU CALL A GAME CHANGER

"I cannot believe you have been so reckless, so selfish," Mother spits out as she paces. "This is completely unacceptable, Malcolm. You need to fix this as soon as possible. This will ruin the family." Her face is pink; I'm shocked to see a thin line of sweat at her hairline. "Think of poor Rachel." I snort. Even when presented with a surprise grandson, her first thought is for that viper they expect me to shackle myself to.

Right after I confirmed Bea's surprise, it took Mother less than ten seconds to spring into action. She immediately slammed and locked the study doors, terrified that the staff would overhear. Rachel's mother, Ingrid, was called, and a mute Rachel was hustled off to her parent's house, where I was supposed to pick her up in the morning to talk and plan. Mother's beleaguered secretary canceled her entire week and called several times to confirm. Now we are all locked in here while she manically paces and nervously spits out instructions.

"Who is this woman? Can she be bought off? Wait, Malcolm, have you done a DNA test? We might be worrying for nothing. After all, your grandmother is old and might be confused. How can we get one without alerting the mother? Hendrix?" She turns to my brother, who has been enjoying her breakdown, and points. "This is right up your alley." Hendrix grins, leaning back insolently in his Chippendale chair. "I don't know if that is a compliment or an insult."

"It's...whatever. What do you think? How am I just now noticing that shirt you are wearing? You look like you are from New Jersey, for goodness' sake. Take it off immediately." If possible, Hendrix's smile gets wider. "Isn't your mother from New Jersey?"

Mother blinks, her mouth opening and closing like a fancy fish. "You know what I meant, Hendrix Elouan Le Laurier," she scolds, resuming her pacing.

"There is no need for a paternity test, Penelope, and do sit down. You are giving me a headache." Grandmother is calmly reclining on a settee, a small glass of sherry in her hand.

"We cannot take some random woman's word, Beatrice. Not to mention, your judgment is to be questioned. You should have come to Percy and I as soon as you had a suspicion. We could have nipped this in the bud. Now we are at risk of humiliation."

"Roman's mother is not random. She is a lovely, accomplished woman, and I am extremely fond of her. Do you understand what I am saying, Penelope? She is under my protection, as is the child." Mother stops and stares, slowly sinking to the couch. "You would side with a stranger over the Clare name?"

"In case you failed genetics, Roman is a Clare," Hendrix drawls. Mother's head turns toward him, and any moment, I expect it to go three-sixty. "No, he is not."

"Yes, he is, Penelope. I am declaring it so. And if it helps calm you, I have already had a test done. And Roman is irrevocably Malcolm's." Father scoffs as his wife stiffens. "It could be any Clare relative."

"I thought you'd say that, Percival. Just like your father, you only know what you want to know. Here are the results." She pulls a stack of papers from her Birkin and hands them to my father. He snatches them, puts his glasses on, and reads them intently, his lips moving. He's long since discarded his suit jacket, and it might be the first time in years that his hair isn't perfectly styled. "This says it was tested against Valentina Clare, Montgomery Clare, and Malcolm Clare. You all knew?" Mother jumps in rage, glowering at her children, who are all grouped on the couch, staring at her. I suspect a plot, but I can't let them take the heat for me.

"Mother...please sit down. The doctor told you that you need to take it easy with your heart," I help her to a chair, swearing that I hear someone mutter, 'What heart?' but ignore it. I sit beside her, trying to warm her cold hands, but she pulls them away, glaring at me. I sigh and start my own pacing.

"I met... Roman's mother in Boston last year. Remember I was closing a deal? I won't go into detail, but we had an amazing connection, and she was stunningly beautiful. We had time together and parted on very amicable terms. She had no idea who I was—we never exchanged names."

"How on Earth can you have a connection without sharing personal information?" Mother scoffs, resettling herself in her seat, grimacing in distaste.

"It's called a one-night stand, Mom," Montgomery chimes in, "In and out." He makes a popping sound with his mouth, and Mother sucks in her frozen breath.

"Montgomery, I do not need auditory details." Hendrix is howling, and Valentina has a pillow over her head. I scowl at his wink and continue.

"I'd briefly thought about trying to find her, but when I got back to New York, Mother had just had her cardiac arrest. Rachel and I... reconciled, and that was that. I never heard from her again until she showed up at my office." Mother pounces on that information. "And just how did she find out who you were? Was she planning this from the beiginning?" I wince; hearing it from her makes what I said to Rory even more horrible.

"She saw his picture in *Persuasion Park,* or rather her best friend did, though it was probably just a matter of time. Thanks to Rachel, his face is all over the place," Monty shrugs. Mother won't even look at him, still upset about his sound effects. "And how do you know that Montgomery Davidson Bancroft Clare?" Ouch, another four-name. She is on a roll.

"I helped deliver the baby. I asked her best friend and got all the deets." Mother's eyes close, and Grandmother smiles.

"*SO*," I get the attention back from Monty, who is probably about ten minutes from being clobbered with a high heel, "She came to my office with a contract for me to sign, which I did." Father's head pops up. "What contract?"

"She wanted me to sign over all parental rights—basically giving up all claim on Roman unless medically expedient. At the same time, she is forfeiting any claim to his inheritance or Clare assets." Mother lets out a large breath, and a relieved smile perks her up. "Well, then, we have nothing to worry about, correct? I'm assuming you were smart enough to have it looked over?" At my nod, her back relaxes, her control sliding back up her spine. "Then this conversation ends here. Mother Beatrice—"

"Have you asked Malcolm if this is what he wants, Penelope? Percy? Have you stopped and thought about this child- your grand-child? Roman is the heir to the Clare fortune, whether you want it to be so or not. He is Malcolm's first-born son. Where is your heart? His mother may not want anything to do with this family, but I will not allow this to continue, and that is that." Grandmother places her glass down, her soft voice coated with steel. She turns to me, a gentle smile on her face. "Malcolm? Is this what you want? Do you want to completely cut yourself off from your son?"

"Of course he does—" Bea raises her hand, silencing my mother effectively. "Malcolm, darling. Live for yourself for a moment. Say what it is you really feel."

I stare at her, the reassurance in her gaze giving me permission. I look at my mother, my intense worry for her health at war with my heart. I glance at Valentina, who has tears running down her face, that touch of hope in her blue eyes. I know what I want- what I've always wanted. I take a deep breath, knowing my next words will alter my life forever. Hell, it was probably knocked off course the minute I spotted Rory across that bar.

"I want my son. And I don't care about the consequences."

21

...AND DON'T LET THE DOOR
HIT YOU...

"Now, just remember to let me do most of the talking. I know Rory well enough to get around that temper of hers. She will be very upset with me for obvious reasons and nervous about you showing up. I will need you to put away your pride, Malcolm. You will want to battle back, defend yourself. Don't do it. She is incredibly smart as well as quick." Bea is ticking off advice as I stare out the window, feelings I've never felt swirling in my gut.

It has been over a week since I have spoken to my parents. Once I announced that I wanted to be a part of Roman's life, my mother stood up and left the room. My father was right behind her, only stopping long enough to tell all of us how disappointed he was with our actions. Montgomery made a half-hearted attempt to speak to him, but dear old Dad just waved him off, telling us to be out of his house and not to come back unless invited. To his mother, he said nothing. We all left as a group— Hendrix leaving for a night of who-knows-what and Cameron, Monty, and Valentina returning to their place. Grandmother agreed to meet me at the office the following day, sharing all the details of how my siblings sent up an SOS and begging her for help. She packed up and arrived two days later. Hendrix had hired someone to follow Rory and learn her habits, and Bea made her acquaintance shortly after. She had been prepared to dismiss Rory but took one look at Roman and knew right away. She was candid enough to tell me how disappointed she had been when she learned I had agreed to Rory's terms, but she understood when I explained my reasoning. She encouraged me to give Rachel a few days to cool down, but I still tried to reach out, only to get the digital cold shoulder: no emails, texts, or even a tag on social media. Valentina sent me some links showing Rachel was not slowing down, still running around going to parties and gallery openings, flashing her engagement ring in every photo. And true to her word, she was seen almost exclusively in Chanteuse clothing, sending me the outrageous bills, which seemed to get higher daily.

"Valentina, darling, you are here as a buffer. Rory is less likely to act foolishly if you are present." Val is jiggling in her seat, two giant bags of toys and clothes in the trunk, a blue and green bear on her lap. Once she heard our new plan, she refused to be excluded, that stubborn chin coming up and her eyebrows knotting together in defiance. I never could resist that face.

"I know, I know. I'm just so excited to see Roman," she smiles, squealing when we pull up to Rory's building. I rarely come to this part of the city, which gives the illusion of the suburbs amidst soaring skyscrapers. "Grandma, what if she doesn't let us up? There's a doorman." Valentina peeks out as a uniformed concierge comes to open the door.

"A valid concern, Valentina, but I thought of that in advance. I bought the building a month ago." Bea steps out as Val shouts out in wonder. For all her claims of being a Clare in name only, Grandmother sure acts like one. The concierge takes the bags from my driver, Val still clutching the bear. Grandmother marches ahead, clearly familiar with the layout. I'm surprised to see a courtyard with trees and a small garden, someone walking a dog towards the back.

We reach an elevator bank, and I thank the concierge, taking the bags and slipping him a large tip. Grandmother presses a button, and I see its for the fifteenth floor. "What if she isn't home?" It's still a weekday, and I know she is busy at Miller-Jones.

"She is. I've confirmed it," she dismisses my concerns. I stare at the old-fashioned paneling, closing my eyes, and taking a few deep breaths.

The doors open, and Bea takes a left. I take in every detail: the clean, blue and red carpets, the pre-war sconces, the patterned wallpaper. Rory's door has a separate mat in front of it, dark grey with an outline of The Strata Center in Cambridge. I smile as Bea rings the bell, her posture straight. She's in a sharp cream pantsuit, her tiny feet in matching suede heels. Valentina convinced me not to wear a suit, so I opted for jeans and a button-down shirt. I hear some muffled sounds, and a tall, good-looking guy opens the door, a light blue cloth thrown over one shoulder and a bottle in one hand. My hackles raise as he smiles, annoying twin dimples popping out.

"Bea?" Fuck, he's got an accent too. I know Bea said Roman's nanny was a man, but I did not expect him to look like that actor, Jacob-something Monty and Cameron love.

"Hello, Julian, dear. I'm so sorry to pop in like this, but I'd love to speak to Rory. Is she busy?" The guy looks at me, eyes squinting, before swinging to Valentina, who is gawking at him with her mouth open. His eyes narrow in interest, and I clear my throat, glaring at him. His grin widens, and he looks back at Grandmother.

"She is on a conference call but should be done soon. I just put Roman down for a nap. Come in, please." He moves back, taking the bags from Valentina. They are having a whispered conversation, and once I hear my sister giggle, I roll my eyes and move away, taking in the space. I know Rory didn't design the apartment, but there are still quirks of her personality around the apartment. The walls are painted in a subtle grey zig-zag pattern and are covered with framed posters and paintings of abstract art and architecture. The living room is sunken slightly, down a single step, and the floors are covered in thick mismatched rugs. The furniture is all custom- fluffy neutral couches and a vintage *biojuterie* coffee table covered in books and baby stuff. I peek around the corner at the modern kitchen and spot a parsons dining table in a light oak and a hallway leading to the bedrooms. Above the living room are expansive, paned windows with a view of the park below. I can hear the murmuring of voices behind a pocket door. The whole apartment feels eclectic and personal—a perfect description of the woman who lives here.

Julian seats Bea and Val, fussing over them, before going into the kitchen to make tea. Val watches his every move, and she fans her flushed face when he leaves the room.

"Oh my god, he is gorgeous! I can't believe he's the nanny!" Val whispers furiously. I roll my eyes, but Bea seems amused.

"Calm down, my dear. You'll catch more fish with a stingy hook," she pats her hand, and I chuckle. Julian comes back with the tea, and we are all sitting silently, Julian watching me while Val is watching him. I meet his stare for stare, guessing correctly that I have been painted the villain.

"Julian is Roman asl—Bea? What are you doing here? Malcolm? What the hell are you doing in my house?" I look up at Rory, a smile threatening to break. She's wearing a pair of old Yankees sweatpants with holes in both knees, while on top, she is decked out in a white silk shirt and a deep green jacket. Her glorious dark red hair is pulled into a slicked-back ponytail, and light makeup makes her already unreal face even more striking. Oh, and she has mismatched socks on her feet. My heart slams, and I take a breath. "Hello, Rory." I hear a bark and see a big fluffball headed my way when Julian quickly cuts him off, herding him out of the apartment.

She blinks, eyes swiftly giving me the once-over before the frown returns. "What are you doing here? And why are you with Bea?" Her head tilts as she looks at Valentina, who has stood up. She's about a second away from leaping on Rory and squeezing her.

"Rory, dear, sit here by me," Bea tells her, patting the cushion beside her. She gives me the stink eye, but I can see her brain trying to puzzle this out. Her hand automatically reaches for Bea's, a habit I doubt she realizes. Her jacket moves, and I see the long strand of black Cavendish pearls, as does Valentina, who grins like a hyena. Rory's eyes narrow at our exchange, and she turns to face only Bea, giving me her back. My lips quirk, and I bite the inside of my cheek to prevent my grin.

"Rory, I will not butter you up or dillydally about. My full name is Victoria Beatrice Demelza Cavendish Clare, or as I am known at home, Lady Holland." It takes Rory a second, but her eyes widen, and she stares at Bea. "Clare?"

"Yes, darling. Malcolm is my grandson—his father is my son. This young lady sitting next to him, about to jump out of her skin, is his sister, Valentina. She called to tell me about Roman and this silly contract you two cooked up. You'll have to keep her in line because she will buy out all of Manhattan for the child. These two bags are after hours of negotiating her down." Val is grinning and nodding. "I can't promise anything, but I won't buy furniture or anything like that without your permission."

"Furniture?" Rory looks horrified, which finally snaps the smile across my mouth. She glares at me, and my smile widens.

"I see that look you are throwing at Malcolm, darling, and I promise you this isn't his fault. He was willing to suffer and follow your plans, but I wasn't willing to once I met you and Roman. Roman is a Clare and Malcolm's heir. There is no need for you to do this alone, darling. I want to know my great-grandson, and his aunt and uncles will surely be pests. Don't deprive him of his family out of pride."

Ouch. Grandmother was laying the guilt on with a finely honed blade. Rory pulled her hand from Bea's and moved back an inch.

"You lied to me, Bea. You lied, Malcolm, lied. Why on earth would I want my baby around a family with a loose hold on the truth." I wince, but Bea is nodding. "That is very valid. But I had my reasons, and I'm sure Malcolm did as well." Rory gives me another salty look, this one filled with sarcasm.

"Uh-huh. So now, suddenly, you want to be a part of Roman's life? Why because your grandmother is putting you up to it? You sure signed that contract fast, though." I realize then that she's right. I didn't even put up a fight; I just went along with what Rory wanted, thinking it was best for everyone, that it was just easier. I never let my own wants and desires factor in— which I told myself was noble, but I'm beginning to suspect was just selfish.

"You're right. I'd like to discuss it with you privately, though, if that's alright." She scoffs at me, shaking her head. I try not to stare at her when she takes off her jacket and flings it onto a chair. Her sweatpants are a gift.

"No, it's not alright, and I don't forgive you, Malcolm," her stubborn chin sets, and I nod slowly. "I understand."

"There is the issue of that ridiculous agreement. I've taken the liberty of having a judge friend of the family look at it. He says that it's a very simple thing to have it invalidated. He is happy to take care of it for us, with the utmost discretion." Rory shakes her head.

"I am certainly not ready for that. I don't think it's fair that the three of you showed up at my house, hoping to distract me with talk of presents and trying to load me down with guilt. That crap doesn't work with me. Roman is the most important thing here, and I will not let anyone dictate what happens with my son." Rory looks Bea in the eye, her voice even but strong. She looks at Val and me briefly, not flinching in the least.

I cough lightly, peeking at Bea, who doesn't seem the least put out but rather proud. I heard stories that my grandmother was a hellraiser in her day, and I can only imagine how much she's enjoying all of this. I think she is magnificent. We rarely get to spar with someone who is not bowled over by our name or money.

"There is much to settle, I agree. For now, I'd like you to open up to the family visiting Roman from time to time. We can set up a schedule—whatever works best."

"I can babysit anytime you want. Like if your nanny needs a break or if you have a date or something. I can do anything." A date? I scowl at my sister, who looks at me with wide eyes and a head tilt.

"Rory, we can start slow. I don't want to take over your life or step out of line. Perhaps once or twice a week?" I ignore the way her eyebrows shot up at my short speech, mocking me, I'm sure. Those plush lips are twisted in a smirk, eyes daring me to push back. Her mouth opens, probably to snark at me, when a wail comes from the monitor on the table. Valentina jumps up, about to tear down the hallway, and Bea smiles. Rory sighs, muttering something under her breath. The wails get louder, and she walks down the hall without saying another word.

22

WHEN LIFE GIVES YOU
LEMONS, SPIT THEM OUT

You have got to be kidding me.

I hurry down the hallway as if demons were chasing me, which, in a way, they are. If you had told me when I woke up this morning that Malcolm would be sitting in my apartment, I would have laughed you out of the city. It's bad enough that I have had next to no sleep with my poor baby up half the night crying and uncomfortable. It's bad enough that I almost forgot about a video call with this damn client who keeps asking for more and more; it's bad enough that Bernoulli broke into the trash can and ate something that had him throwing up and...other things all over the apartment. But this fool has to show up wearing the identical outfit he wore the night we met? Like I will swoon at his feet and do whatever he wants? I don't care that he looks like some fantasy with that tall, muscular body and chiseled face. I don't care that his longish hair is a bit messy, with one side tucked behind his ear and the other falling in his face. I DON'T CARE.

I push open Roman's door, schooling my scowling face. I melt as I see him kicking his feet, his face wet with tears. His cheeks are pink with discomfort, and his blue eyes are limp with exhaustion. "Ah, my poor little bug. Come here." I pick him up, kissing him all over. I quickly change his diaper and wipe his face. Part of me wants to lock the door and have Julian deal with the Clare family, but I've never been a coward, and I won't allow these people to chase me out of my own apartment.

"Okay, Roman, here's the thing. There are some folks out there that want to meet you. Say the word, and I will kick them clean across the room. 'K?" I kiss him again, and he sniffles, crying a little and rubbing his face in my chest. His breath hitches, and I feel awful for putting him through this. I take a deep breath, walk slowly down the hallway, and hear Bernie slobbering into his food bowl in the kitchen. I stop briefly before I scold myself and walk into the living room. Malcolm stands automatically, his eyes riveted on Roman. His sister is crying, and she stands too, seemingly torn between bum-rushing me or letting Malcolm greet his son first. I take the decision from her and walk straight to him, trying not to be affected by the look on his face. Nope, nope, nope.

"Malcolm, this is Roman. He is fussy because he's trying to grow some teeth, but he's still a good boy. Roman, this is...," I stop not wanting to give Malcolm a title he wouldn't be comfortable with.

"Your daddy. I'm your daddy," Malcolm says, his eyes glassy and hands already reaching. I hand him over carefully and maneuver him around until Malcolm has a good grip on him. Roman automatically starts crying, not used to strangers, but Malcolm shushes him gently, leaning him back so that he can see his face.

"Hey, there, little boy. What's happening, hmm? Your mama says that you're having some tooth issues. That's what happens when you are growing up to be big and strong. Sometimes, we must be uncomfortable with things before learning from them. But you have an amazing mama, and we will both take care of you, right?" He just sways Roman, who traitorously has stopped crying and is just staring at his father, a confused look on his face. Valentina is taking a video, tears flowing down her cheeks, and I hear a sniffle, realizing she is not taping but has called someone watching on FaceTime. Malcolm pays no one any attention, just walking Roman around the house.

"And this crazy girl is your Aunt Val. She is a pain in the butt, but she will love you with her whole heart. She also likes to shop, so hide on those days." Valentina laughs and peeks over Malcolm's shoulder, cooing. "Oh my god, he is even more gorgeous than I thought. Look at all of that hair! It's kind of red, huh? He's got the Clare blue eyes, too." She leans in, kissing Roman, who gurgles a bit, making them laugh. "Oh, I love him," she sniffles again. "Can you say hi to Uncle Monty? He's at work, but he loves you." She holds the phone up, and I see Dr. Clare in his white coat, waving at the screen.

"You have another uncle, Rix, but you are not allowed to hang out with him until you are eighteen." Bea laughs, and I frown—I thought there were only three of them. I ask Bea, and she nods.

"Penelope, Malcolm's mother, was briefly married to a complete hellion for less than a year. He died while she was expecting Hendrix. My late husband Cyrus stepped in and snatched her up for our son. Hendrix's family, the Le Lauriers, are a rather unruly bunch. They refused to allow Hendrix to be raised as anything but one of them. He spent the majority of his childhood between the two families, mostly on the other side. He is not my biological grandson, though I've always considered him such. He's a bit of a cad but a good boy." I raise my eyebrows, vowing to look him up when they leave. Roman is completely calm now, and Malcolm sits with him, smiling at me.

"He likes to be able to see—he's nosy. Speaking of nosy," I nod toward Bernoulli, who is slinking around the corner, staring at all the strangers. He ambles to Bea, nudging her hand for some scratches but staring at Malcolm. "This is Bernoulli. He's Roman's best friend." Bernie edges closer, sniffing and side-eyeing Malcolm, checking on Roman, who kicks at him. He sits at Malcolm's feet, staring at him, a giant puppy glare on his face.

"I swear he's friendly, but he's trying to figure out why you are holding his bestie. He will probably stand like that the whole time you are here." Malcolm holds on to Roman with one arm while holding a hand out for Bernoulli to sniff. Valentina kneels next to him, and Bernoulli woofs at her softly, allowing her to love on him. She takes something from behind her back, and I roll my eyes at the Kong toy she rolls to his feet. Bernie— a treat monster, barks and picks it up automatically, tossing it in the air, making Valentina laugh—another traitor.

"Rory, come sit. You are hovering," Bea says, and I realize I am standing in the middle of the room, ready to leap at any moment. I sigh and sit next to her, rubbing my forehead.

"This is a lot for you, I know," she says in a low voice, though no one would be able to hear us above the play between Valentina and my puppy. "I promise you it will be worth it in the end. A baby can never have too much love, no?" I nod, annoyed to see Roman gumming down on Malcolm's hand, drooling and happy. I refuse to acknowledge how good they look together.

"Now, the worst days are ahead. I will be frank with you, darling girl. Malcolm's parents are not happy about these developments—they are mortified, to be precise. The Clares— on the whole— are an extremely rigid family. They are very steeped in tradition and appearance. My daughter-in-law, Penelope, has made being a Clare her life's work. They hand-picked Malcolm's fiancee, Rachel, when she was thirteen. Rachel herself is a xerox copy—she is very invested in being the future Mrs. Clare. Frankly, I don't know how these children came out as lovely as they did, but that's neither here nor there. Navigating this next storm will take a lot. I am here until things are settled."

What? "I don't know how to take that, Bea. I will never force my child on anyone. If they don't want to be a part of his life, then screw 'em. Pardon my French," I tack on at the end. She laughs, twining her fingers with mine. "The most important part of this is that Malcolm is willing to do whatever he has to to be in Roman's life. Trust me. Just look at them." She smiles at her grands, Malcolm staring at his now sleeping son, who his besotted aunt is holding. My mean little heart relents. A little.

"Now, darling, let's discuss the family tree. Did you know we were once related to the king?"

23

THE ROMAN EMPIRE

"Let me get this fucking straight—Bea is Malcolm's grandmother? And she's what a countess or something?" Saige, who has been gone forever (a week), is lying on the floor of my apartment, Roman beside her, playing under his floor gym. His little tooth popped out overnight, and a whole ton of his suffering eased down. I'm lying on the couch, a bottle of wine in my hand that I keep swigging from. Julian stepped out for the night but promised to be back later. Bernoulli is napping with his paws in the air, snoring like a furry buzzsaw.

I nod miserably, taking a long swig. "Yup. Fooled us all." I've spent the past few days being inundated with visitors—all that talk about a schedule, a giant bunch of crap. Montgomery and his husband showed up the next day, bringing dinner, some educational toys, and a tiny doctor's coat with his name embroidered on the pocket. According to Julian, Valentina has been by every day, bogged down with bags of clothes and toys. I came home last night, and Bernoulli was wearing a blue sweater with a "B" on it. And Malcolm...

"It says here that her older brother is the Earl of Danby, and she's a Viscountess. She married Cyrus Douglas Clare and had three kids, one of whom is Malcolm's dad." She continues reading off the family tree, most of which Bea told me about, even though I zoned out after about the fifteenth 'cousins of cousins of marriage to the duke of this who was the whatever of whichever King.' I keep nodding.

"Yeah. I guess Malcolm's brothers and sister called her up, and she came running to the rescue. She knew all about me before I ever laid eyes on her. She lives on one of the daughter's estates and rarely comes to the States anymore."

"I mean, that's sweet, right? They want to be a part of Roman's life." Saige sits up, her shiny blonde ponytail fanning behind her. "I can't believe you didn't call me, though. I would have come straight home."

"That's why I didn't. I don't need your mom mad at me, too." Saige laughs, knowing I'm right. Saige's mom, Pam, is the definition of a proud mama. She has a shrine of her daughter's achievements on a wall in the living room and sports Miller-Jones sweatshirts all over their small New Hampshire town. Her husband is just as bad, calling us every Monday morning, checking in, and giving us advice. It's a big deal when she goes home, and I'd feel like a whole shithead if I pulled her away. I tell her everything she missed, including Bea's warning about Malcolm's parents.

"That's scary. I mean, it sucks that his parents aren't supportive of his life. I give him props, though. It can't be easy for him." I snort, not interested in giving him any sympathy. "Has he been by to see Roman?"

I pull a pillow over my face. "Yeah. He comes over after work, normally around Roman's bedtime." The day after the AMBUSH (that's what I've been calling it,) I'd just finished with Roman's bath when my doorbell rang to reveal Malcolm. I stood there, a wet shirt front and messy hair, blinking at him. His mouth quirked, and I moved back silently to let him in. He took the naked baby from me, ignoring my mute state and asking a ton of questions about Roman's routine. He did everything I directed perfectly, which was fucking annoying, and rocked him to sleep while reading him a story. Roman went down like a champ, and once he tucked him into his crib, he kissed him softly and left. This has happened for the last three nights, but I don't expect him to show up tonight since tonight is a Friday. I've seen plenty of pictures of his fiancee recently, decked out in Chanteuse (uh-huh) with her moon rock engagement ring threatening to cause an eclipse over Manhattan.

"And?" Saige is bouncing around, making Roman laugh. I roll my eyes at their antics. "And nothing. He gets Roman ready for bed and then leaves. We barely talk. Wipe that look off your face." I point at the pout/scowl her pretty face is sporting.

"I mean, that's not awkward? You two should be having conversations and planning stuff, Ro. You can't communicate by note or whatever the hell you are doing." I shrug, taking another sip of wine.

"It works for now. All of this makes me uncomfortable, Saigey—I can't just jump into a relationship with these people because they want it to be. And they are like dysfunction junction over there. I have to think about what's best for Roman." She nods, but I can see she disagrees. I've been without a family for fifteen years now, and it's overwhelming to have so many people in my business, stopping by and texting constantly. Montgomery sends me baby articles, and Cameron shares fun stories about the kids he teaches. Valentina is just everywhere. Texts, phone calls, visits, deliveries. She always asks before coming over, and I always say yes because being mean to her is impossible. I was leaving for work this morning when my phone started pinging like crazy. It took me a second to catch on to the text thread Valentina had started, naming it "The Roman Empire."

Montgomery: Rory, does Roman have a bank account?

Valentina: Ohhhh yes! Does he?

Valentina: Wait, did you see the pictures I took yesterday? (j.peg) (j.peg) (j.peg) (j.peg)

Cameron: LOL, that's adorable! Where did you get those pants?

Valentina: I ordered them from the collective

Hendrix: I haven't even gone to bed yet, why
am I in this?

Cameron: No one cares, fool.

Malcolm: ?

I NEVER ANSWERED, BUT LATER THAT DAY, I GOT AN ALERT FROM THE
bank that a deposit had been made in the baby's account despite my
not giving them a lick of information. I've been too nervous to look
at it.

"Wha—" The doorbell rings, and I sigh. Even though Wallace
monitors all guests, the Clares are on the permanent entry list. It's got
to be one of them since Julian has a key. I stand up, wishing I had
thought more about what I was wearing. Saige and I are in grey sweatpants, except she has a matching tank top and a cute cropped jacket.
Her ponytail is perfect as always, and her makeup still looks fresh after
a day's work. I have on a ratty Brown University t-shirt and my hair in
a crooked bun. Oh well. I look through the peephole and grimace,
unlocking it. Bernoulli, now wide awake, is nudging me, trying to get
to the visitors.

"Uhhhh, hi?" I look at Malcolm, moving to the side. I give the man
with him the stink eye, which does nothing except make his hazel eyes
gleam. "Hello, sweetheart. Good to see you again." I close the door,
crossing my arms over my chest. "I guess the Yankees game wasn't a
coincidence?" He laughs, chucking me under my chin and giving
Bernie a good scratch.

"Rory, this is my brother, Hendrix," Malcolm shrugs in apology.
He's already holding Roman, and I'll have to get Saige a towel because
she is drooling like a fountain.

"Yeah, I just put two and two together. The living statue next to
you is my best friend, Saige Marchand. Saige...well, you know," I make
a sweeping motion with my arms. Malcolm nods at her, but Hendrix
slinks forward, lifting her hand and kissing the inside of her wrist and
then the palm. I swear I hear Saige's heart disintegrate into a million
pieces and snicker, though I don't think a woman alive wouldn't fall at
his feet. I don't know the last time I saw a man wear jeans and

suspenders, but with his tall, muscular frame and wild hair, he works it. Seriously.

"Miss Marchand," is all he says, turning her face flaming red.

"Enough of that, you idiot, come and hold your nephew," Malcolm says, shaking his head. Hendrix winks at Saige, holding his arms out for Roman, who ducks his head in Malcolm's neck before peeking at his uncle. He's been a trooper about all the new people in his life, and I shouldn't like the way he turns to Malcolm for comfort.

I really shouldn't.

Hendrix laughs, leaning forward and taking Roman anyway. He fusses a bit, but before long, he is full of smiles as Hendrix throws him in the air and catches him with silly noises. Saige looks at me, eyes wide, mouthing "holy shit."

"Have you eaten yet?" I look up at Malcolm, who is studying me quietly. My mouth opens and closes, the wine making me foolish. "Um, no?" His dark eyebrow quirks at the bottle in my hand, and I quickly hide it behind my back. Hendrix laughs, and Saige sidles next to me, easing it out of my hand and hiding behind her instead. Rix is still snickering while Malcolm struggles not to laugh.

"I'll call for delivery. Any preferences?" My brain is still as red as a traffic light, but I shake my head. I try not to notice how his light grey suit fits him, how his hair waves into a mess, how his blue gaze lasers on me. I gulp and close my eyes, not noticing how he's watching me, the wolf behind his eyes. I count to five in my head, cursing that damn Rioja that Cameron and Monty brought over.

"She's a meat eater, for sure," Saige adds unhelpfully, and Rix chokes back a snort. Malcolm's face twitches as I glare at her.

"That I do remember. How do you take your steak?"

❧ 24 ❧

LET THE WAR BEGIN

"That might have been one of the best nights I've ever had."

I look at my brother, who has a slight smile on his face, and see that he is serious. Rix has always led a ridiculously privileged and adventurous life. He's had the world at his fingertips since birth, traveling extensively and living to the zenith. He's never still, always flying off somewhere, sailing here, driving there. My mother says he is just like his father, River, who was a constant stream of motion and energy.

"It was just dinner," I say, not wanting to admit that it was almost perfect for me, too. I'd been cutting my days short at the office, racing to the West Side to see Roman each night. The first night I showed up, I was a wreck, worried that Rory wouldn't let me in, wouldn't let me make amends. I mean, she didn't make much conversation, just giving me quiet instructions and then letting me be alone with my son until he fell asleep. I thanked her to silence, going home every night determined to break through. The next few nights were better, her face not as grim, her voice not as dry. I even think her plush mouth smiled—a little.

"Yeah. But a relaxed dinner with two gorgeous women, watching the Yankees game, and playing with my nephew? Perfection." He does the chef's kiss motion, and I smile. I ordered dinner from a Thai place that Saige recommended, which perked Rory right up. They started bickering about dishes, and I ordered a ton more food than we could eat. Before the food arrived, I showed Hendrix how I got Roman ready for bed, with Saige cracking up at his expression and taking photos. When he was down for the night, Rory turned on the game, talking smack with Rix about Baltimore, our division rivals. The food arrived, and the girls set up a buffet on the living room table, bringing out more wine and beer. It was a close game, with Rory yelling at the umps and Saige rating the player's hotness on a scale of one to ten. I'm not sure what I enjoyed more, the sight of Rory's sublime ass shaking at every homerun or the way her thin t-shirt molded to her breasts. Rix certainly got a kick out of Saige, who recovered from his outrageous flirting and sassed him to death, putting him in place several times. Once the game was over, I wanted to linger, but Rory gave us a pointed look, tucking away all of the goodwill from the night. I peeked in on Roman, stroking a stray strand of his dark hair and patting his rump, which was popped in the air. I shook Saige's hand and nodded at Rory, shaking my head at Rix, who grabbed both of them and gave them over-the-top kisses and hugs. I murmured that I would be by the next day, and though she sighed, Rory saluted me, giving Saige the side-eye.

"Have you heard from Mother and Percy?" I shake my head.

"No. I've tried to call a few times, and Elena just tells me she will take a message. I'm sure if I showed up at the brownstone, she'd tell me the same thing. It's been total radio silence."

"And Rachel?"

I snort. "Not a word. I'm sure she and Mother are trying to wait me out. Her shopping bills sure haven't shut up."

Hendrix is thoughtful. "So you are still going through with this stupid wedding? Not to use Roman as an excuse, but there's no reason to. Rachel's entire existence is predicated on her giving birth to the Clare heir. It's the only thing she has ever wanted. Now that the baby is here, what else is left for her? You don't love her, and she isn't capable of loving anyone, sooooo...." My phone rings before I can respond.

Speak of the devil. "Hello, Rachel." Rix makes a face and rudely sticks out his tongue.

"Malcolm, where are you? I am at the apartment, and Boone will not tell me where you've gone." Her voice is ice cold, and I hear Boone in the background, snarling something. No one would be happier than him if Rachel just evaporated into a cloud of dust.

"I'm with Hendrix. I should be there shortly."

"Fine. And do be quick. I don't like waiting." I raise my brows at the sudden silence.

"You know, I own a pharmaceutical company. I wonder if they can develop an anti-bitch vaccine." I bury my face in my hands, laughing.

"She might need a booster or two as well."

⌘

MY DOORMAN LOOKS SYMPATHETIC WHEN RIX DROPS ME OFF AND reminds me to call him if I need him. My phone has been pinging, meaning he updated the rest of my siblings.

> Montgomery: I have the shovel ready
>
> Cameron: You've been at our house all night.
> ALIBI
>
> Valentina: Can I be there when you tell Mom?
> Pleeeeease?
>
> Rix: Just show her a picture of Rory. She'll
> fold like a lawn chair
>
> Valentina: Can I be there for THAT 😊

I shake my head as the elevator opens to the marbled foyer. Boone meets me, hurrying. "She's been measuring the bedrooms and the gym, just a heads up." He takes my jacket and hands me a full glass of vodka with ice. "Good luck." I walk the long yards to the east side of the penthouse, where the windows face the Hudson. I hear the slamming of drawers and take a breath. I peer around the corner and see a large mound of clothing on the ground, some with the tags still attached. "Rachel?"

"Oh good, you're here. So I had the design firm on a call today, and they promised that they could finish the gut and remodel by Christmas. Of course, we'd have to pay extra, but that's no problem. Then, we could have the magazine shoot us for the spring re-design edition. Sounds perfect, yes?" I take in her short white leather skirt edged in ridiculous silk white roses and a matching crop top showing off her flat stomach. Her five-inch heels don't even wobble as she struts across the thick Berber carpet. Her glossy hair is pin straight, the ends a symmetrical wonder. I notice the diamonds in her ears and wonder if I paid for them, too.

"There will be no remodel, Rachel. We discussed that."

"And I think that if I can't get the furniture I originally wanted, we can have *Boca do Lobo* do something. I already called them, and the *cavalhiero* assured me he would love to work with the Clare family," she continues, adeptly ignoring my words. She's always been good at that— brushing off whatever doesn't please her, ignoring you until you forget why you were saying no in the first place.

"There is an incredible *Lapiaz* set that is to die for. It's cream and gold; we should get all the matching pieces. Speaking of, these clothes need to be thrown out. I don't know what I was thinking—the designer is passé now. A whole scandal, dahling," she laughs meanly. I cock my head at one of the tags. "These pieces are thousands of dollars. We would be better served donating them."

"I don't want a poor person touching my old things! What would they do with them anyway? It's not like they have balls and cocktail parties to go to." I wince as her voice raises, and I pray none of the staff hears her. Val has worked with a charity that auctions off luxury donations and uses the proceeds for shelters. I'll contact her in the morning.

"Rachel, we are incredibly fortunate, but that doesn't mean I approve of money being wasted this way. If you don't want these things, I will have Val work on them." She snorts, muttering something I don't catch. "And back to my decision. The only remodeling will be a room for my son—he needs a nursery here." The temperature in the room drops about fifty degrees, the silence as thick as the carpet.

Have you ever watched a horror movie where the killer does a slow turn to the victim before they start chasing them with a hatchet?

Yeah.

"You think I am going to allow that, that CHILD, into my home? That I will just go along with this stupid fantasy of yours? I gave you some time to figure out how you will make this all go away. Is this what you think is acceptable? It's bad enough you cheated with some WHORE, and she couldn't even get the birth control right, but now you think we are going to be some happy blended family? I. Will. Not. Here's what is going to happen. Malcolm. You will pay that woman off — I don't care how much it takes. We will hire the most bulldog law firm in New York to intimidate her into agreeing. Then she and that child are going to move far, far away. You will forget about him, and my child will be the heir. Period. This is what I want, and it's what your parents want. We've discussed it. Now, when can they start construction? Next week?" I stare at her, the twisted, ugly look on her face, the venom in her voice. I haven't moved from my lean on the doorway, though she is a blur of fury, flitting from one side of the room to the other. Can I really spend my life with this?

"That is not going to happen. None of it. This is my home—not yours. You have no say in what I do; we aren't married; you can wheedle all you want, but my decision is final. And the fact that you are more interested in yourself and your fucking selfish plans for a closet instead of working on being a stepmother to my son is very, very telling. It may be time to reconsider this whole engagement, don't you think?"

The invisible hatchet swirls over her head. "No, I don't think, Malcolm. You have room to talk about being selfish. We've been engaged since we were teenagers, yet you've spent your whole life running away from your commitments. You've broken my heart a million times, humiliated me, and made me the laughingstock of Manhattan. Now you pop up with an illegitimate son you insist on making your heir, despite your family traditions. It's all about what you want and what you need. Not this time. YOU. OWE. ME." Her overfilled lips twist and curl. I almost chuckle when I see a few clumps of smooth hair standing up on her head. She'd freak out if she knew.

"I don't owe you my life, Rachel."

"No, but you owe me your mother's life." I pause and stare at her, triumphant arrogance on her face. I always knew that she was capable of it, but facing it was something different.

"Are you that evil?" She scoffs, waving a slim hand, her engagement ring winking in the light.

"Oh, please, Malcolm, spare me the theatrics. This is a business deal, plain and simple. We can both benefit if you just fall into line. Now, I am going to call the designer in the morning and tell her that we are a go. Then we will visit your parents and tell them the wedding is intact. Your father already has a lawyer lined up. I hope you didn't get attached to that child— it will be easier if you just cut off contact. Cream and gold are exquisite, don't you think? Maybe a teeny hint of black, just for drama. After all, a little drama never hurt anyone, right Malcolm, dahling?"

✦ 25 ✦

WE'VE BEEN GHOSTED

There's something weird going on.

Malcolm has disappeared for over two weeks; his nightly visits over as quickly as they began. I kept expecting the knock on my door, the dreaded (maybe) interruption, but it never came. At first, I thought that perhaps it was work-related—he was the CEO of a giant company, after all. But then the pictures started popping up: Malcolm on Broadway previewing a new show, Malcolm at the opening of a new exhibit at the Guggenheim, Malcolm at the Yankees game, presenting a charity with a giant check. Saige even found one of him and Valentina shopping on Madison Ave. In ninety-nine percent of them, his fiancee was hanging off his arm, smiling brightly at the camera. I'd think the whole clan dumped us if every other family member didn't keep showing up as usual, including Bea, who didn't mention Malcolm but gave me long speeches about appearances and smoke and mirrors, whatever that meant. Valentina and Monty have been texting all morning, but Malcolm makes no comment.

Valentina: Today's the day! Yay, Rory!!!!

Cameron: Wait, what's happening?

> Montgomery: She's going on-site to the restaurant
>
> Cameron: Yay- This means what exactly?
>
> Valentina: It means she gets to the real work. It's exciting!!!
>
> Montgomery: Can you stop using so many exclamation points?
>
> Valentina: !!!!!!!!!!!!!!!!!!!!!
>
> Montgomery: I hate you
>
> Valentina: Take that back!

Nothing from Malcolm.

I wasn't pressed.

Really, I wasn't.

I'd planned on raising Roman on my own, anyway, so the sudden mini-loss of his father didn't factor in, though if he did show back up, we would be having a conversation about it. I won't allow him to jump in and out of Roman's life, especially not when he is old enough to remember. Saige was angrier than I was, encouraging me to get the scoop from one of his siblings, but I refused. I don't want anyone to get the wrong idea.

"It's not the wrong idea if your baby's father just up and stops visiting him. It's a valid concern!" Saige is pacing in my office just after the last morning meeting. I have a site visit to the Schillings new venture, where I will spend most of my time for the next few weeks. Saige will run the office for the most part, and the rest of the team is busy with other projects. I've already changed out of my dress and happily into jeans, a T-shirt, and my old Timberlands. Saige French braided my hair into a single long plait, smoothing all my curls and tucking them tightly. This is my favorite part of any project and where I am the most comfortable.

"Saige, I don't care what Malcolm does, okay? Maybe he realized that attempting to be Roman's father was too much for him. I told you what Bea said—his parents don't even want to meet Roman. I don't blame him for taking a step back because he's disrupting a huge part of his life. Not to mention he is planning a wedding to his childhood sweetheart; she's got to be devastated," I pull on my baseball hat, transferring my wallet and stuff into my ancient knapsack, tucking my fancy briefcase away into my coat closet.

Saige snorts. "Sweetheart my ass. That chick is known for being a witch—I've heard stories that would make a nun blush. She's got a reputation for being nasty to everyone in her path. I doubt she is devastated as much as she is pissed." I frown, wondering why Malcolm would marry someone like that, then shrug.

"Well, that's their business. All I care about is Roman."

"It is your business too, Rory. Stop burying your head in the sand; it's driving me crazy!" She yanks at her freshly highlighted hair, pulling off one of her stilettos and throwing it across the room. "I swear you have to be one of the most stubborn people I have ever known." She takes off the other one and tosses it in the same direction.

"I'm not being stubborn; I'm being practical. He didn't ask for any of this—he's got a right to decide how his life will be led, including whether or not he wants to be in Roman's life. Malcolm signed that contract, Saige. The only reason we are here right now is because his brother and sister wanted to get involved. Not Malcolm, remember?" I roll my shoulders and bury my face in my phone.

"So you are just going to ignore how much Malcolm seems to love Roman? Are we going to totally disregard that? He's head over heels for that kid. Don't you think it's strange that he just disappeared but is all over the city like a mad hatter?" I say nothing, flipping through old messages, my lips glued together.

"Alright, you want to be that way, fine, I'll go for it. I think the real reason you are being such a fucking donkey is because you don't want to feel anything yourself. Did you think I forgot how much you whined and cried about the amazing man from Boston? How much did you regret not exchanging information? That he might have been 'the one?' And maybe you refuse to acknowledge it, but he looks at you like a thirsty man in the desert coming up on a frozen margarita."

"No, he doesn't, and I don't want him to, Saige. He is engaged to be married, dammit. I am not the OTHER WOMAN!" My voice goes up twelve octaves, and I glare at her. She storms over, slamming the door and whirling around with a finger pointed at me. The last time we fought like this was our first week of college. We were chosen to be roommates, and on the first day, we circled each other like wild animals. Pam was bouncing around, decorating the room, offering me snacks, and just being a mom. I was a resentful little crap, missing my mother, and couldn't take the outpouring of kindness. I snapped at Pam, who had offered to take me for bedding, and Saige let me have it. She called me an ungrateful brat and a weirdo, and I called her a spoiled idiot. We went back and forth until Pam intervened and made us talk it out. Once I confided that my mom was gone, Saige eased down, giving me a huge hug and a coveted bag of BBQ chips. I was mortified at my behavior and apologized twenty times. We've been besties since.

"Who says you have to be the other woman? There is something between you two, Rory, and it is not just sharing a child, which itself is a big tether. Anyone with eyes can see it, except maybe you. I only saw you two together for a few hours, and it was right there. He couldn't take his eyes off of you."

"I don't want his eyes or anything else on me. Drop it, Saige, I mean it." She growls, kicking at a pillow she'd grabbed and dropped.

"Fine. Don't fight for what you want. Let him marry that gold-digging beetle. Maybe they will invite you to the wedding." I'm barely managing to keep my face neutral when the phone rings and the GC updates me about some deliveries. I answer a few of his questions, not paying attention when Saige leaves the office. I hang up, rubbing my face and grabbing my bag. Maybe I can sneak out and avoid Saige for the rest of the day.

"Need a ride, gorgeous?" I spin around and see Hendrix leaning in the doorway, for once dressed in a spectacular black suit, his honey-colored hair pulled into a simple ponytail. He's got a little scruff on his jaw, and despite his serious face, his eyes are sparkling. I should have expected something like this, this family is nothing if not *involved*.

"Um, sure, if you want people to think you are giving one of your maids a ride to work." I wave my hand down his form, grinning. His laugh bounces off the walls, and for a moment, I swear there is a brief silence as the sound stops every living thing in its tracks.

"They will think I am the luckiest man alive, trust me. My sister tells me you are going to your newest project. May I tag along?" I squint at his face, suspicious. "Why?"

His grin only deepens, which even makes my concrete heart patter. "Because."

"Because?"

"Yup. Now let's go before you are late." He winks over my shoulder at Saige, who is still giving me an evil eye, arms braced like an MMA fighter. "I'll make sure she gets there in one piece." Saige nods at him before whirling around and closing my office door behind her.

"Bye, Saige!" I call out and hear nothing in return. I sigh, knowing she is still mad at me and it will be a while before she forgives me.

THE CONSPIRATORS-
HENDRIX

I let Rory walk in front of me, mostly because I am admiring her butt in those tight jeans.

Dayum.

I'm tempted to take a photo and send it to Malcolm, but he is already on the edge and about to kill me. On second thought, I take a snap and send it off to him, hoping it will push him into action. I don't put any caption in case that raging she-wolf he is marrying checks his phone. I won't need to anyway—Rory has a world-class ass, and he won't mistake it for anyone else. (And just in case you think I'm a perverted fool, I delete it right away. I've got plenty of not-off-limits asses on my phone. Like Margit, the chick I brought home last week, who orgasmed so hard she passed out.) My driver, Winchell, does a double take when I walk out with Rory and not from shock. Rory is objectively one of the most beautiful women I have ever seen. She's got the whole package: eyes, a rare metallic pewter with a touch of copper and thunder, that suck you into a vortex, lighting you up with cool heat. Hair a deep red, almost black in some lights, and a curvy voluptuous body, with tits for days. It's nothing but a bonus that she is smart as fuck and oblivious to her traffic-stopping looks. No wonder my poor brother is so gone for her. Winchell hands her into the back of my Maybach SL Monogram, and she gives him a big grin, enough for my stoic driver to falter and smile back. I roll my eyes at him and sit opposite her, giving Winchell the address and smirking at her raised eyebrows. Poor girl has no idea how entwined our lives are and will be forever.

Valentina called me one morning this week, frantic over Malcolm's absence. Apparently, after I dropped him off a few weeks ago, he stopped visiting with Roman, effectively ending all communication with Rory. When Val asked him about it, he changed the subject, cutting her off in a way that sent off alarm bells. I immediately called him and was informed by Eve, his (sexy) assistant, that he was indisposed. I messaged Val to let me take care of it and thought about how to set some stuff in motion. I was in the middle of a large brand takeover, twenty men seated in my boardroom staring at me. I drummed my fingers on the table before shooting off a text and then giving them back my attention. Once the paperwork was signed, I checked my messages and read the one from Boone. I frowned at the information and called Wicker, the same lawyer I'd sent to Malcolm. I gave him explicit instructions, telling him to use what he needed to make my demands happen. He was still working on it but assured me he would get everything done. My next step was to meet with Bea and tell her what Boone overheard. She was livid, and we devised a plan that would stay between the two of us for a while. Now, here I am, envying my brother and his future. He better thank me when this is all over.

"I visited with Roman just before I came to get you. He's getting bigger every day. Those two teeth are adorable." Rory beams, the first genuine smile I have seen from her. I warned my family that they were about to disrupt this poor woman's life, taking away her peace, but like always, they bulldozed ahead, promising to fix it as they went along. Rory has mastered a blank face, keeping her feelings close, except a few times when her usual spunky attitude comes out. This smile—a real fucking one—is stunning. This is the woman Malcolm met in Boston, the one he could never forget.

"He bit me the other day when he was, um, feeding. So now I'm weaning him..." Her face turns red, and I laugh out loud. "I wonder if that happened to me too, because do I love nibbling." She buries her face in her hands, shoulders shaking, which makes me laugh harder. Malcolm is a fool. A well-meaning one. But a fool. Time to make some magic happen.

"Val tells me that Malcolm has done a disappearing act. That true?" Her laughter stops that blank mask back in place. Pity.

"Yes." She seems to be struggling with more words, though they aren't necessary since I heard her entire argument with Saige. I wait for more, then sigh inside. I swear she and Malcolm are perfect for each other—both stubborn and moral with little care for their own wants.

Fuck that.

I sigh dramatically, taking my hair out of its ponytail and winding it into a bun. "I guess he's just trying to protect you again. I tried to tell him not to, but..." I shrug, peeking at her from under my lashes, stifling the urge to fist pump at her concerned frown.

"Protect me? From what?"

"Well, from that barracuda, he is being forced to marry. She is trying some shady shit, and he's doing everything he can to make sure you and Roman stay out of the line of fire. She's always been a piece of work, obsessed with being the next Queen Clare, but all that is out the window now. If Malcolm weren't worried about how our mother would react, he'd call this whole shit off." I watch that adorable frown deepen, wishing I could speak straight to her, but knowing I have to stick to the plan. "Forced?"

Gotcha.

I cover my mouth, exaggerating my dismay. "I shouldn't have said anything. It's Malcolm's business." I look out the window, doing everything I can not to look at her.

"Well, I think if it concerns Roman, I should know. He is my son, and if someone is trying to pop shit, I need to be prepared. I can handle it. And I don't care what street this chick is from; no one threatens my son." I keep my voice even though I want to give her a high-five. This is one mama bear I would not want to cross.

"Well, as of right now, she has no idea who you are. Mal has worked double the time to protect your identity, so he's staying away." I think.

I'm making this up as I go, but I know my little brother well enough to know his thought process. "I don't put it past her to have him followed."

"Followed? Is she crazy?" Rory looks horrified, but I continue.

"Yeah, she's off her rocker. They broke up last year, and Malcolm just couldn't take it anymore. She refused to accept it and ran around trying to make everyone believe they were still together. He was out of the country and then in Boston, so he had no clue. Shit went down, and the engagement was back on—she's been making him pay for it every since. Now this? She's probably got a tracker in his car, in the office, and all his shoes. She's ruthless." I stop, not wanting to go too far, just giving her stuff to think about. A nibble, if you will.

"But what could she possibly do to me? It's not like I'm running around New York telling everyone about my business." The bad part of me wants to bite that pouty mouth, her ire making her even hotter. Then I remembered she would be my sister and sighed.

"Maybe not, but she could start rumors about your business—she's adept at going for the jugular." Those silver eyes flash, her cheeks spotted with anger. "I wish she would try. I'd wipe the floor with her." I keep a grave expression on my face, nodding.

"Well, we will let Malcolm take care of it. Poor guy. All he wants is to be the dad he always wanted. Oh well. Maybe someday." I wince, hoping I'm not laying it on too thick, but she doesn't seem suspicious.

"So, we are almost there. May I have a tour? I'd love to see you in action." She smiles, a small one, but real. I can see the wheels spinning in her head, and a small wrinkle is etched between those fine brows. She nods, slowly telling me about the restaurant's progress, her voice picking up a happy tone as she gets excited. I listen with half an ear, well-versed in the construction, quietly tapping out a message on my phone.

Rix: Your move

$\maltese$ 27 $\maltese$

THE CAT IS OUT OF THE BAG,
AND GALLOPING AROUND
THE ROOM

When I bought this penthouse, it was the talk of Manhattan. *33336 East* was one of the most expensive properties in New York at the time—always a coveted building, the top four floors had been tied up in probate for years, the previous owner's heirs fighting tooth and nail over rights and percentages. When all the smoke cleared, and the decision was made to sell it, I was first in line with an outrageous offer that far surpassed what the family was looking for. I immediately had Clare Construction combine the four separate apartments into one giant dwelling. It took three years, lots of work, and planning, but it became a dream space. Of course, Rachel wanted to put her stamp on it, butting into the designer meetings and demanding all kinds of crazy shit that almost made the interior design firm quit a few times. I put my foot down on some of her more outrageous demands, ignoring her pouting, sneers, and scowls. She wanted my home gym to be smaller, her make-up room bigger, and two ballrooms. Instead, I made my gym bigger, adding a pool and indoor racquetball court. I haven't been to a public gym in years, ever since a group of drunk bridesmaids tried to get into the locker room when I was changing. I spend a lot of time here, working off frustrations, punching through problems, and swimming away the emptiness. Tonight, I am hiding, avoiding Rachel like a pothole in the street. With twenty-three thousand feet of space, you'd think it would be easy, but she finds me almost immediately every time. If I hadn't found that people tag in my briefcase, I would have thought it impossible or even scary. Thankfully, I found it the day after our big blow-up when I was going to see Roman. I had no idea what else she was up to, but the one thing I could do was protect my son and his identity. For now.

"Malcolm? Your parents are on their way up." I nod at Boone, staring out the wall-to-wall windows overlooking Central Park and most of Manhattan. If I squinted, could I make out Rory's building?

"I'll be there in a few." Rachel got some bug in her ear about having them over for dinner, an 'amends' she called it, though I had already apologized to my parents weeks ago, pretending to fall into line, until this morning when my plan was finally ready.

"Well, you-know-who is..."

"Malcolm? Why are you hiding in here? We have guests coming, you should be out here with me, waiting. Boone, why aren't you wearing the uniform I asked all the staff to wear? I've told you that what you wear is unacceptable—go change immediately...where are you going? Get back here, Boone; I will not be ignored. Malcolm, help me!" Her run-on sentences and speeches seem to get more shrill as time passes, and I don't blame Boone one bit for hightailing it to the other end of the house.

"I swear he needs to be replaced! I will not have the help disrespecting me like this in my own home. I don't care if his family has been attached to the Clares for years—he is an insolent ass." I run my hands through my hair, praying for patience and maybe for a crack to open up on the floor and swallow me up.

"Rachel, Boone is going nowhere. Maybe if you were nicer to him, he would listen more." I might as well have said she should wear fake diamonds because the way her face creased up (as much as it could—because, as Val says—that Botox is kicking her ass) was almost comical.

"I do not have to be nice to the help—their role is implied in the name. H.E.L.P." I stare at her face, ten thousand words climbing up my throat, but I push them down. I take a deep breath and paste a smile on my face.

"Let's go see my parents." I hold out my elbow, and she sniffs, her nose in the air, though she takes it. As usual, she is wearing white, this time a high-necked short-sleeved sweater with matching wide-leg pants.

We arrive in the foyer just as my parents do, Boone escorting them to the largest sitting room. One of the maids is already serving them drinks and light appetizers. Before I can even get Rachel seated, Boone announces that my Grandmother has arrived. My mother mutters something under her breath, and Rachel looks like she's swallowed a live snake. I direct the maid to set another place setting, and Mother's chattering gets a little louder. I consider postponing my plan, but realize it might be easier with Bea here.

"Malcolm, I thought it was just the four of us tonight," Mother says tightly. Ever since I gave her the groveling she wanted, she has looked about ten years younger. Too bad it's only temporary.

"Mother, I didn't invite Grandmother, but she is more than welcome in my home anytime." She sniffs (oddly identical to Rachel) but says nothing, knowing there is only so far she can push with Father listening.

"Penelope, I hope I'm not intruding. Shall I leave?" Boone brings Bea into the room, his lips tucked behind his teeth. These two are always trouble together, and I know he wants to howl at her sarcasm. With her soft British accent and manners, she can confidently put anyone in their place—especially my mother.

"Of course not, Mother Clare. I should have considered inviting you, but I didn't know your schedule."

"Well, it's not your home, is it? Don't worry, Malcolm, dear. I'm deliberately gate-crashing. Boone, a bit of sherry, please. The Macallan." Boone bows, rushing to do her bidding, which is about to set Rachel off because she knows Boone would have pretended to hear his mother calling him if she tried the same thing.

"Rachel, how is the designing going?" Mother jumps right in, as usual, ignoring everyone else in the room, and Rachel starts babbling about her colors and other bullshit. My father has wandered away, gulping down some of Rix's new whiskey, and I phase out for a moment, my future as clear as a polluted river.

"Tell me, dear, how is Roman dealing with his teeth? Rory tells me that he's up to two now. Valentina sent me the pictures." I pause with my glass in mid-air as Rachel and Mother's conversation ends abruptly. Father comes back as well, all of them staring at me with different levels of anger.

"Rory? Who is Rory?"

"I thought you said you haven't seen that child in weeks, Malcolm. What is she talking about?"

"Valentina? Why is she involved?"

I stare at my grandmother, who has a devilish look in her eyes, though her face remains perfectly British-placid.

Well done, Bea. Corner. Painted.

I take a deep breath and remember that this was my plan all along.

"I haven't seen Rory or Roman in a few weeks, Bea. I've been very busy. I plan on remedying that tomorrow, however. Perhaps after dinner, you can show us all the pictures."

"Malcolm, do not ignore me. Who is Rory? Is that the child's mother?" Rachel asks, her sharp nails tunneling grooves into her palms.

"Oh dear, Rachel, are you not up to the time? Yes, Rory, a dear girl. Percy, you know of her, don't you? She owns that lovely architecture firm you are always going on about. Miller-Jones? To think we shall have two firms in the family is just fortuitous. And that little dumpling, Roman, looks just like Malcolm. Mayhap a little of his mother in the hair and mouth, but otherwise, a dead ringer. When is he coming over, Malcolm? I assume soon? I'd love to be here." Bea sips serenely as she throws bomb after bomb. The air has thinned to a mountain-top level, and I hold my breath, waiting to see who breaks first.

"Are you telling me that you had a child with one of our competitors? Is that how she keeps stealing projects out from under us? Are you giving her information? A bit of pillow talk?" Father has a line of sweat across his upper lip, and his face is a mottled purple. I stand up slowly, placing my glass down carefully. I don't even notice when Boone swoops in and removes all of them, always thinking about his pantry.

"Father, are you accusing me of sabotaging my own company? Did I hear you correctly?" I ask him quietly, waiting to see if he realizes his fatal error.

"You're damn right—"

"Of course, he isn't Malcolm. Your father is just in shock."

"I don't need you to speak for me, Penelope. Conveniently, we lose several bids to this... person, and then Malcolm throws her child in our face. I want an explanation. Immediately."

I tuck my hands into my pockets, staring at him. "I refuse to be called to the carpet as if I am a child. I am the CEO of Clare Inc., per tradition, and the board. What I hear is the prideful ranting of a man angry at his fading influence."

"Malcolm! Apologize at once!" My appalled mother points her finger at me. I ignore her, still waiting for my father to retract his accusation.

"You forget who I am, Malcolm. I'm still the senior Clare of this family. I can have the board remove you if I see fit. I've been wondering why no law firms were willing to take our retainer, and now I know it's because of you. I'll be calling a meeting for the morning." Rachel gasps, and I give him a half-smile. "Okay."

"Malcolm, stop this. Don't you see what that woman is doing? She is tearing this family apart. This was probably her plan all along." Rachel places herself between me and my parents, and I look over her head at them.

"The only people damaging the family are you, Mother, Father. I wish you could step outside of your arrogance for a moment to see what I see. I have a son. A beautiful, healthy baby, who I am very proud of. His mother is brilliant and strong, and all I want is to raise him and love him. But you are so tied up in this bullshit—this awful sacrifice you expect me to make, that you can't even give my son a little love, a little consideration. You aren't normal parents; you're something else altogether." My phone vibrates, and I see two words on the screen.

"It's done."

I smile and nod to myself.

"I have never felt so disrespected in my life. Malcolm, you are forcing us to choose sides, and I fear you don't recognize the repercussions." My father signals Boone for his overcoat, and my mother's face is pale but set. Rachel is on her phone, fingers flying, an unattractive red creeping up her neck. Have they always been this awful? Rhetorical, of course. I've known their limitations forever.

"Oh, I know exactly what I am doing. If you check your email, Father, you will see I tendered my resignation to the board two minutes ago. I've also sent out a press release announcing my leaving and the formation of my own company, MDC Holdings. I'd make sure you are in the office early, as I'm sure the press will be hounding you since you are now CEO. Again." I smiled at him politely, the high color he had draining out of his cheeks.

"You can't do that! You're the oldest—the heir!" Rachel spits out, moving closer to my silent mother, who radiates anger, twitching, and cold. I can tell Rachel is holding back, not wanting my parents to see her real nature. Rachel has always been careful to hide that demonic temper, only going as far as my mother would, saving her worst impulses for the staff and me.

"Yeah, I can. See, I have two other trust funds— one from the Cavendish side and one from the Deveraux side. If I never even look at my Clare inheritance, I am still well off—several lifetimes over. I can care for my family—meaning Roman and his mother—very well."

"Not to mention, he will have everything I have when I pass. I have quite a portfolio, as you can imagine," Bea chimes in, and I hide my grin.

"Is this what you are choosing, Malcolm? Because I will never forgive you for this. You will not be welcome in my house ever again. I have raised you to respect the Clare name and the traditions and customs we have kept for hundreds of years." My mother threatens, and for a small teeny moment, I turn back into the son who wants to make his exacting mother proud. But then I picture a red ponytail and wide silver eyes, and that boy disappears.

"I know, Mom. But I forgive you." She gasps, taking my father's arm.

"We have waited years for you to grow up, Malcolm. We let it go when you kept postponing your engagement and then the wedding. We forgave you when you went gallivanting off to Europe, avoiding the chaos you left behind. We thought you were finally getting it together, and now this. I have never been so disappointed in you."

"Well, that makes two of us because I'm disappointed in you too." I wave a finger between them. Mother snarls, dragging Father and hurrying out of my house. Bea watches them go with a snort, and Rachel is still standing there, fists curling and uncurling.

"If you think I will take this lying down, another thing is coming. This is the last time I will let you humiliate me. Malcolm. Do you have any idea what that announcement is going to do to me? I will be the laughingstock of Manhattan. Your own company? With no clients? With no reputation? You'll be a failure, a joke. And don't think that whore is going to get out of this unscathed. I will make sure everyone knows exactly what she is. When I am through with her, she won't be hired to design a subway car." She storms out of the room, hollering for Boone, who is hiding behind a silk screen in the foyer, his eyebrows waggling. She reappears a few minutes later, a bag with some of her things in it on one arm. She stabs the elevator recall, her back to us, only giving us an evil look when she pushes the button for the lobby. The silence is a blessing before Boone steps out, reaching for the phone.

"Hello, this is Boone from the penthouse. Going forward, Miss Van Pyke will be removed from the visitors and tenants list. Any deliveries, packages, and inquiries will be returned to the sender or redirected to her personal number. Is that clear? There will be no exceptions. Yes? Thank you." He turns to us, a giant smile on his face.

"I have been waiting decades to do that. So what's next?"

❧ 28 ❧

THE WAY TO MY HEART

"Rory!"

I look across the room, seeing Saige hurrying over to me, stepping over wires and open boxes, high heels wobbling around the mess, about to give me a heart attack.

"Saige! Hard hat!" I yell from the top of the ladder. One of the electricians hands her one, his fist over his chest in a love declaration. Only my best friend would show up at a job site wearing skintight navy blue pants and a clingy pink silk blouse. I will probably have to pay overtime to about thirty people—who are all watching her frantic stumbling with stars in their eyes.

"Get down off that ladder right now!" She stands at the bottom, waving a newspaper around like a windmill. I roll my eyes, tucking my screwdriver into my back pocket, before descending. I blow a strand of hair out of my eyes and squint at her. "What are you doing here?" Saige rarely comes to sites; instead, she runs details from the office and waits until the end to make her suggestions on decor and lighting.

"Girl, have you seen the paper this morning?" She waves it again, her pretty face slightly sweaty and shining. September in New York can be up and down: cool and fall-ish one week and hot and humid the next. "No, I left early and came straight here. What's up?" I'm distracted by a hanging cord and call out for it to be furled.

"Rory, focus! Everyone is talking about it! Malcolm resigned from Clare Inc. and is starting his own company. He sent out a statement last night. Gurlll, it's about you and Roman. Check this out," she starts reading the press release.

"Clare Inc. has been part of my lineage for as long as I can remember. I am proud of everything I have accomplished as CEO and hope my contributions have made my family proud. As of this morning, I am no longer a part of Clare Inc.'s executive suite or future. Instead, I will be starting a new venture, MDC Holdings, which will embody my vision of real estate and technology and prioritize time with my newborn son. We have already signed a major partnership with Grant-Alloy and look forward to sharing more details soon. For press inquiries for Clare Inc., please contact the Public Relations department on the website. For inquiries about MDC Holdings, please email the address below."

My son.
My son.
Holy. Shit.

"Social Media is going CRAZY. I think it took a minute for everyone to realize he dropped a baby in the middle of a business report, but now that's all anyone can talk about. The speculation is wild, and everyone wants to know who the baby mama is. His office is not commenting, and apparently, that chick he's engaged to was seen leaving her building with three thousand suitcases. Everyone knows it's not hers because she has always been skinny as a stick. Plus, they aren't married yet, and that's a big no-no up there on Park Ave." She rambles on while I sink onto an old folding chair. What in the living hell is Malcolm thinking?

"Girl, I cannot believe he didn't tell you about this. Well, wait, maybe I can—this guy isn't predictable. He basically announced to all of New York, 'screw my family, I got my own shit and my kid.' I just hope we can keep a lid on who you are for as long as possible. The gossip pages are ruthless when they want information."

I wince, thinking about all the photos I've seen of Malcolm, dozens and dozens each week, breathless coverage of every move he makes. Intellectually, I understand the fascination- a man so rich, handsome, and successful from a family full of earls and billionaires; people want the fantasy. But then I think about what Rix said—about Malcolm wanting to be a good dad and that dragon having him followed. My phone pings, and I see the missed text icon climbing. I have the Clare family thread on mute, but Julian's text comes through first.

> Julian: Just a heads up. Malcolm Clare is on
> his way to you

"Oh no." I show Saige, who starts squealing and clapping. "Will you stop it? First of all, there are wires and stuff everywhere, and if you fall, I will have a whole world of issues. Second of all, you are going to cause someone to nail themselves to the wall if you keep jumping around like that." I roll my eyes as she starts whisper-yelling and jiggling quietly. I peek at the Clare thread, almost dreading what I am going to see.

> Valentina: Malcolm CLAREEE!!!
> Whatttttt??????
>
> Montgomery: OMG. I am knee-deep in a
> vagina, but what the HELL
>
> Cameron: Rory! Are you okay?
>
> Cameron: Mal.. I'm proud of you.
>
> Montgomery: Waaaait! What about Rachel??
>
> Valentina: Malcolm don't make us hunt you
> down! What is going on?????
>
> Hendrix: How can I buy into MDC Holdings?

I stopped reading, and my chest started to get tight. He didn't even tell his family about this?

"Rory!" Sagie hisses, pointing. A uniformed man stands near the entrance, his hat in hand, staring at me. He says nothing and makes no moves, but I know he is there for me.

"I'll be right back. If anyone asks..." Saige snorts.

"If anyone asks, you are in a meeting. You don't need to tell me how to cover your ass. I've been doing it for over ten years." She waves me away, and I walk swiftly, not wanting to draw any more attention. The man is standing outside now, and I walk up to him, looking around for a cameraman to jump out from behind a food truck. I pull off my dirty hard hat and tuck it under my arm.

"Miss Miller-Jones? I'm Tam. Please follow me." He gestures a few feet away, and I notice the dark-tinted Bentley idling at the corner. It's a gleaming deep burgundy with black accents—flashy but discreet. Tam opens the back door, and I grimace at the state of my dusty clothes. Talk about Cinderella.

"Rory? It's okay, come in." His deep voice comes from the darkness, and I climb in, staring at the plush leather seats and mahogany paneling before finally focusing on Malcolm, who is smiling at me uncertainly. I stare at those true blue eyes, and my shoulders come down from my ears, recognizing his nervousness. I let out a deep breath and let a smile slip over my lips. "So, how has your day been?" His startled laugh, combined with that glamorous grin, settles me down further.

"Well, let's see. I just announced to the world that I quit my job. I started my own company, which is currently running out of my apartment. I saw my son, who bit me, and now I am riding around New York hiding out in a new car, and my new driver probably thinks I am crazy. You?"

I smother a laugh at Roman biting him. The little sucker has been trying out his new powers and is nipping at everything in his path. He even got Bernoulli, who just laid there and yawned. "That's all?"

A lazy smile blooms on his mouth, and I gulp silently. "Well, now I am sitting across from one of my favorite people. So my day is looking up." I ignore that weird look on his face and rub my dirty hands on my pants. He says nothing, just watching me. *He is not that handsome, Rory. Get a grip.*

"So, um, do you want to talk?" I wave at the air while he still stares.

"I brought you lunch." Wait, what?

"Julian says that you tend to work through all your meals and then go home and eat out the refrigerator. I don't like the idea of you being hungry, so I had my chef make you some pasta and chicken. I've been to your office, then your house, where Julian finally told me you were here." He hands me a fancy glass container with a gold and silver fork that I swear is real. "Um, thanks."

"Take a few bites for me. I have a feeling you will still not eat it if I don't keep an eye on you." I blink at the command but automatically open the lid and shove a few forkfuls in my mouth.

"Oh. This is delicious." I wolf down more, the slightly spicy chicken merging perfectly with the lemony pasta. A bottle of sparkling water appears in my peripheral, and I gulp it. I finish the whole bowl before realizing who I am sitting with. I peek at him and see he is laughing silently. I scowl, handing him the empty container and poking him in the ribs. "I was hungry."

The chuckles finally come out, and I fight my own amusement. "I see that. I'm glad you ate something. I know you will be working late, but can I come over tonight to talk? You must have a million questions." I nod at him and look at my watch. "I've got to get back."

"Text me when you are leaving, and I will meet you there. Unless you want me to pick you up?"

I shake my head. "I'll text you. Wait, do you have my phone number?" His dark brow quirks. "I've had it, Rory." Oh.

"Do I have yours?" My brain isn't ticking with the way he is studying me.

"You do, but I will message you to make sure." His head tilts as he peruses, a lock of thick black hair sliding forward and over one eye. God help me.

"Um, okay. See you later?" He smiles at me again, and Tam opens my door right on cue. He hands me out, not flinching at my grubby fingers. "Thanks."

"It's my pleasure, Miss Miller-Jones." He tips his hat, and I run inside, hiding behind the scaffolding, and listen to the car purr away.

"What did he say?" I yelp and jump at Saige, who's been hiding behind the other wall. "You scared me!"

"Whatever bitch. What happened?" Her eyes are wide and excited, and I shrug.

"He brought me lunch."

❧ 29 ❧

FOOL ME ONCE

.

I hope you didn't think I would go along with my parent's plans.

C'mon now. They threatened my son and his mother. You had to know that was the last straw.

After Rachel told me all about how she and my mother and father had gotten together and planned on chasing Rory and the baby out of town, I snapped. It was a quiet snap, a cavernous invisible crack in the iceberg of my soul. I'd spent so many years following the rules, bearing through the weight of being the 'Clare Heir,' setting the example for my younger siblings while being the antithesis of my part-time older sexcapade brother. I did everything right, refusing to acknowledge how underwater I was and not looking at how happiness was an abstract concept I would never have. I put up with a woman who wasn't fit to be any sane man's wife, who only wanted me for what I was giving her, waiting for her to realize I didn't love her, but who never did or cared. I watched from an emotional distance as my parents prioritized their own wants and expectations, forsaking loving their kids and ignoring our disappearing acts, sometimes to the other side of the world. I would have gone on that way for the rest of my life if Summerlin hadn't invited me out to that bar in Boston. Sure, I'd had a pure lustful moment with Dr. Cassidy Masters, her dimples and curvy body helping me realize that Rachel had never been my type. But I knew it wasn't long-lasting because once Ayden St. Devane gave me that possessive I-will-execute-you look, I never thought about her again.

No, Rory, with her laughing sensuality and overflowing affection, turned me into a human pretzel. I left her that morning, feeling like I was leaving behind essential body parts like I was losing my senses. I've never told anyone, but I went back the next week, desperately knocking on the door, only to receive a phone call that threw me back into my personal prison. I even went back to the bar, but no one knew anything about her, though I don't think they would have told me if they did. Bostonians are protective by nature, and as far as they knew, Rory was one of theirs and they were not going to let some rich suit chase her around. I left Boston with a stomach full of panic and a head full of sorrow. I let my mother's health wash away all of my progress and buried my could-have-been deep in my heart's dungeon until a few months ago when my once-in-a-lifetime came storming in, giving me everything I wanted on an unobtainable platinum platter.

Yeah, I signed that contract. I wanted her to have peace of mind and salvage a last-ditch effort at being what everyone wanted me to be. But once Montgomery showed me my son's birth pictures, I knew I couldn't do it. I spent the next few months exploring options, going back and forth until I called the one person I knew would understand.

"Malcolm! What's going on on your side of the palace?" Nicholas Grant's green eyes crinkle at me from the screen, and I finally felt myself relax.

"Conquering lands and building castles as usual." It's an old college joke, a shared humor only a few could appreciate. Nicholas' family is as old and rich as mine, staking a claim in Chicago, where he runs his family's company, Grant-Alloy. His dad retired a few years ago after some health issues, and Nick has already doubled their business, mostly venture capital and hedge funds.

"Is that one of your legion of children in the back?" I ask, knowing by his happy expression that I am right.

"Yes, it's Remy, our youngest. Kenna took Kian and Erik to a comic book store, so I've got baby duty." He turns in his seat and gives me a better look at a small body asleep in a playpen. I see a headful of dark hair and chubby pink cheeks. My smile falters, and Nick frowns.

"So what's up? I somehow don't feel like this is a call about our latest deal."

"It's not. Nick, I need your help." I tell him everything, starting with more details about my teenage tether to Rachel and ending with my parent's latest ultimatum. It feels like an avalanche of information, but he listens to every word, even taking notes, without a hint of judgment. A few years ago, Nick and Kenna, his now wife, went through their bullshit, with MacKenna even taking off with their oldest son, Kian, leaving Nick a broken-down mess. He fought hard to win her back, and now they have a big family and a world of joy. He is so far from the arrogant lady-killer he was in college that it's almost a joke. Today, he is wearing a hooded sweatshirt with a Star Wars character on the front and what suspiciously looks like spit-up. Old Nicholas wouldn't be caught dead in that, but now he's a man deeply in love whose sole goal in life is to make his family happy.

"Well, the first thing we need to do is get you some independence. Aside from your Clare Inc. Stock, what other assets do you have?" I sent him my portfolio, which is much more vast than he anticipated. We spent the next hour strategizing, and he gave me some homework with a deadline to match. I confided my plans to Eve, and she jumped on board and helped me with my assignments. I spoke to Nick four more times, the last when I was ready to change my life forever. His wife was in the room at that time and chimed in with some advice at the end.

"Mal?" MacKenna's adorable face popped onto the screen, and I gave her a wide, flirty smile, chuckling when her eyes rolled at Nick's growl. "You sure have some hot-ass friends, Nick. OW!" A loud smack echoes through the speakers, and I see her rubbing her butt. "You better kiss and make it better, Nicholas Grant. Anyway, I want to ask if Roman's mother is part of this equation?" I'd sent them a bunch of pictures, proud as can be of my lookalike son. In one, Rory was laughing while holding him, and Nicholas gave a low whistle.

"If he's smart, she will be. That is a drop-dead gorgeous woman. And a native New Yorker? You know how I feel about those." He nips his Bronx-born wife's ear, whispering something that makes her freckled cheeks blush.

"All I'm saying is that if you want her, you've got to show her. It can't be baby, baby, baby—she's got to feel wanted too. Don't let her mistake your attention for anything but your attraction. If you fall into the co-parenting trap, you may never get out. Nicholas, if you don't move your hand, Malcolm is going to get a show," her husky voice goes whispery, and I see him kiss the back of her neck. "Oh, and nip that Rachel shit in the bud, asap. I know women like her, and let's just say she will be the hardest part. Piranhas come to mind."

"Call us when you need us. I'm proud of you, Malcolm. Going your own way without your parent's support can be hard, but I promise it will be worth it." I salute them both, with Kenna blowing a kiss as the call ended.

And now here I am, on my way to Rory's apartment with a (mostly) clear head and a boatload of determination. She texted me a few minutes ago, letting me know she was finally leaving the job site hours after she expected. Roman is long asleep, but at least I'll get some time with his mother before the night ends. Tam, my new permanent driver (and new head of security), drops me off just as Rory walks up to the lobby of her building. She looks wiped out but beautiful. It's on the tip of my tongue to tell her so, but I hold back.

Not yet.

"Fancy meeting you here," I smile at her, and she gives me a tired grin back. We walk to the elevator, and she taps the brim of my base-ball cap. "I almost didn't recognize you with that crap on your head." Even though I've been here before, Tam suggested I mix up my wardrobe when visiting Roman. It only takes one person to tip off the press.

"I figured if anyone were paying attention, they wouldn't think it was me. All of New York knows I wouldn't be caught dead in Mets hat." She chuckles as she unlocks the front door, the quiet of the apartment and dim light somehow soothing. I hear padded footsteps, and Julian peeks out from the corner.

"How was he, Jules?" Rory asks him, toeing off her dusty Timber-lands and dropping her old backpack to the floor. Julian smiles, and I suddenly want to poke him in the dimples. With my fist. I shake off my unexpected anger and hold out my hand for him to shake. "He's quite the little solider. Put on his jim-jams, had a bottle, and down he went, not a spot of trouble. You're in for the night, then?" Rory nods, giving him her schedule for the next few days, a grueling pace that I know is necessary with the restaurant deadline fast approaching.

"Brilliant. I'm off to my flat, then. I'll be here before Sir Roman wakes up. Have a good night." He gives me a pointed look with a raised eyebrow. I give him one back but with narrowed eyes.

"Malcolm? You want to peek in on Roman?" I snap to attention and follow her to the nursery, where the moon and stars projector Valentina bought him softly lights the room. Rory is leaning over the crib, covering up his little rump, which is pushed into the air, his chubby arms and legs tucked under him.

"He always kicks off his blankets in his sleep," she whispers, pure love and pride in her voice. On cue, he stretches, the blanket falling off before he resumes his little hedgehog curl. She chuckles as I tuck it back over him, smoothing his wild, dark curls. I touch the skin on his neck and ears before leaning in and giving him a soft kiss. "He's so perfect. Thank you for my son." I stand up straight, giving him one last pat before following her out of the room, the door closing silently behind us. I step over Bernoulli, who appeared out of nowhere, ready to guard his friend.

"Can I get you anything? Coffee? A snack?" I shake my head as she digs in the fridge, coming out with a sandwich and bottle of water. She takes a huge bite, puttering around until she settles down on a cushioned stool. I watch her every move, fascinated by the way she chews, by the way, her long braid swings above that delectable ass, and by the warm musk scent that wraps around the room.

"This is awkward as hell, isn't it?"

I burst out laughing, nodding my head while leaning on the wall. "It is. I wish it weren't. I feel like I know you and also feel like you are a complete stranger." She waggles her eyebrows, finishes the sandwich, and turns in her seat until she faces me completely. Her silvery eyes study me, and she sighs. "Tell me what's going on."

"You read the papers, right?" At her nod, I continue. "Well, I've been planning this for a while. I always wanted Roman, Rory. I've spent a lifetime doing what was expected of me, of being the perfect son. When you showed up with that contract, my automatic response stepped in before my heart could. I'm sorry for that—that's not who I am." I stop, struggling to continue. Her face is impassive, but I see her eyes slightly softening. "I've known that the only way I can have a real relationship with Roman is to kick my parent's brainwashing out all at once. So that's what I did. I went public before they could spin their own narrative or devise another plan. They know who you are, by the way. Bea snitched." She laughs with a shrug. "I'm not afraid of your parents, Malcolm."

"They are not nice people—they are set in their ways and stuck on the power of their name. It took me a long time to say that out loud. I won't let them do anything to you or Roman, trust me." Nick's wife already advised me that the way to win against my parents was in the press. I already have another statement going out tomorrow. That's when the shit will really hit the fan.

"So now, what?" She yawns, and I feel bad for springing this all on her when she's been at work for the entire day. I would love to tuck her into bed, but it's not time for that offer. Yet.

"So now, I'm here for Roman. I want to be the best father I can be, better than the one I have. And I want to get to know you, really know you." Her eyebrows shoot up, and another yawn pops out.

"I've laid enough on your plate for one night. I want you to get some rest, Rory. I'll come by to see Roman tomorrow. Just know that my only priority is you two, okay?" She stares at me but says nothing. I pull her out of the chair, her small frame swaying with exhaustion. I wrap an arm around her back, guiding her to the front door. She grunts at my manhandling but doesn't pull away. Her puppy follows us, still giving me a suspicious glare. I unlock the door and turn to her, tucking a disobedient curl behind her ear.

"I'd love to have you and Roman over this weekend if you get a break. There is a back entrance to my apartment. I can have Tam pick you up?" I realize I'm still holding her head in my hand, but then she is leaning in, so I say nothing.

"He will need a car seat," she says with a slight frown. I stroke one finger behind her neck, fascinated by the color that spreads to her cheeks.

"Boone already bought one. It'll be installed tomorrow." I smile at the thought of the giant pile of boxes that appeared in my foyer. Boone had shoved dozens of websites in my face until we picked out a bunch of baby paraphernalia, which seemed neverending and all necessary.

"Who's Boone?" I laugh, dragging my thumb down to her stubborn chin.

"He's my house manager, therapist, brother, bodyguard. You'll love him." I brush my mouth against her forehead and step back. "I'll call you." She nods, and I take one last long look at her before heading to the elevator and down to my waiting car.

Step one: Freedom. Check.

Step Two: Infiltration- Commence

FROM THE OFFICE OF

NY Times Post:
"I'd like to thank everyone for the well wishes and congratulations I have received over the last twenty-four hours. Transition can be challenging, but the support of my peers and the community can preclude normal complications.
I hope this same sentiment can be mimicked with the announcement of the dissolution of my engagement to Miss Rachel Van Pyke. Rachel informed my family and me of her intention to travel for an unspecified amount of time while we separate and tie up loose ends. We are committed to remaining lifelong friends and ask for privacy at this time."
—Malcolm Deveraux Bancroft Clare, Founder and CEO of MDC Holdings

Persuasion Park Blog:
...Does this mean he's single????

Post International News:
Again? How many times can this couple break up? Just throw in the towel already!

The Big Apple News:
WHO IS THE BABY MAMA?

TimesUp New York:
We don't believe it. Rachel, what's good?

WakeUpWithSeth:
NYC girlies, it's time! Who will be the lucky girl to bag the Most
Beautiful Man in New York?

❧ 31 ❧

WELCOME TO HEAVEN

"I can't believe he lives here," I hiss at Saige, who is just as gagged as I am. Her mouth hasn't closed since Tam picked us up this morning in a sleek navy blue Aston Martin SVU, the windows mob-tinted and mysterious. Sure enough, there was a brand new car seat, which Roman snuggled into perfectly. Tam drove expertly through the gnarled Manhattan traffic, asking us what we needed for our comfort, whether the temperature was good enough, and whether we wanted him to stop for anything. I half expected Saige to start demanding outrageous things while hanging out of the window and hollering, but thankfully, she just sat there, fingering the fine Italian leather, eyes wide and gleeful. Tam made a few turns onto a back street, driving down a discreet ramp that ended in three security checkpoints. We pull up to a well-lit foyer, and Tam hops out, handing us out while gathering Roman's two thousand bags and equipment. I take him out of his car seat, his little feet swinging, while he grins at Tam, who chucks him under one of his chins.

A doorman came out of nowhere, pressing a gold card to the elevator in front of us, and Tam herded us on. Saige whistled at the burgundy silk-covered walls, and I said nothing, noticing that the panel only had one button labeled with an illuminated "C." The ascent was quick, and before we knew it, the doors opened, where a handsome blonde guy wearing a black polo shirt and jeans was waiting for us.

"Miss Rory? Miss Saige? I'm Boone. Welcome to 33336 East." He gives us both a slight bow before stepping forward and grinning at Roman. "And I am thrilled to meet you, Sir Roman. You have your father's ridiculous good looks but your mama's sweetness." He picks up the baby's hand, shaking it, disregarding the drool. "Please follow me. The rest of the family should be arriving in about an hour."

Rest of the family? I glanced at Saige, who had the craziest look on her face. We follow Boone, and I try to keep my cool, but holy fuck. Malcolm's house is insane. The entire east and west walls are windows, giving unfair views of the city all the way to the Hudson. There are archways into every room, gorgeous potted plants everywhere, and I recognize the floors as a rare bronze marble that closed out an entire quarry. I'm overwhelmed and grip Roman a little closer. As an architect, I can be easily seduced by etched stone pillars and thick custom carpets. But this is a whole other level.

"I have set up the whole room around Roman's needs. As you can see, there is a playpen and toy area, and behind that screen is a changing station. Roman's rooms will not be ready for a few weeks, so we must make do. The rug is certified allergen-proof and has been professionally cleaned, so it is safe to place him on it. It's not part of the original decor, but we bought it specifically for him. Now, what can I get for you? Our chef is pleased that you liked her pasta. Would you like some more of that, or perhaps something else? Just drinks?" I stare at him, torn between wanting to run away and wanting to move in.

"I'd love some coffee," Saige says sweetly, elbowing me out of my trance. I glare at her while placing Roman on the fancy allergy-rug. "Um, maybe some tea?" I'd really love a roast beef sandwich, but don't tell him that.

"Very good. I'll be back shortly. Please make yourself comfortable. This is your home." He smiles while hurrying out of the room.

"Holy. Salami. Rory! I knew Malcolm was loaded, but this is another fucking level!" I poke around, seeing other baby equipment: swings and walkers, even a giant stuffed Yankees baseball bat.

"It was all over the papers when these apartments were sold. No one knew who bought them. I won't even tell you what the asking price was." I remember laughing at the real estate listings in the newspapers. "I can't believe he lives here."

"Look how sweet all of this is. He really tried to think of everything." Saige touches a humidifier that is puffing out a slight lavender scent. After Malcolm and I had our 'talk,' I wasn't as startled as the rest of the Eastern seaboard when he dropped his engagement press release. Saige called me hyperventilating, and I could barely get a word in edgewise. I told her about his visit the night before and had to tolerate her squealing and breathless commentary. Saige is addicted to gossip blogs and sent me screenshots of the manic hype around Malcolm's announcement. To his credit, he called me early that morning, sounding harassed but checking to make sure I got enough sleep and saying he would see Roman later that day. He kept his promise and has spent the last week carving out loads of time for our son and having his chef make me delicious lunches that Tam drops off with a Mona Lisa smile.

"I'm so sorry. I have potential investors crawling out of the woodwork. They don't always have the best sense of time." Malcolm hurries into the room, a wide, white smile on his face.

That. Face.

I give him a quick once-over, turning around so he doesn't see how his black sweatpants and v-neck t-shirt make my face hot. He's got to work out every day because no human should have biceps like that. And let's just say his six-pack is six-packing, if you know what I mean. I've had unwilling fantasies about his body for the past year, but I don't think my very vivid imagination did him any justice. "Uhhhh, I think we can forgive you, Malcolm. Hey, maybe you should buy a bigger place, yeah?" Saige sasses him and he laughs, the deep sound dancing up my spine like silk spiders.

"I'm a big guy, Miss Marchand. I need my space." To her credit, Saige turns beet red, and I chuckle. That's what she gets.

"How's my boy?" He kneels on the carpet, picking up the baby, who had been enjoying the mobile Saige had dragged above him. He kisses him all over, growling and getting Roman to make the rusty giggling sounds he's been trying out. Saige eyes me meaningfully, making silent explosion signs near her ovaries. I roll my eyes and smile at the two of them, snapping a few discreet photos.

"Rory? What do you need? Did Boone offer you any refreshments?" He stands up, balancing the chunk-butt on one arm while coming over to touch my face. His black hair is a wild mess, and he looks more like Roman than ever.

"Uhhh, he did." I will myself to ignore the chills his fingers produce, biting the inside of my cheek to stop myself from taking a bite out of him. He smiles, and Saige coughs lightly, the sound suspiciously close to sounding like "sexpot."

"Well, whatever you want, okay? A blanket, a nap, a circus, whatever. I want you to feel at home here." I nod, swallowing hard. "Now, let me take you on a tour. I want you to see Roman's rooms and tell me what you want. Saige? Coming?" He looks at my best friend, who is already halfway out of the room. "Are you cool if I wander around on my own?" She winks at me, not even trying to be discreet. Malcolm's lips twitch.

"Of course. There is an intercom in every room," he points at a small video monitor on the wall. "If you get lost or need anything, just press it, and Boone or one of the staff will help you out." She salutes while scurrying away, making little yelping noises. I shake my head, sighing dramatically. "I found her on the side of the highway." Malcom laughs, which makes Roman laugh, his identical blue eyes squishing up at the corners. "Let's walk, shall we?"

Boone must be a psychic because after Malcolm took me through his apartment—all ten bedrooms and pool/gym/garden— we returned to Saige to chow down on some finger sandwiches and cookies. I went to grab a plate, but a smiling, apple-cheeked lady with the same polo on as Boone insisted on doing it for me, starting with delicate but thick roast beef biscuits and a small bowl of pasta salad with a handwritten note that had my name on it. She placed a personal tea set in front of me, spreading a napkin on my lap and patting me on the shoulder. Roman had fallen asleep, and Malcolm placed him in the pearl-inlaid crib I'd just noticed. Boone pulled the screen around him just as Malcolm's brothers and sister arrived. Hendrix immediately leaned down to hug me and kiss me, ignoring my chewing and full mouth, settling himself closely next to a scowling Saige. Valentina peeks at Roman, and Monty and his husband exclaim over all of the baby stuff Malcolm bought.

"Did you buy a baby store? Like a chain or just a standalone?" Hendrix drawls, stretching his arm across the back of Saiges's seat, leaning over and nosing about her plate. She elbows him, playing keep-away with her food as he tries to snatch some of her snacks.

"Leave him alone, Rix. He's a daddy now; he's allowed to go over the top for his son." Valentina scolds him, taking pictures of every-thing and probably mentally calculating what she needs to shop for, even though there is absolutely nothing. "It'll be better when the nursery is done. It just seems like a lot." I admire her loose caftan-style dress; the swirling colors a perfect compliment to her dark hair and blue eyes—Clare eyes, she told me.

Rix snorts, successfully stealing some fruit from Saige, who angrily screeches. "Will you just go get your own plate? There is a ton of food." She points out the spread that items are still being added to, and he grins at her pretty face, a lazy, overtly sexual promise. "But what if there is nothing I like?" She rolls her eyes, unsuccessfully trying for space. "I doubt it. I know your preferences."

"Oh? What are my preferences, pet?" That smile is wicked, but my best friend gives him a skeptical look. "Anything. You like anything."

"Yeah, the blogs call him a Vagitarian," Valentina pipes in, and Cameron immediately starts howling. "A what?" Monty spits out his drink, choking on his laughter. "Vagitarian. You know, because he eats so much pus-"

"Valentina Diana!" Malcolm has his hands covering his face, shoul-ders shaking. I fall over on the couch, burying my face in the cush-ions. Of course Malcolm would have a Sarah Ellison Float Sofa, my dream couch. Sucker.

"Thanks, sis. You're really helping my cause here," Rix gripes at her, though there is no bite behind his words. I think he likes to rile Saige up because I'm positive if she crooked her little finger, he would've been panting at her feet. Not to mention, for all of his perfection, he's not Saige's type. I think.

"Valentina," Malcolm says her name once more, but she grins at him, shrugging her shoulders. "I didn't make it up. And you know his reputation." Malcolm drops his head between his shoulders, pushing his fists into his pockets. "You're terrible."

"Is Bea stopping by?" Cameron interjects, trying to change the subject, though his face is still pink from his laughter. His green eyes sparkle, and Monty gives him an adoring kiss.

"She is having lunch with some friends from England this afternoon," Valentina tells them, coming to sit next to me. "She said she would call us later." She leans forward, eyeing her brother. "Malcolm, have you heard from Rachel after your announcement?" He shakes his head, giving me a look that I can't decipher. I've been wondering the same thing, though I've also been trying to mind my business. I can almost see Saige's ears perk up because she doesn't want me to mind my business. She wants me to be all up in it.

"No. It's been radio silence, though I've heard she's been in Paris," he says, making a weird face.

"Well, that ain't good. If she hasn't been beating your door down, then she is planning something. We all need to be on the lookout. We have to protect Rory and Roman." All of the siblings nod, and I frown.

"I don't need protecting— I can take care of myself. Besides, how bad can this chick be?"

Valentina huffs and pats my leg. "How much time do you have?"

$$\textbf{32}$$

HOW BAD CAN SHE BE? PULL
UP A CHAIR

"What do you mean our permit was pulled?"

This morning, I had a quick staff meeting before heading to the restaurant. Just before I hurried out the door, my project GC called me frantic, cursing a blue streak and threatening the whole city.

"It's just what I said. We had just started on the kitchen when an inspector walked in and shut us down. Handed us a complaint someone had submitted and another laundry list of violations. It's all bullshit, but he threw me a card and then stuck his nose in the air and left. We have ninety days to respond."

Ninety days? This won't take me ninety minutes. Part of this business is a lot of city bureaucracy and red tape. You need a thousand signatures and approvals, so many submissions, revisions, fees, and taxes to construct one square inch. We'd had all of the paperwork squared away for months, so this was completely unexpected.

"Send me everything he gave you. Then I'll meet you down at the DOB on Broadway or have Saige call up some favors." A couple of years ago, Saige dated a lovely guy named Derek, who worked for the city. I thought he was good for her, and for a minute, so did she, but he called it quits abruptly, citing his intimidation of her looks and the attention they got. They remained friends, though, and they sometimes meet up for coffee.

"Tell the guys they will be paid fully for every day we miss, but if they want to stay busy, I've got a new project that could use some help." He agrees and hangs up, and I wince at the cost to the budget, a huge amount that's going to eat in my contingency. I compose an email to the PM at one of my associate's job sites, telling him he may be getting extra help and copying the rest of my team. I also email the Schillings group and let them know we are on top of it. They respond immediately, and I wince at the curtness laced through the concern.

"Have you read this shit? None of this is true," Saige says, frowning at the iPad. "Inadequate hazard communication? Scaffolding violations? Zoning issues, fall protections— this is like a Construction-101 checklist. I'm going to call Derek." She sends him a text, attaching pictures of the report. "He says he'll get back to us in a few. I sent him all the approvals and the most recent pictures, too." The phone rings off the hook in the background as I nod absently, my phone pinging insistently with incoming text messages.

> Malcolm: What can I do? Call me

> Valentina: Rory! Are you okay? I just read the news!

> Cameron: What news?

> Valentina: <attached>

> Hendrix: What the fuck

> Valentina: Rory call me!

I frown and click on the attachment Valentina sent over. My breath catches in my throat, and I let out a horrified scream.

STAR ARCHITECT CITED FOR HEALTH VIOLATIONS AND HARASSMENT

Underneath is a picture of me, holding a wrench and grinning like a fool. I'm not wearing a hard hat. I remember that day—It was taken just outside of an older project before we got the keys to the space. I was making a joke about loving my tools, and I'm wearing an old T-shirt, but with the new company stress-eating, it's about ten sizes too small. My hair is a mess, and I have dark circles under my eyes. Where on earth could they have found that? I don't even have a copy. Kill me now.

"Rory." I look up at Saige, whose face is a combination of rage and sorrow, an echo of my own. She's standing with her hands at her sides, the iPad dangling from her fingertips.

"They're making me look like an idiot. Unprofessional and incompetent." She swallows and holds the tablet up. "There's more, Rory." She taps the screen and flips it around.

HOME-WRECKER! MEET THE CONSTRUCTION HOE WHO BROKE UP THE KINGDOM

CLARE FAMILY NO COMMENT ON ACCUSATIONS

"THEY FOUND OUT. PROBABLY NOT BY ACCIDENT EITHER." I sit down and skim the page. The first paragraph is my personal information, high school pictures of me in Scarsdale, and my first project after establishing Miller-Jones. The rest of the article is just a bunch of innuendo and false gossip, but it's enough to make it sound like I slept my way into my projects and may not even have a college degree. They give a history lesson on Malcolm and his ex's relationship and try to tie together a timeline where I was the catalyst for their first break-up. They even list Roman's whole name, including his date of birth, which unfortunately dovetails with their accusations. I feel a stone in my heart, and my stomach bottoms to my toes. An anger and helplessness that starts a hurricane in my soul. Saige's voice comes from a million miles away, and I feel a pair of strong arms lift me off my feet.

"Baby? Look at me." I blink a bunch of times and focus on Malcolm's perfect face, one inch from mine. "I'm here."

"I...I don't know what to do first." He pulls me closer to his chest, and I bury my head in his neck, the familiar smell of cloves and vanilla battling with the salty sting of my tears. I hear him bark some orders at Saige and another soft voice answers. Eve. He brought Eve with him.

"It was her, wasn't it? Rachel?" I know his family tried to warn me. Valentina even pulled me aside and told me the girl going silent in the face of such a public break-up was a huge red flag. And like an idiot, I brushed all of their concern aside, thinking that stuff like that only happens in movies and books, not real life. Malcolm's arm tightens, and I feel him nod from above. I pull back and stare at him, wallowing in shame.

"I'll kill her."

Malcolm grunts sympathetically, his eyes searching mine intently. "None of it is true, Malcolm, I swear it."

"I know that, Ace. And while I admire your bloodthirsty nature, there are better ways to deal with this. Will you let me help you?" I wipe my face, hating the tears, the weakness. I squash down the red-hot need to lash out, to blame him, but it drains away as quickly as it comes.

"She brought my baby into this, Malcolm. I could've stayed calm if it was just me, just my business. But not my kid. I won't stand for this." His plush lips twist into a smile/snarl.

"I already called Julian and had him vacate your apartment before the press discovered your address. Tam picked them up, and they are at my place. You two will stay with me until this blows over." I ignore the small sound Saige lets out because it sounds suspiciously like a 'yay.'

"Unfortunately, we were not so lucky here—they showed up just after I did." He chuckles at my look of horror. "I'm very experienced in this, Rory. I've been dealing with the press for years. Trust me, okay?" I nod and stand up, my head already hurting. I want some cheese fries, a beer, and a dark room. Stat.

"Saige, is there a way out of here?" Malcolm is firing off messages on his phone and ordering my best friend, who is torn between staring at his long, sculptured form and wanting to jump into battle. She shakes it off when Eve coughs lightly while standing to her side.

"Yes. There is a tunnel that connects to the building next door. All the delivery services use it to shuttle packages." Her cheeks are a little pink, and I glare at her. Talk about timing.

"Okay. Here's the plan. Tam is going to pick up Rory and me up in fifteen minutes. You and Eve will close down the office—have all your employees plan on working from home for a few days—drop that look on your face, Ace. We have to let things cool down and counter the allegations. It's not fair to your associates either." I shut my mouth and cross my arms over my chest. "I could've done all of that," I murmur, annoyed.

"Uh-huh. I remember well how you don't like to listen, Rory. Let me do this, alright?" My face colors, and he grins at me, his messy curls tumbling over his forehead, making him look like a boyish dream.

Nope. Nope, nope, nope.

"Rix is sending someone for you two at the same spot. He will bring you to my house. Saige, I think you should stay with us for a few days. You and Rory are a package deal and everyone knows it. They will harass you, too." Saige shakes her head. "Eve and I already discussed it, and I will stay with her. It will be easier for us to coordinate." He nods after a moment, not noticing the evil smirk on her face. I narrow my eyes at her, promising silent retribution, like hair-pulling and possible burglary of her Son of Anarchy DVDs.

"Everyone is going to meet us this evening. Try not to worry, okay?" He touches my chin, stroking his way up to the back of my ear and tugging gently. He gives Eve more instructions, and Saige leaves to give the team the new orders. The phones have gone silent, probably being sent to an already overloaded voicemail system. I sigh and slowly pick up my abandoned backpack, turning in a small circle and staring at my office. When will I be able to come back here? I spent years building up my business, and it all went up in smoke in an instant. What a bunch of bullshit.

"Rory?" I look over my shoulder to Malcolm, leaning in the doorway. There is a worried look on his handsome face.

"I feel like I am running from my problems, and that's not me. My parents raised me to fight for what I want, and I feel like a failure." The words come out in a rush, involuntary and necessary.

"Despite being parents to the same child, I'm still learning things about you, Ace. And with the little I know, I can guarantee you that 'failure' will never be a word I associate with you. Stubborn, yes. Talented, yes. Determined and brave. Gorgeous, without a doubt. But never a failure. We are regrouping; we are strategizing but not retreating. None of this is your fault, so how can you be failing?" He doesn't move toward me, but I can feel each word like the slap of a feather against my face. I'm also gonna ignore the 'gorgeous' comment. Hard.

"Tam is here, and we are going to make our escape. Are you ready?" He holds out his hand, and I stare at it, a sigh as deep as the Mariana's Trench erupting from my chest.

"Yeah. I'm ready. Let's get out of here." I sling my bag over my shoulder and grip his fingers, holding my heavy head high.

GET TO THE CHOPPA!

I shake my head at my brothers messages, not knowing how Hendrix manages to disrupt all of our phones with his constant contact information changes. Last year, it was "Ten Inches of Fun," and none of us would answer him until he fixed it.

Brothers Of Sex Machine

Montgomery: I smell a rat

Sex Machine: I called Bea she is furious

Sex Machine: What time are we meeting

Montgomery: How is Rory? Should I bring a sedative?

Sex Machine: More like a tranquilizer. She's probably pissed

Cameron: What the hell is this thread? Who is Sex Machine? Monty?

Sex Machine: My eyes! Gag!

Malcolm: I hate all of you

"They are both asleep. Julian has left to return to his flat, and Valentina is having tea in the garden room with Sir Bernoulli. Is there anything you need me to do?" Boone was already in action when I arrived at the penthouse. Valentina happened to be visiting with Roman when the nine-one-one went out, so she jumped up and packed a bunch of Rory's things while Julian gathered up Roman and Bernoulli. Tam took Valentina and Roman while Julian loaded up his car with the puppy and all the bags. Boone said it was like a cuteness circus came into town, between Bernoulli running in circles and yelping and Roman giggling and yelling (a new thing he started this week) while Valentina laughed hysterically. Luckily, Romans's room was about finished; the Yankees mural I had commissioned was done a few days ago. All his furniture moved from the living room to his nursery, every drawer and little hanger full of clothes that Valentina and Camreon had been non-stop buying. Knowing Rory would want to be near the baby, Boone set her up in a lovely room, all swirled, luscious Koa-wood furniture (which matched mine) with pale green silk upholstery and thick vintage Persian rugs. Her things were tucked neatly away, and he had vases full of Arabian Nights Dahlias delivered for every surface. Conveniently, her room was just a few feet away from mine, but I'm sure that wasn't his intent. Probably.

Rory was mostly silent after leaving her office, and I watched her expressions worriedly, cataloging every frown, sigh, and snarl. She was equal parts pissed and sad, and I cursed Rachel to an eternity of wrinkles for the hell she was putting us through. I'd known her silence meant bad shit was on the way, but the viciousness shouldn't have surprised me. Eve has been messaging me non-stop with link after link as the stories grew and twisted. I even got texts from Nick and MacKenna, both furious. MacKenna was ready to storm New York, babies in tow, but Nick had other plans. He managed to calm his wife but told me to look for his support within the next few days. We arrived at my building, and I've never been so glad for a private entrance. The front driveway is overrun by the press, two news vans, and a bunch of looky-loos. The concierge team has them pushed to a corner, and the security team stands ten deep, glaring at the crowd.

Luckily, the other tenants have had some issues of their own, so they don't blink at the disruption.

I guided her limp form upstairs, and Julian met her at the door with Roman, who squealed when he saw his mama. She took him mutely, and Boone led her straight to her room, Valentina waiting to push her into a hot shower. She came out with her deep-fire hair hanging in wet curls down her back, wrapped in baggy sweats and thick socks, looking like a fantasy despite the sadness on her lovely face. Boone brought her a tray of food loaded with a crispy Monte Cristo sandwich, fries, and a tall glass of chocolate milk. She took a tentative bite, holding Roman possessively with one arm, before giving him up to me so she could scarf down the rest. Roman settled for a bottle, his eating matching his mama's pace. Once she was done, I handed him back over, leaving them both with a kiss, and closed the door.

"No, Boone. Thank you for everything. Please inform the staff that they should not disclose that they are staying here. I'm expecting one hundred percent discretion. This is my son and his mother—I'm not fucking around. Anyone who breaks this will be immediately terminated." Boone's eyebrows shoot up, but he nods.

"Understood. I will drive home the message." His watch pings, and he glances at it briefly. "Hendrix is on his way up."

"Hendrix is already here." I look up at my brother, who, for once, doesn't have a smirk on his face. "Where is Rory?"

"Asleep," I sit back and point at the whiskey decanter before me. He pours a glass and sits back, crossing one foot over his thigh.

"In your suite?" One dark eyebrow raises, and I take a sip and shake my head.

"Of course not. Boone has her set up in her room near Roman's nursery. Fuck Rix, you should have seen her. She was so devasted and lost. I've never been so angry in all my life. Rachel has gone too far this time." I slam my glass down, running my hand through my hair and pulling. I'll be bald before the weekend. "This is all my fault."

"And just how is that?" Rix drawls, sinking lower into his chair.

"If she had never met me..."

"None of that shit now, Mal. If you hadn't met her, you wouldn't have Roman. You'd still be stuck at Clare Inc. and about to marry that crazy bitch. You both gained in that meeting, Malcolm. You gained freedom and a fucking bright ass future with a phenomenal woman and a perfect son. And she's now got the world at her fingertips. Stop beating yourself up. If anyone is to blame, it's Mom and Percy—they picked that demon out, not you." His voice is harsh, almost commanding.

"Rix is right. Sometimes Fate steps in and takes over," Valentina says, Bernoulli at her heels until he sees Rix, who he runs over to drool on. He gives him a ton of attention before flopping down, ignoring me. Rix gives me a shit-eating grin, and I growl at him. I'd gone from never seeing my brother to seeing him several times a week. I'd almost forgotten how much he gets on my fucking nerves.

"I know you are right. Deep down in here," I point at my head, "But in here, I feel like an asshole," I slap my chest.

"Well, that shit go because we have things to plan," Rix tells me, pulling out his phone and nodding. "Wicker is preparing a cease and desist, it should be ready soon."

"Won't that look desperate?" Valentina muses as Hendrix shakes his head. "No. Not when we pair it with a statement from Malcolm and the rest of us. I'll wait until Cameron and Monty are here before I plan more."

"Grandmother is on her way over also. You know, she is such a lady that I forget that she can curse like a truck driver. I almost thought I had the wrong number," Val laughs. "I'd always heard stories that she used to give Grandfather Cyrus the business. I guess it was true."

"Yeah, I vaguely remember them going at it for a time or two. She never raised her voice, but she could make him see red. She's always been a spitfire," I smile. "Rory reminds me of her a little bit. She's got the same spine." I remember our first meeting and how she shot the middle finger at all those booing Boston fans, not caring that she was in enemy territory. I'd been scared, and she'd been fierce. Today, the business she'd worked so hard for was jeopardized, but her first thought was about our son. A warrior through and through. I hear Rix and Valentina muttering and frown at the whispers. "What are you two gossiping about?"

"Nothing."

"The weather."

"It's supposed to rain, right, Rix?"

"Sure is, Squirt."

"See. Nothing." I narrow my eyes at those two owl-eyed fools, both staring at me with the fakest innocence known to man. I'll have to keep my eye on them.

⁂

"JESUS, SHE REALLY THREW GRENADES DOWN EVERY STREET, DIDN'T she?" Cameron says, shaking his head as he and Monty read every dirty article printed about Rory. They arrived on the heels of Eve and Saige, who came armed for battle with multiple computers and file folders. Bea was the last, clad in a light pink suit with a matching hat, ears, wrists, and neck decked out in layers of jewelry as if she would intimidate the shit out of anyone who stepped out of line.

Eve printed every article she could find, and Saige had all the blog posts bookmarked. Each and every one is damaging to Rory's company as well as to her spirit. She and Roman came out of hiding, both with messed up hair and sheet wrinkles, though Roman squealed and bounced when he saw all of his favorite people. Rory looked like a wrung-out dishtowel, but her silvery eyes were dark with anger. She and Saige holed up alone while they called all their employees and clients. I eavesdropped on half of the conversations, ready to charge in and take off some heads, but most of them were sympathetic and supportive. She was brutally honest, telling clients that someone twisting facts started the rumors. She promised to tell them the truth in person once things had blown over. In the meantime, work would resume on all projects since Saige's ex-boyfriend had come through, and all their permits had been reinstated. The only one who had more questions was Chandler Schillings, who asked her point blank if the rumors about Roman being my son were true.

"Yes. Roman is Malcolm's son. But it was while he and... that lady were apart. There was no affair." She gave him a thumbnail about our meeting, and he went silent for a while.

"So Percy and Penelope know that you are their grandson's mother?" Rory took a breath, battling some internal morality. "Yeah. They do."

"I see. Well then, I'll stop by the restaurant myself tomorrow. We are still ahead of schedule?" Rory assured him they were, the deadline being a few weeks away. They rang off, and Rory's breath came out in an exhausted sigh. Now, she is seated beside my grandmother while Boone fusses over her, bringing her a thick cashmere blanket and tea with snacks. Another maid caters to the rest of us, but Boone won't leave Rory alone, hovering and giving her worried looks. She grins at him, giving him that fucking smile, brilliant even with her worry. Roman is sitting with Monty, who won't give him up despite everyone growling at him for their turn. Even Bernoulli is calm, gnawing on a rawhide bone that Boone had produced out of nowhere. Who was this guy?

"Well, Rachel is nothing if not thorough. So now we have several obstacles to tackle. The first thing is Rory's business. What do we need to do?" Grandmother says, tapping an invisible scepter. Rory opens her mouth, and Bea snaps it shut.

"Dear girl, do not bother with your obstinacy. That Irish in you is rearing its head, and I'm telling you to put it to rest for now. You are our family, and we rally for our family—something my son and his wife have never learned. Saige tells me that you only lost one project, and the rest are standing with you. Brilliant. That's one less thing to think about for now. Future projects may be a bit of a rough go, but we will worry about that later."

"I was planning on hiring her for one of my Long Island projects," Rix says, winking at Rory, who looks confused. "I was going to tell you in a few weeks, gorgeous."

"That's lovely, Hendrix, but it will look like charity, and we don't want that. Let me think on it. The next issue is Roman. The secret is out, but it means he will need security. The paps will be clamoring for pictures of him—it won't be safe."

"What do you mean not safe?" Those thundercloud eyes flash, and Rix whistles low with their threat.

"Well, those vultures will go to extraordinary lengths for exclusives.

Dig through your trash, pay people off; the whole lot of them are awful." Bea waves her hand in front of her face as if she smelled something foul.

"I've already got Tam on it. Obviously, he is fine here, but if we take him anywhere, protocols must be put in place. Don't worry, Ace. I'll never let anything happen to either one of you."

"Protocols?" Rory asks, a frown on her lips that I'd like to bite off. Wait...

"Yes darling, one of the drawbacks of all of this lovely money is the risks that come with it. Everyone in the family has some protection, invisible as it may be. A terrible thing, but there it is. Roman and you will be no exception. Saige, we will add you as well." Rory looks like she wants to run away, while Saige seems thrilled. "Might as well just accept it, love. Consequences of that one night and all." Her face turns beet red at this, and I struggle not to laugh.

"I say we give them what they want," Cameron says slowly.

"How so?" Valentina snatches Roman while Monty's head is turned, doing a little triumphant dance that makes the baby laugh.

"Well, let's look at the rumors. Malcolm cheated on Rachel and had a secret baby that we have been hiding. The family is mortified and wants nothing to do with him. I say we turn that on its ear. Here's what we are going to do..."

❧ 34 ❧

ANIMAL PLANET

You know that meme, "I bet you wonder how I got here?" Well, that's my life right now.

I've been at Malcolm's apartment/house/palace, whatever, for over a week. Malcolm didn't want us to return to my apartment until our 'plan' succeeded and we were guaranteed a measure of peace. Julian rode past, and poor Wallace, our doorman, was busy yelling at a bunch of reporters, so my apartment was still a no-go zone. It took a few days for me to settle, to feel any sort of belonging, despite Malcolm's excellent staff bending over backward to accommodate me. I tried to fend for myself at first, skulking around the massive penthouse, trying to sneak into the kitchen, making my own bed, and attempting to take up as little space as possible. That lasted about two days until Boone caught me hiding out in the garden room with Saige and gave me a firm but gentle lecture.

"Rory, one day, a very long time from now, this whole place will be Roman's. He's Malcolm's son, and this is his home. I know it's hard for you, but my job is to care for you. Both of you. With everything you have going on, it would be much easier to let down your shoulders a bit." I stared at him, his eyes twinkling.

"I just dont want to be a burden. I'm used to taking care of myself."

His smile grew, and he laid a warm hand on my arm, shaking his head. "Rory, you could never, ever be a burden. I swear this place felt like a mausoleum until you and Roman came along. Now, part of my job is asking what you would like for lunch. Cook is chomping at the bit to make you her special salmon croquettes." I relaxed and agreed to the croquettes, now my new favorite. I tentatively began venturing further into the house, even taking the baby to swim in the giant heated swimming pool. Roman splashed and squealed, his little feet kicking, his floaties keeping him buoyant. I looked up to see Malcolm watching us, a soft smile on his face, phone in hand, taking pictures. That night, we started having dinner together early enough that Roman could join us before we paired up and put him to bed. I loved his nursery, a large, airy space in cool blues and creams with a Yankee stadium mural, tons of stuffed animals, and custom burl wood furniture. His new play rug is right in the middle, and most often, he's spread out on it, Bernoulli keeping watch while Roman yelps and coos at the shapes painted on the ceiling. Julian has had no qualms about his new accommodations, making friends with the staff, and not being intimidated by the sheer size. I asked him how he could stay so cool, and all he did was wink at me.

I woke up this morning and was greeted by the sight of Malcolm talking to Roman, shirtless and barefoot. I stood there for a full five minutes, watching the play of his muscles as he held our son, the way his sculpted back ended in that spectacular ass, how his thick black hair waved and curled around that perfect face. I was so frozen I didn't notice that he'd turned around and watched me check him out with a smug grin on his face. Remember when I said my parents taught me to stay and fight?

Yeah, I ran.

So I've been trying to avoid him most days, though he manages to find me every time, probably because Saige makes as much noise as a freight train. Boone gave us this lovely room to work out of, and it only took us one day to fill it up with a ton of stuff. I have been teleconferencing into every job site, and the Schillings project is back on track and still ahead. I'm worried, though, because while we only lost one project (and I'm not even mad because it was the one that kept asking me for more shit), none of our new inquiries were returning our calls. We are booked for the next year, but after that...nothing.

"It will pick back up soon. Right now, everyone is trying to figure out what's going on. Once we drop our get-back, you'll see. Not to mention, *Discovery* is opening soon. That'll gin up people's interest."

I sigh, shaking my head. "I can't even go to the opening, Saigey. It'll be a circus, and my popping up will detract from the project."

"That's bullshit. You are going come hell or high water, as my mama would say. And you are going to wear a FEA dress, and that's that."

"An FEA dress?"

"Fuck 'Em All. I'm going to start looking now. Valentina will help me. Eve, too." She shot off a text message, and her phone chimed immediately. "They're down—leave it to us. Now, what are we doing about the Chanteuse project? We are still gonna go for it, right?" I snorted. The news was all over the place that Chanteuese had finalized a prime spot on Fifth Avenue, right on the main luxury strip. The building was a tear-down job—an old department store that had seen its heyday a century ago. Now, they are opening the door for design bids—just no one knows when.

"Hell yeah. What's the worst that could happen? They laugh me out of their office, and I get humiliated? I won't let that...wench win." I'd done my own digging into Miss Rachel Van Pyke and didn't find anything to like. She's a phantom in a way—someone who floated through life, terrorizing everyone for no reason. According to Saige (who heard it from Boone), Malcolm's staff avoided her like the plague. She was rude and demanding, and something happened in the kitchen that almost caused a revolt. I can admit that she is beautiful with a rocking body, but that's where it ends. I still couldn't believe Malcolm was engaged to her.

"Good. The Moaner will be back in town next week, and I'll get the details from him. I can take one for the team." I crack up. "I'll buy you Moaner-proof earbuds."

"Who the hell is The Moaner?" I look up at Malcolm's perfect face and grin. Saige fills him in, and his face morphs from anger to hilarity on my behalf. He gives me an amused look, shaking his head. "You two are mayhem, aren't you?" The plain affection in his voice makes my toes tingle, but I ignore it.

"Yup," Saige tells him, emphasizing the' p' loudly. "Better get used to it, Mally Mal." He grimaces at her nickname, but the smile still stays in place.

"Ace, I just came to see if Saige is staying for dinner." He looks at me and then at Saige, who checks her watch and starts dramatically scrambling. "Look at the time! Eve and I have a date in front of the TV tonight. Gotta go! See ya tomorrow." She's gone in a flash—a flurry of blonde hair and clattering heels—yelling out for Eve, who yells back, her ordinarily soft voice excited.

"Was it something I said?"

I crack up at Malcolm's dry tone, shrugging one shoulder. "She's a weirdo. I've tried to put her up for adoption, but I got no takers." He smiles, leaning on the door frame, and my eyes—those damn traitors— struggle not to eat him up. Since working from home, he's traded in his power suits for more casual wear: knit pants, crew neck sweaters, and today, a navy cashmere hoodie covering a pristine white V-neck tee. I can feel my face heating and turn my back to him, faking pulling papers together and straightening invisible stacks.

"Are you ready for tomorrow? It's going to get a little crazy around here." He moves closer, and his rich clove scent with its hint of vanilla curls around my nose. I gulp and try to scoot away, but I've run out of room. "Ace?" His voice is low, like a whisper of a caress, a tiny flick of affection.

"Why do you call me that?" I peek over my shoulder, coming face to face with his broad chest.

"Because that's what you are—an ace. You are the highest of the high, the most important, the best of the best, the number one starting pitcher," he says calmly as if he isn't paying me a sweet compli-ment, as if my face weren't fire engine red.

"Oh. Thanks." *Great job, Rory.*

"So...tomorrow? What can I do to make it easier for you?" *Take off your clothes? Wait..shut up, Rory.*

"Nothing, I guess," I shrug. "Like Bea said, 'consequences of our one night and all that.'"

"I wouldn't change anything, Rory. If I had a chance to go back, I'd do all the same things. Except I would have gotten your name. I wouldn't have left like that. I'd have taken more of you with me." His breath is on the back of my neck, the delicate hairs standing up at his warmth. I close my eyes, willing my legs to stay strong, to not buckle. "I went back for you, you know? I got desperate and went back to that apartment. I even went back to the bar—no one would tell me anything." My eyes screw tighter, my skin pulling at me to face him. I turn slowly and look into his eyes, trying to keep his gaze without leaping on him like a willing antelope lying down for a lion. "Why?"

"Why? Why do you think?" His hands, which had been tucked into his pockets, slide up my face, tilting and pulling at it until our mouths are an inch apart. "The same day I went back for you, I got a call that my mother had a heart attack. I spent months thinking about you, trying to get you from under my skin. And then there you were, like a dream you have to be forced to wake up from." His tongue slips out, touching my bottom lip with a gentle tap. "And now here you are again."

"Ooops! I guess you forgot that you invited everyone to dinner?" The iceberg that hit the Titanic couldn't have caused a bigger crash. I jumped back two football fields and ran out of the room, pushing past Valentina, almost careening straight into Hendrix, who steadies me. "Whoa, girl. What's chasing you?"

"I caught her and Malcolm kissing," Valentina says excitedly. I cringe and glare at her over my shoulder. "We were not kissing."

"I saw tongue. That's all I'm saying." She grins at my embarrassed face. "And Malcolm is back there trying to tame the beast if you know what I mean," she smirks. I hear choking noises that sound suspiciously like Cameron.

"You know I'm an only child, and I've never been more grateful for that in all my life. If you'll excuse me, I'm going to go dig a tunnel in my room and hope I pop up in Australia." I pull away from a hysterical Hendrix and run as fast as I can.

Being brave is overrated.

35

DON'T START NOTHIN', WON'T BE NOTHIN'

EXCLUSIVE!! FIRST PHOTOS OF THE CLARE HEIR! PAGES 2-8

WE'VE GOT HIM, AND OF COURSE, HE'S GORGEOUS! ROMAN CLARE MAKES HIS FIRST APPEARANCE!

'KNOCKED ME OFF MY FEET' MALCOLM CLARE DESCRIBES MEETING HIS SON'S MOTHER

HE IS A 'HONORABLE!' LADY HOLLAND DECLARES NEW GREAT-GRANDSON A CAVENDISH

RIGHT NOW, HE'S MY HEIR—IS ROMAN CLARE THE RICHEST BABY IN THE WORLD?—HENDRIX LE LAURIER MAKES A STATEMENT

MOST BEAUTIFUL BABY'S MOTHER IS A GENIUS! CHECK OUT HER DESIGNS!

GRANT-ALLOY HIRES CLARE BABY MAMA FOR NEWEST SKYSCRAPER—"IT WAS A NO-BRAINER"

"Jesus. This is insane." Rory whispers to herself, a stack of newspapers in front of her. "Roman dude, you're famous." She bends down to our son, who is rolling over, trying to pull himself into a sitting position. We've been cheering him on all week, but so far, he just flops over, giggling. Saige takes a few videos of his efforts, laughing as Bernoulli nudges him over so he can start again. Eve darts in with some things for me to sign before scuttling off to my home office, in her element with deals to be made and the phone ringing non-stop. Rix's PR manager is here too, pleased at her efforts, and handling the calls with Eve. Saige stayed over, and this morning, it took everything in me not to laugh at her pajamas, which had Rory's head printed all over them. I did lose it when Rory walked in with matching ones, but hers had Roman's face, while my little man's had mine. I took a few pictures and sent them to the family group text.

Valentina: OMG, that is the cutest!

Hendrix: I'd like them better if Saiges were shorter

Saige: Dream on, hoe

Cameron: SHOTS FIRED

Montgomery: Children…be nice

Montgomery: …but for real, where can I get those

Rory: The Internet

Montgomery: Why thanks, how original

Rory: What?

Valentina: LOL

Valentina: I just put it on my socials. Comments are going wild!

> Hendrix: Saige, I love you
>
> Saige: Gag

CAMERON'S IDEA WAS BRILLIANT. HE SUGGESTED THAT INSTEAD OF going the legal route—injunctions and C&Ds with lawsuit threats- we do what Bea said: we rally. We put all the information out while showing Roman off, taking the urgency out of the paparazzi's sails, even just for a little bit. Valentina took it a step further, hiring one of her college friends to take professional but candid pictures for the press. Rory didn't like the idea, but she relented when I snuck her downstairs and showed her the frenzy outside of the building. We had a stylist come in to ensure we looked our best and spent hours reviewing which photos to release first. LLC, Rix's company, loaned us his PR manager, and she made the final choices, reaching out to contacts and promising them all kinds of goodies if they gave us front-page prominence. She could've saved all that because not one blog, paper, or website turned her down, all of them jumping at the chance to break some exclusive.

Everyone's phones started ringing off the hook, and with our pre-planned responses, we managed to defend Rory and Roman without defending them at all. The only iffy part was I was questioned about how and when I met Rory, and I cleared that up swiftly. I refused to let anyone accuse her of any impropriety and made sure I carefully laid out the timeline until everyone was satisfied. I was candid about my makeup with Rachel, letting the press know that the reconciliation was due to my mother's health—her one wish was to be able to live for our canceled wedding. Without spelling it out, I alluded to Rachel using it to keep me in a relationship, which I'm sure will go over well.

"Most of the comments are positive. There are a few haters here and there, but it seems like it's working." Saige pulls her laptop over and shows Rory some things on the screen. "They seem determined to call the baby Roman Clare. Are you guys going to change his name?" I look at Rory, who is frowning, a stubborn look on her face. I want to grab her chin and bite it. And then maybe her butt. When Valentina interrupted us yesterday, it took everything in me not to chase her down and taste her all over. She was out of sight most of the night, only coming out this morning, her face pink whenever she looked in my direction. If today weren't so important, I'd kick my whole household out and challenge her to a game of hide n' seek—with specific body parts.

"Is that something you would want, Malcolm?" She asks me quietly, chewing her bottom lip. Her eyes look wary, and I sigh inside, knowing only more time and patience will get me what I want.

"Yes, it is. We don't have to change anything else; we can just add Clare at the end. Is that okay with you?" I'd like to change her last name, too, but I don't think that would go over too well right now.

"Ummmm. Is it okay if I think about it?" I smile at her and nod. "Of course it is. Whatever you want, Ace." She relaxes and gives me a grateful look.

"Ace?" Saige asks with a wicked look on her pretty face. Rory gives her a glower, her cheeks turning red. I have a feeling Saige knows it all and is giving her a hard time. I say nothing, just winking at Rory, who is still wishing bad things on her best friend. "What else are they saying?" I nod toward the stack of papers, noticing that the one with my interview is on the bottom and folded in half.

"It's all pretty much what we wanted, I guess. There's enough in here to keep them talking for weeks. The only, um, issues I can see on repeat are a few trolls still trying to make this sound like you cheated on Rachel. But I'm sure that will die down." I grimace and look at Rory, who has a weird look on her face. Saige glances at her with a wince, and that's when I know I'm missing something. The look doesn't ease, and it takes me a moment to realize she is in a rage and trying to control it. Uh-oh.

"Rory? What's wrong?" I watch as she takes several deep breaths, clenching her hands into tight fists. Saige rubs her back, and she shakes it off, standing up. "I'll be right back." She hurries out of the room, and I take a step after her, but Saige's voice stops me.

"One thing you need to learn about Rory is that she hates to seem weak. If you go after her all soft and sorry, she'll bury her stubborn head deeper." I pull on my hair, pacing a bit.

"She's upset, Saige, and I don't like that. I'm doing my best to fix this, but I can't if she doesn't talk to me. What can I do?" I drop my hand and stare at my son, who is happy and gurgling, oblivious to all the drama as he should be.

"She's been on her own for a long time, Malcolm. Both of her parents died when she was in high school—first her dad and then her mom. She has a hard shell around her because she had to have one—things were not easy for her, even before that. She's a big softie underneath, but this whole situation is hitting every one of her panic buttons over and over. Rory still thinks she has to take on the whole world by herself. If you want my advice—and judging by that look on your face, you do—you've got to push her. She will clam up, march those feet behind a wall, and keep herself there, shutting you down at every turn if you don't push her. Give her no space. Demand more. She's such a little boss; she'll be shocked. Then you'll get to the core of her. And I don't mean the one in her pants either." I shout out a laugh and feel my face get warm for the first time in my life. "Believe it or not, I don't need help in that department, Miss Marchand."

She gives me a long look, grinning like a bandit the whole time. "Oh, I know. I heard every single detail about your time in Boston. I guess you would have skills to go along with all of that," she waves her hand at my face. I grin and step closer to her, bending down and lifting her delicate hand. "I've never had a complaint," I murmur, kissing her hand while looking deep into her eyes. I make sure to let my hair fall over my face, and she gulps loudly before swatting at me.

"All that game must be genetic. Go dump all of that on Rory. I'm immune." I stand up, winking at her as she holds a cold glass of orange juice up to her forehead. "Malcolm?

I turn around and smile at her pretty face, thinking someone is going to be very lucky when they finally tie her down. "Yeah?"

"Do you want her? I mean, really want her?"

"More than anything in this universe. Watch out for my son, hmmm?"

I KNEW I WOULD FIND HER HERE. SINCE SHE AND ROMAN MOVED IN (and in my mind, it's moving in, not visiting), she has gravitated toward the garden. In all of my apartment's splendor, this seems to be her favorite room. I stare at her for a moment, my stomach knotting up at the sorrow painted across the tightness of her shoulders. Something set her off and I need to get it out of her before it burrows deeper. I see her let out a deep sigh and realize Saige is right—and it's time I use my gifts to get what I want. I've been the nice guy for too long.

"Rory? What's wrong?" I step toward her, watching her spine close up sharply like a zipper. Nope. Not gonna work this time, Ace.

"Nothing. I just needed a minute." I can see the silhouette of that chin lifting, probably hoping I'll leave her alone and let her stew.

"Bullshit." She whirls around, her pink lips parted but snarled. "What?"

"I said bullshit. You were perfectly fine until you weren't. So tell me what set you off." I take another step, crossing my arms and across my chest. She looks at my stance and gets the most adorably obstinate look. I wanna bite her again.

"No."

I smirk. "No?"

"Yeah, no." She matches my stance, crossing her arms and facing me. "I don't want to talk about it." I take another step until our arms touch. Her scent, which I learned was an old eighties perfume she has to special order, a musky light seduction, makes my mouth water.

"Well, I do. I can't help you if I don't know." She scoffs, and my fingers itch to spank that sass right out of her. "I don't need your help."

"That so?" I uncross my arms and yank her to me. She yelps, off balance, but I hold her tight, almost lifting her off her feet. She keeps her arms pretzeled, which works in my favor because she is trapped. She struggles a bit, but I hold firm.

"Tell me." I lean down and brush my lips across her forehead, inhaling the sweet scent of her hair. "Let me be here for you." Her shoulders finally drop, and the saddest sound comes out of her, one that stabs me in the heart. I hold her tighter and wait.

"My dad cheated on my mom." My eyes close. Dammit. "I was a kid, and I was so wrapped up in my own crap that I didn't notice that he was never home. Didn't notice that my mama was fading away." I stay silent, feeling the hot splash of her tears.

"The lady's name was Mandy. She worked with my dad. She told my dad she was pregnant, and when my mom found out, she made him leave. I confronted him one day and said nasty things, stuff I will forever wish that I could take back. He died in a car crash before we could make up." I rub my face against hers. "I'm so sorry, baby."

"Mandy died, too. And she wasn't even pregnant. She just wanted my dad and did whatever to keep him. My poor mom was humiliated, and right after my high school graduation, she died—probably of a broken heart." She buries her face in my chest, her words muffled. "I hate cheaters. And I hate that they are saying I'm the type of woman who would do that to someone." I dig my hands into her hair, gently pulling until she looks at me.

"I would never cheat on anyone, even Rachel. She and I were genuinely broken up when we met. And we would have stayed that way if my mother hadn't gotten sick. Unfortunately, our timeline is so close that people will always speculate and wonder. But I swear to you, I will beat up anyone who even thinks about saying that." She snorts, wiping her wet face against my shirt, snot and all. "You're gonna beat them up?" She looks skeptical, and I smile. "Yup. What do you think I have all these muscles for?" I flex one bicep, and the little brat rolls her eyes.

"To torture women with. To fill out your shirts. To..." I swoop down and bite her mouth while digging my fingers into her ribs, causing her to scream in laughter. I tickle her while holding her tight with the other arm, enjoying the feel of her squirming against me. My dick, which was close to jumping her yesterday, recognizes its favorite person in the world and decides to say hello. I pull her closer, and her laughter suddenly stops. Her mouth, which is open with silent surprise, is too much for me to resist. I bend down and smooth my lips over hers, slipping my tongue against hers with a moan. It takes her a millisecond to respond, her toes raising to give me more, hands grip-ping my hair and pulling me closer. I back her up against the wall, never taking my mouth from hers, giving her a dance, a symphony of just my tongue. I can feel the hard points of her sweet nipples through her pajamas and slip my hand down her silky throat, skirting to her ribs and just under her breast.

"Can I?" I ask against her mouth, and she moans and nods, putting her hand over mine.

"So I guess this isn't kissing either, huh?" I growl at my sister, peeking over my shoulder at her shit-eating grin. I move to cover Rory, who looks like a ravaged dessert. No one gets to see her like this.

"Valentina... can you give us a minute." She snorts, and the damn kid just sits in a chair, crossing her legs at the ankle and examining her nails. I'll kill her.

"Nope. And you won't kill me because you love me so much. So what's next? Besides, you two losing your pants?"

36

FRIENDS— HOW MANY OF US
HAVE THEM?

"Ummmm, hi?" The stupidly handsome man on the screen bursts out laughing, his green eyes crinkling at the corners. Even through the tiny monitor, you can tell he is big—really big. Saige, who is sitting next to me, hasn't said a word, just staring at him with a dumb look on her face. I almost want to record it because I don't think I've ever seen her this still—not even in her sleep.

"Well, um, I guess you know I'm Rory Miller-Jones? And I guess you hired me?" Yesterday, a week after all of the press stuff had been released and the frenzy died down (a little), Malcolm reminded me that I had a new project, a buidling I was supposed to be designing in Chicago.

"But I thought that was just a press thing," I asked him, wringing my hands nervously. I thought I was years away from tackling the Chicago market, with its strict architectural standards and rich history. It's been one of my dreams to leave my mark on that magnificent city, and I'm almost afraid to believe it's true.

Malcolm snorted, his handsome face needing a shave, which I secretly enjoy. He's usually groomed to his teeth, but lately, he's been more relaxed, which makes him even hotter—if possible. "Nick is one of my best friends, but he puts all that aside for business. If he says he's hiring you, he means it. He called me last night asking when you planned to reach out." He handed me a post-it note with an email address, kissing me lightly before whistling for Bernoulli, who still won't give him the time of day. I watched him leave, cursing all of the annoying obstacles that have gotten in the way of any more kissing time. Like the one sitting next to me.

"Hi Rory, I'm Nicholas Grant, but you call call me Nick." Saige finally snaps out of her stupor and starts scribbling on the notepad, long abandoned in her lap.

"Big Dick Nick?"
"Lick me, Nick?"
"Send Me Home Sick, Nick?

I SOMEHOW MANAGE TO KEEP A STRAIGHT FACE, KICKING THE FOOL under the desk. "Til my hips dislocate," she whispers, and my breath comes out in a whine.

"Malcolm tells me you are your wife and have three boys?" I give her an extra hard thump, which makes her yelp and scowl at me. Nicholas, to his credit, doesn't seem to notice, though there is a smile hovering at the edge of his mouth.

"Yes, we do. Kian, Erik, and Remy. I'm sure you will meet one or more of them before we wrap up. Now I've seen your work, and this is what I'm thinking." He continues, and Saige finally calms down enough to take proper notes, and I listen as I sketch out some ideas. Though there will be restrictions to the design, I can still put my stamp on it. "What do you think of something like this?" I flip my pad over so he can see it, and he leans forward, staring. "Jesus, yes. Maybe make the windows a little bigger?" I quickly make some revisions and show him. His smile beams across the screen, and he nods excitedly.

"So what's next? How do you normally proceed?" I will send him more ideas and a rundown of what he can expect. He tells me that the land on which the building will be built is already cleared—it was an abandoned project that he snapped up. "I'm looking at seventy-five floors with three executive floors not included. I'm also considering making part of it residential since commercial real estate can be risky. Is that possible?" I blink hard but shake off my excitement. "Yes, of course."

"Fantastic. And you'll send me your quote sheet as well?" I agree, though I have yet to learn how to scale a project this big. Grant-Alloy also has a partnership with a British company that will provide sustainable materials, which a friend owns.

"We like to keep it all in the family. I'll include their contact information in an email. Saige?" Her head snaps up, and he smiles at her. "My assistant will send over everything you need. Please feel free to include me in all correspondence, though. She's expecting a baby and may go any minute." Saige agrees, and there is a slight commotion in the background. "Day-ee!" A little dark-haired tornado hurls himself into Nick's side, and Nick catches him with the reflexes of an experienced dad.

"Sorry. I did warn you." He kisses the top of the little gremlin's head, who has twisted himself until his adorable little face is full on the screen.

"Hi!" He waves, and I snicker when I see how dirty his hands are. He's got wide, brandy-colored eyes and a host of freckles across his cheeks. I want to squeeze him.

"Hello. I'm Rory. Who are you?" He looks back at his father, who shrugs with a smile. "I'm Rix."

"Rix? I have a very good friend with that name. He's a little bad. Are you a good boy?"

"Nope! I bad too." He looks proud as can be, and I laugh harder. "His name is Erik, but it should be a Cyclone. He's never still." I hear a feminine voice, and Erik squirms to get down.

"Mama! I gots a fren!" He jumps down and disappears before a beautiful woman who looks exactly like her son comes behind Nick's shoulder.

"Hello, sorry about that. Rix likes to interrupt his father whenever he can. Oh!" She leans closer, a brilliant smile on her generous mouth. "You're Rory!" She scoots until she is sitting on her husband's lap, his arm automatically wrapping around her. He kisses the back of her dark head, the love he has for her plain as day.

"I'm MacKenna Grant. "I'm so happy to meet you!" She leans forward, shaking her head. "Your pictures don't do you justice—you are stunning." She peeks to the side and grins. "Is Roman around there? I would love to see him." I tell her he is down for a nap, and she pouts. "Damn. Malcolm sent us so many pictures, but I bet they don't compare. All the ones he sent of you barely scratch the surface."

"Of me?" I point at my chest, and she nods. "Oh yes. He is so very proud of you, both of you. I hear you're from Scarsdale. We're neighbors!" We start chatting like old friends, listing places we've both been to and what high schools we attended. We chat for a while before Saige clears her throat and taps the calendar reminder in the corner of my computer.

"Damn, I've kept you, I know. But I don't get to talk to someone from my 'hood very often. I'm so glad you and Malcolm have worked it out together.

"Oh, we're not..."

"You need to have more kids so they can grow up together. Remy and Roman are close in age, but you need to have a few more, huh? Can I call you? I'll get your number from Malcolm. I'll try to remember that time difference, though. I don't want to interrupt sexy time." She winks at me, and I cringe.

"We don't..."

"Though if Mal is anything like Nick, he won't care what time it is. Whenever, wherever, right playa?" She nudges her husband, who puts his hand over her mouth, which she promptly bites.

"Let me know if you need advice on keeping all the vultures away from Malcolm. Even after three kids and all kinds of publicity, I still get chicks who try to push up on Nick. Of course, with all those articles about how Malcolm feels about you, it should die down, and after you are married, it will be even better."

"Married? I..."

"Just make sure you invite us to New York before the wedding. I wanna hang out first." MacKenna's smile is infectious, and even though I think she is crazy, I smile back. She climbs off her husband's lap and leans in for a kiss that quickly turns a little heated. Nick tugs on the hood of his wife's sweatshirt and nuzzles her, murmuring in her ear. She pats him with a sassy grin, running off at the sound of chaos from her boys.

"Sorry about that. My house is a zoo on its best days. I look forward to working with you, Rory—you are extremely bright and talented. Have Malcolm call me." He signs off, and I sit back and stare at Saige, who has a similar expression. "Seventy-five stories with three executive floors?? Holy shit!" We jump up at the same time, screaming and carrying on like teenagers. I throw some papers in the air and jump on the couch.

"What in the world?" Boone is standing in the doorway, a tray in his hands. His eyes take in Saige, who has one foot on an antique Germain Boffrand chair, and me, standing on a ten-thousand-dollar couch, its cushions everywhere. I quickly tell him about the project, and a giant grin spreads across his face. "Well, that is cause for celebration. I'll have Cook pull some champagne out of the cellar." He sets the tray down, filled with sandwiches and delicate soup bowls, and hurries off.

"I hear we have champagne coming?" Malcolm grins at me and walks over to steady me. I jump into his arms unthinkingly and wrap my legs around his waist. His arm comes up under my butt for support, the other brushing my hair out of my face. Saige gives him a rundown, and his grin widens. "Wow, that sounds amazing. I'm proud of you, Ace." I swallow back some stupid emotion and lean toward him.

"I have to do massive comps, but I don't know how much to quote him. I don't want to undersell myself, but I don't want to rip your friend off."

He snorts. "He can afford it. What's the address?" Saige rattles it off, and Malcolm closes his eyes, muttering. "So it's the heart of the financial district, right off the river—lots of visibility and construction headaches. You'll have to hire a preservation architect and a green building architect. Your staff will be huge." He names a figure, and I thank the universe he is holding me because I would have fallen on my ass. Saige almost does, and he quickly steadies her with his free arm. "Seriously?"

"Yup, and that's probably conservative. Real estate is what I do, Ace. I'll help you with your comps, etc." I shift a bit and automatically feel a thick and hard greeting. My brain tells me to jump down, but my body tightens my legs and moves closer. The pupils in his true blue eyes blow, and his other hand automatically buries into my hair.

"Uhhhh, I think I hear Boone calling me. I'll ummmmm." I don't even hear the rest of what Saige says before Malcolm's mouth takes mine, a hot silky caress that makes parts of me I've tried to ignore, tried to strangle into submission, sit up, and cheer.

"Is this a bad idea?" I ask with a moan as his tongue swipes at a sensitive spot on my neck. I tilt my head back to give him more access, his chuckle tickling my skin.

"This is the best idea I have ever had in my life. Hold on." He walks swiftly and locks the door, a wicked smile on his face. "I swear if we get interrupted one more time, I'm calling the police." I burst out laughing and his handsome face creases in mock seriousness. "Off," he plucks at my shirt, and I pull it over my head in one motion. He growls, burying his head in my boobs, which are covered in a rose pink lace that Valentina made me buy. I feel him dip, and then I am lying on the sofa; it's missing cushions, giving us a ton of room.

"So tell me, Rory, what's off the table?"

37

ARE YOU THAT SOMEBODY?

Her face is flushed, that wild auburn hair in waves caught under her shoulders and spilling onto the cushions. Her breasts, which are larger than I remember, spill over the cups of her bra, twin temptations. I wish I had more time, could worship her the way she deserves. But by my calculations, I had maybe twenty minutes before someone came looking for one of us, banging on the door or deliberately making some noise. They know exactly what we are doing in here, and if I didn't know better, I would think our whole family is conspiring to torture us.

"We will have to be quick, Ace. Just a little taste." I lean over her, bracing on one arm as I brush my mouth over her lush, soft pink lips. I nip the top one first, sucking it gently, then the bottom. "This mouth." Her lips part on a deep shudder, and I dive it to take advantage, dancing my tongue with hers again, a deep desperation washing over me, a feeling of relief of homecoming. The taste of her, the way her body moves under mine, pulls at something primal in me, my body almost shaking. I kiss her for long minutes, her hands moving restlessly along my back, tangling in my hair and pulling. "Malcolm," she moans against my mouth.

"I know, baby." I flip us over until she is braced on top of me, pink nipples in my face. "Let's see how much you can take." I grab her hips, keeping her pinned, my dick, hard and demanding, pushing into the heat between her legs, thanking the universe for sweatpants

"What? Oh..." I lean up, teeth and tongue, nibbling and licking, biting and sucking. Her hair falls on either side of my face, sliding over my chest like a silken sheet. I pull at one hard peak, letting my teeth give a little dig. Her head falls forward with a jolt, lips and sweet breath touching my neck. "Do you like that, baby?" I slide my hands from her hips to her ass, cupping both supple cheeks hard, grinding into her pelvis, feeling her heat, craving it. I flip us over again, taking a moment to admire the obscene redness of her nipples, the swollen flesh sensitive and tortured. I want to beat my chest, howling while I drag her back to my cave. I rest on my knees, pulling off my shirt, watching her eyes glitter with greed. Yeah, I need a cave.

"Give me this," I pluck at the drawstring of her sweatpants, sliding my hand between her legs and squeezing. "Now." A sassy smile graces that mouth, and I can't help but smile back.

"Come and get it."

I throw my head back, laughing. "You got it, Ace." I pull her pants down slowly, snickering at the reveal of her panties, bright blue with hammers all over them. "Are these an invitation or a demand?" Her beautiful face flames up, and she howls, covering her eyes with both arms. "They're comfortable!"

Have I ever laughed with a woman right before I intended to devour her? I don't think so. I run a finger down the cleft of her pussy, reveling in the dampness, and then back up, pressing on the part of her that throbs for me.

"Here's what's going to happen, Rory." I tug her panties to the side, staring at the glistening flesh, my tongue coming out in anticipation. "I'm going to spend a little time right here," I gently probe until I am at her opening, swirling my finger slowly until I'm almost halfway in. Her eyes close, her back arching slightly. "It's going to feel good, but not quite enough. You'll want more, and you'll need it harder and deeper. But I'm not going to give it to you." I drag my finger in and out slowly, twisting it from side to side, watching her face go slack in pleasure. Her hips twitch with every thrust, and I smile, knowing I am driving her to the edge. I reach over and pinch a nipple, pulling and keeping time with my finger. "You like that, don't you? Maybe it feels like a little too much. You're getting wetter." I put my finger in my mouth; her flavor like a honey bomb on my lips. "Jesus, you taste better than I remember." I smooth my hand down her stomach, using two fingers to stroke her lips, bypassing her clit, which is begging for attention. "Two fingers now."

"Malcolm, please," she breathes, pulling at my arm. "Please." I flick my fingers lightly, her moans louder, the begging more piteous. "What is it you want, Rory?" Her silvery eyes open and lock onto mine. "Harder, I want it harder."

I smirk and shake my head. "Nope. You'll take what I give you." She's almost dripping now, the deliberate pace of my fingers leading her where I want her to go. "Trust me, baby." I watch my fingers disappear into the sweet hole, my dick twitching like mad, desperate to get to her. But this isn't about me. This is me showing her that no one on earth can make her feel this way.

Except me.

"I think you've had enough," I whisper, ignoring her whine. "I'm going to take these all the way off now." I withdraw from her heat and tug her soaked panties down to her knees, then pull them off one leg at a time. "Let me see." I push her knees apart, staring. "So pretty." I lean down until I am on my stomach, draping one supple leg over my shoulder while holding the other wide open. I take a deep breath, my eyes almost rolling back from her scent. "Rory?" Her eyes shoot open, unfocused and blurry with pleasure. "Yes?"

"I'm going to use my tongue now," I touch the tip of my finger to her clit, tapping it. "Right here. I'm going to lick it slow at first, then I'll suck on it. Then you'll come." Her tongue slides out to wet her lips, eyes closing again. I stare at her a moment, wanting to capture this moment, her hair wild and sweaty, lips puffy and bitten, her whole body rose-flushed and trembling. Wanting me.

Grrrrrrrrrrrowl.

The first flick causes a loud moan to jump out of her throat. The second has her digging her hands into my hair, alternately pulling and running her hands through it, pushing her pussy further into my mouth. A tangle of words flows out of her mouth, some pleading, some cursing. I lick her slowly, making small circles, before stopping and starting again. I think she's had enough. I slick my whole mouth over her mound, pressing down and sucking hard. A scream begins, and I slap my hand over her mouth, part of me wanting to howl, the other part knowing if anyone heard her, she would probably blame me and move into a closet for eternity. I use the other hand to slide three fingers into her, rapidly fucking her with them, feeling her walls finally begin to pulse, letting my tongue finish before she pushes my hand away, gasping. "No more. I can't take any more." I give her one more lick before pulling my fingers out, sucking every drop of her wetness off. She watches for a moment before pulling a loose pillow over her face and making screaming noises. I crack up, looking at the time, happy to see only forty minutes have passed, though I'm shocked we had that long. My dick is going to break through my zipper, so I hurry to get dressed and get a little distance. I can smell her pussy in the air, and I don't know how much more I can take.

"How do you feel?" I ask her, shrugging my shirt back on, watching a deep blush start from her chest and spread to the little I can see on her face. "Mmmrph."

"What was that?" I tug at the pillow until I stare at her perfection, an arrogant wave flushing over me. She looks like a woman well fucked.

"I said I feel fine." She sits up, embarrassment written all over her. Her head swivels as she looks for her shirt and pants, realizing too late that I am holding both in my hand. "Rory, look at me." She shakes her head, holding her hand out for her clothes, which I hold in the air, too high for her to reach. "Look at me, Ace." That stubborn chin sets, and she stands up, hands on hips. "Give me my stuff."

"I will after you look at me." I admire her nudity, wondering if I could get away with another thirty minutes and knowing I am pushing my luck. She huffs and snaps her head up, fake anger and annoyance twisting her mouth. Okay, maybe the annoyance is real.

"What is that face for?" I lean down close enough to kiss her. She glares at me, eyes wandering over me before she sighs.

"Because!" I hand her her shirt, which she puts on, holding her hand out for her pants, which I still hold hostage. "Because what?"

"Because I promised myself I wasn't going to give in!" I grin wolfishly, and she gives me the finger, making my grin break into laughter. She scowls, poking me in the stomach. "Where are my underwear?"

"In my pocket, and no, you can't have them back. I'm going to start a collection." She scoffs, shimmying into her sweatpants, covering up all that deliciousness.

"Well, I don't know how you are going to do that when we aren't doing any of that stuff again." I snort, and even her pretty face can't fix itself to believe that bullshit. She keeps her eyes down, fussing with putting the pillows back on the couch. I grab her chin and force her to look at me.

"We will absolutely be doing that 'stuff' again and more. You can run, Rory, but I am running right behind you this time. And when I catch you, then you'll see."

Her eyes flash, the gold flecks glowing. "See what?"

"What's right in front of you, girl. Me."

38

DO THE HUSTLE

"I love a generous King," Saige whispers, pushing the custom banquet along its railings until it faces north.

"Hush it, fool." *Discovery* is finally done with construction, and this is the best part: angling lights, setting up the decorations, and, in this case, trying out all the different combinations of seating and artwork. Interiors are Saige's specialty, and she has been having a blast. I'm always in awe of her talent, but I want to strangle her this morning.

"What? Any man that looks like the creator of sex who wants to spend time just worshiping you is fucking royalty. What's higher than a king? A god? Zeus?" I say nothing, just glaring at her as I tighten the screws on one of the tables with a slightly wobbling leg. I should have never told her about me and Malcolm's, um, sexcapades. She commented how relaxed I looked despite all the crap going on, and I blurted out that orgasms are a cure for anything. Her face looked like an owl, wide-eyed and with an open mouth, and I just wanted to kick myself. I should have known she would dig all the details out of me, and sure enough, I told her almost everything, and now she won't shut up.

"What I want to know is when you are going to start reciprocating.

I mean, I'm all for his.... proclivities, but girl, you gotta turn the channel too, you know?"

"Keep your voice down," I hiss, though with all the activity going on, I doubt anyone can hear her. Still, the press is hovering around, trying to dig up stuff on us, and you never know. "I don't need to start any more stories, especially since we are saying that Malcolm and I are just co-parents." She snorts and fusses with some pillows, turning and fluffing them.

"Rory, no one believes that shit. Look at you. Look at him. You guys are like a porno waiting to happen," she points at my boobs, then my ass. "I think people would be more shocked that you weren't playing hide the baguette than if you were. Shit, I'd be shouting from the rooftops if Malcolm Clare was chasing me around the house, trying to tongue me to death."

"SAIGE MARCHAND!" I don't know whether to laugh or cry. I might put an ad out for a new best friend, preferably one who isn't a hornball. "And he isn't trying to tongue me to death." Okay, that's a lie. A big one. Ever since the day that we had our first (second) uhhhh, interaction(?) Well, after that, I tried reallllly hard to avoid being alone with Malcolm for anything longer than a minute, and it backfired. Big time. Because he could do things in a minute that could make your head spin. And true to his word, the more I tried to run, the quicker he would find me. In one of the biggest apartments in the country, he could track me down within seconds. And each time he did...

"You ready for me yet?" He whispered in my ear, his fingers sliding in and out of me, his thumb pressing hard on my clit. My hands are gripping his shoulders, feet dangling over his arms. He's got a thing for picking me up against the walls, probably because I can't get away. I could feel my body about to let go, another massive orgasm binding me closer to the man I was doing my damndest to resist. "All you have to do is say it, Rory, and I will give you what you want." I shake my head, mute with pleasure but desperate to give in. This is all he will do—drive me crazy with his hands and mouth but never take it any further. I might die soon. "Say it, Rory. Say you want me."

"Uh-huh. He's got you sprung, girl. You have a dreamy look on your face and are trying to hammer with a screwdriver." I blink hard and grimace at Saige's grinning face. "Shut up."

"I don't know what you are so afraid of. You know the dick is amazing." She lowers her voice, which does nothing for my embarrassment.

"It's not that. Trust me, it's not easy saying no. I don't want to start all that up, when Roman and I are going home soon. I ain't gonna be the booty-call baby mama." She stares at me for a full minute before busting out laughing. I'm talking, tears running down her face, she can't breathe, and she's slapping her leg--laughing. Several of the workers in the kitchen step out to see what's so funny, half of them falling over each other to watch Saige's pretty face lit up.

"Rory, you still think you are going back to that apartment? Girl, you live with Malcolm now. Aside from the fact that it'll never be peaceful at your place again, do you really think he will let you go? He's got everything he has ever wanted: his son, the woman he loves, and his own company, all under one roof. He hustled you, girl." Her phone beeps rapidly, and she pulls it out, ignoring my horrified stare. She reads the message, sighing and gesturing to me.

"You gotta admire her creativity and tenacity." I pick up my phone slowly, already dreading what I will find. It's been relatively quiet, with only a few articles here and there and a ton of pictures of Malcolm's ex, still wearing all white and her engagement ring.

SHE STOLE MY DREAMS- RACHEL VAN PYKE SPEAKS OUT ON HER WISHES FOR MOTHERHOOD AND HER LOVE FOR MOST BEAUTIFUL MALCOLM CLARE.

The accompanying picture shows Rachel, almost makeup-less, sitting in a luxury nursery with a sad look on her face while she holds a blue bear—the same one Valentina gave Roman. "You know she borrowed that nursery." My phone rings as I skim the article. "Hello."

"Ace? You alright?" My smile tics involuntarily at the nickname and the deep timbre of his voice.

"Yeah. It's not every day I get called a womb-raider." His laugh makes the smile smile bloom fully, and Saige rolls her eyes, making heart shapes with her hands.

"I'm working with Hendrix's PR team on a response. We might not say anything, though. Val just posted a video on her social media of

Roman trying to eat bananas. It's already got more views than Rachel's crap. Are you sure you are alright? I'm sorry about this," he sighs. "This is a big week for you, which I'm sure Rachel knew." The coverage of *Discovery's* opening is at a fever pitch; the private soft launch is in a few days before they unleash to the public. Chandler pulled me aside and told me that he had so many requests for press passes to the opening party that he had to create a lottery system. I apologized, but he brushed it off with a smile. "*Honey, all press is good press. Our reservation system went down yesterday. We are booked for the next two years except for contingency seating.*" He laughs. "*You want my advice? Show up at the party with that gorgeous head held high and Malcolm Clare on your arm. The press will eat it up.*"

"I contacted Schillings and told him I am sending two guards to the restaurant. They will be there shortly and will prevent the press from trying to get at you. Tam will pick you and Saige up when you are ready." I nod, though he can't see me. My shoulders ease down when I realize he is taking all my worries off my plate.

"I also left a message for my parents. Though they've stayed out of most of this, I warned them that if they co-signed on this bullshit, I would never speak to them again, though they won't have time since my dad is swamped at Clare Inc., and my mom is fighting the Park Avenue brigade."

"I don't want you to fight with your parents because of me and Roman, Malcolm. Even though I was mad at my dad, I would give anything to have a few more minutes with him. And I miss my mom every day."

"I'll fight anyone who hurts you or tries to hurt you. That includes my family—it's non-negotiable, Rory." I ignore how my stomach twists and my heart sneaks an extra beat or two. *Get a grip, girl.* "Now, what are you having for lunch? Shall I have Cook make something to drop off?"

"The kitchen staff is here, and they're trying recipes all day. Saige and I have volunteered to test everything. We've already had a bunch of brunch items. Tam might have to roll me home in a wheelbarrow."

"Alright," he laughs. "Don't give this article another thought, okay?

I'll take care of everything. Promise me you'll call me if anything happens: don't be stubborn and try to handle it yourself." I stay silent

"Rory."

"Alright, alright."

"Tell Saige I said hello and to behave."

"I heard that!" He laughs again. "I peeked in on Roman a moment ago, and he almost took on a little knee-step, but then he fell over again. I think his belly is holding him back." I crack up because despite being weened off of my boobs, Roman still eats like he's competing in the Formula Olympics. He's a big baby, but his dad is six foot four. I hear a knock and see the delivery driver holding up another invoice for me to sign. "I gotta go."

"Okay. I miss you." I hold the phone away from my ear, eyes wide, but he's already hung up. I look at Saige, who shrugs.

"I'm telling you. Hustled."

PARTY CITY— ONLY COOL KIDS ALLOWED

"Stop pacing, you're making me nervous."

I flip Montgomery off and keep walking in a meandering circle around the living room. We are supposed to leave for the opening party for *Discovery* in a few minutes, and I'm torn between being worried for Rory, excited for Rory, and proud as fuck of Rory. I tell Montgomery this, and he smiles at me, taking Cameron's hand. "It's going to be amazing, Mal. We will all be there supporting her, and with that look on your face, no one will even think about stepping out of line." I frown at him, pointing at my head. "What look?"

"Well, you've got this whole broody thing going on, scruffy face, messy curls, all-black suit—very Byron. But those eyes. A threat mixed with a lot of emotion. You're wearing your heart on your sleeve, kid," Cameron says, pointing his free hand at me. I don't reply because he's right. I feel so many things for Rory; a dark possessiveness is at the top of the list, a deep sense of her being MINE. I'll destroy anyone who tries to come for her. I take a breath, trying to push these new feelings down.

"Well, they better hurry up. We are already going to be making an entrance as it is." I insisted on a show of force, and the only one not here was Rix, whose plane was late coming from Texas. Even Eve is here, all the women camped out in Rory's suite getting ready like its prom.

"You can't rush perfection, Clare. She'll be out in a few. "Saige breezes into the room looking phenomenal in a short emerald green mini dress, with tons of gold necklaces and sky-high gold heels. "She was putting up a fight, but Valentina got her together." She kisses both Cam and Monty, sitting primly next to them, lowering her voice to gossip— probably about me.

"We're here!" Valentina rushes in, a flurry of swirling fringe and long legs, pulling Eve, who chose a classic black mini dress. Her blonde locks are smoothed into a tight bun. She hugs Monty and Cam before dancing to me, her twin Chagall-blue eyes twinkling. "Try not to freak out."

"Why would I freak out?"

"Holy shit! Rory!"

"Oh no. Someone get the tranquilizer gun."

I turn around, my heart seizing in my throat. I blink hard twice and step toward her, wiping my hands down my face. "You've got to be fucking kidding me." I feel like a cartoon, like my eyeballs will shoot out of my head and then pop back in. "Rory, my God." I don't know where to look first, so I focus on her beautiful grey eyes. "You look..." I shake my head, words failing me.

"Is it too much?" She asks nervously, and I smile. Her thick, dark, auburn hair is full, flowing over her shoulders and back in a riot of luscious curls. Her dress—if it could be called that— is all black lace, sheer and ridiculously sexy, long-sleeved and high-necked except for a thin black band that barely covers her breasts and a teeny pair of black panties that gives her some modesty but almost none. The dress stops just under her knees, and a pair of spiky black heels gives her an illusion of height. Her make-up is all smoky eyes and glossy pink lips with matching polish on her fingers and toes. I walk in a slow circle around her, almost having a heart attack when I see that the panties only cover half her sublime ass. I'm actually rubbing my chest—I may not make it.

"No, it's not too much. He's just contemplating murder in

advance." Val elbows me, scowling. "Say something nice," she mouths at me, and I take a deep breath.

"Nothing on earth can compare to you, Ace. I got you a little something." I face her again, wanting to howl at her perfection, just barely resisting the urge to lock her up and fuck her into submission. Thank God for this black suit, which is concealing how hard my cock is. I pull a red box out of my pocket, and her eyes, studying me closely, look confused until I flip the cover open. "I didn't know what you would wear, but diamonds go with everything." I pluck one earring out and step forward, inhaling her sweet musky scent, brushing her silky hair aside before screwing the two-carat stud into place. I repeat it with the other ear, leaning down and brushing my lips against her forehead. "You look like every wish I've ever had," I whisper, and she tilts her head back, smiling.

"Are you sure it's not too much?" I shake my head and step back, taking her hand and lacing my fingers through hers. "Never. Let's go."

❧

I CRANE MY NECK AND SEE THE CRUSH OF PAPARAZZI OUTSIDE OF Discovery, earning their bonuses with snaps of celebrities and socialites. The line of cars is blocks long, and our three cars are behind each other, with Rory and I last. "The press is thick. Remember what we planned?" Rix's PR manager loaned us an associate for the evening who was already there, waiting to usher us past the wolves and through the red carpet. I'm still holding Rory's hand, which is a little cold and clammy, though her beautiful face is serene.

"Yup, Cameron and Monty will go first, then Saige, Eve and Val. We will be last. Keep my head up, smile, and wave. Don't acknowledge any shitty things they call out." She lists our instructions off, and I can't stop staring at her perfect mouth as she speaks. Valentina had already warned me not to mess up her make-up, and it was taking everything in me not to suck all that gloss off her lips.

"That's right. If any of the paps get out of hand, let me answer for you. I don't think it will be that bad, honestly. According to Rix's team, the sentiment has firmly swung in our direction." Rachel's friends were still leaking gossip to the blogs, mostly about me, but instead of constantly fighting it, we took a different tack—releasing photo Roman, articles about Rory's new project with Nick, and MDC's fast-growing reputation. My parents have been radio silent, still not speaking to any of us kids. Bea, who slipped back to England for a birthday party, claims that Dad won't answer her calls either.

"Do you think we'll be able to go out in public soon? I feel like a prisoner. I'd love to take Roman to the park. Feel normal, you know?" I squeeze her hand, not wanting to tell her that her life will never be 'normal' again. But if my girl wants to take our son to the park, I will make it happen. Tam thumps the wheel to let us know that we are next, and I point at Saige and Val, who are vamping for the cameras. "The worst thing we ever did is get those two together." Tam pulls up, and the valet opens the door.

"Take a breath, baby. It's our time now." I step out, and the cameras go wild, shouting and screaming my name. A trim, no-nonsense girl with a clipboard is waiting, a stack of press releases in her hand. "Mr. Clare. I'm Sissy. I'll be your guide tonight." I turn around and hold my hand out for Rory. She pauses, and I see her eyes close on a silent prayer before she slides her palm onto mine, and I pull her out, the lights of a million flashbulbs highlighting her smooth skin and turning her hair into a flame.

"It's Rory!"

The yelling turns into a deafening roar, and Sissy walks firmly forward, pausing every few feet and directing us to pose and how. Dozens of questions are being shouted at us, and Sissy passes out the press releases listing out the designers for our outfits, down to the scents we are wearing. The paps ask for a few of each of us alone, and they almost explode when Rory makes a complete turn, the bright lights showing the transparency of the lace and her perfect heart-shaped ass.

"Rory, how's Roman?" Her head whips around, and a wide, unexpected smile stretches across her face. She zeroes in on the guy who asked and steps forward, pulling her phone out of her clutch. I watch as she flips through photos telling the reporter something, flashes going off. She laughs and dances back, her hand stretching for mine, and I can't help but kiss her forehead, my pride spilling over. Sissy guides us to the end of the carpet and through the doors, where the yelling is replaced by loud music and chatter. "You were amazing, Ace," I whisper in her ear. She beams at me and pulls me along, waving her hand. "Welcome to *Discovery*."

⚜

"I CANNOT GET OVER THIS, RORY. HOW DID YOU EVEN THINK OF this?" Cameron pushes a table with a finger, watching it glide into a different position. All other tables in the space are locked, but Schillings decided to leave a set loose so the press could see how the concept worked. Currently, the chef is serving a Mediterranean fusion, so the decor has a ton of Morrocan influences courtesy of Saige, who I learned is a talented designer. The food is fantastic, though I barely get a chance to try it as dozens of partygoers have been approaching our group, all wanting to congratulate Rory and get an up-close look at the two of us. I haven't left her side, the messaging as clear as glass.

"I wish I could tell you, Cam, but sometimes the ideas just come to me. I like to let my clients talk a lot, and the concepts usually flow from that." There are a few guests hovering and listening, and I see some of them texting. Spies, I assume. There are quite a few rival architecture firms in the building, and I'm positive they are taking notes and 'ear hustling,' as Saige says.

Valentina, who has been working the party with Eve, pops up, jiggling in her high-heeled shoes. "Rory, where is the restroom? The champagne is too good." She slings back another glass, and Montgomery snatches it out of her hand before she can break it.

"I'll take you," Rory laughs.

"Ohhh, girl trip!" Valentina does some sort of drop-it-down dance, and Rory whisks her away, cracking up. They get stopped a few times, and Valentina, with that charming smile, interrupts, saying God knows what.

"She's a fucking star, Malcolm." I turn at the sound of Rix's voice and grab him into a hug. "It's about time." He shrugs, accepting a glass from a server, giving her a wink and smile. Like me, he's in all black, but instead of a black button-down and tie, he's bare-chested with a giant gold medallion hanging off a diamond chain —the insignia the Le Laurier crest.

"Damn weather coming out of Texas and then a jam at Teterboro. This place is killer." He looks around, nodding at some people and smiling at others. "How long did Schillings say the reservation list is?"

"Two years. But Rory says there are seats they leave some tables off the list for VIPs." I see Saige working through the crowd, her mouth smiling but her eyes worried. I frown as she and Eve come hurrying over, keeping their faces calm, but their energy urgent.

"Where's Rory?" She says in a low voice, conscious of anyone who may be eavesdropping.

"She took Valentina's drunk ass to the bathroom. What's wrong?" Monty asks as he and Cameron crowd in.

"Remember that guy I told you about, the Moaner? The one who works for Chanteuse? He's here." She gives us all a little backstory, and Rix shrugs.

"Well, what's the issue? This will do nothing but give her an edge over the other firms—they'd be idiots not to consider her designs. Why the dramatics?" Hendrix smiles at her, giving her long legs a thorough once over.

"He brought a date," she glares at Rix who smirks at her expression.

"Jealous?" She shakes her head, flipping him the finger before smirking.

"It's Rachel."

...MEETING IN THE
LADIES ROOM

"Ohhhh, it's nice in here," Valentina whispers, and I crack up. I've never seen her this tipsy, and I'm enjoying it a lot. She closes the stall door, and I wait to see if the noise cancellation fan works. I did a focus group on what women loved/hated about public restrooms, and one thing they complained about was the lack of privacy with all the cracks in the doors. I not only eliminated those, but I also added the machines that pipe in an ocean sound. I'm happy that once Val locked herself in, her voice was totally muffled. I stand at the custom agate sinks and squint at the mirrors on the wall, mentally measuring the heights. This had been a pain point for me as the Schillings group wanted them higher while I advocated for lower. I still think they need to come down a few inches, so I take pictures and text them out.

I put my phone away and touch up my gloss. I'd been horrified when Val and Saige pulled this dress out of my closet, asking them where the rest of it was while they laughed at me. I might as well be wearing nothing because the dress was totally sheer, and Saige pulled out some very small undergarments that cover up (some of) the goods. I know the style is fashionable right now and that I needed to make a statement, but good grief. The one thing that convinced me is that

Valentina got the dress from an up-and-coming designer who was not only a woman but also from a small town in Congo where Val volunteered. This would be her first big dose of publicity, and I'm thrilled to help. The look on Malcolm's face was worth it—once he got past his shock. I lean forward and stare at the giant diamonds in my ears, part of me praying they are fake and the other part knowing that red box meant they were very real. Saige is already calling them my push present, whatever that means. The door opens, and I straighten up, preparing for small talk, when the face in the mirror stares at me in disgust.

"I can't believe he thinks you are fit to follow behind me. Look at you." Rachel closes the door behind her, leaning her long body on the wall. She's wearing a bright red, short silk dress that fits her perfectly with everything else matching: lips, nails, shoes, the rubies in her ears. I turn around and give her a dismissive once-over, counting to ten in my head because she might catch the beatdown of the century, and I don't want to mess up my hair.

"I am looking. At you. And the fact that you are still wearing that ring is a joke." I point at her hand, where the forty-thousand-carat ring still rests on her skinny finger. "You've been publicly dumped, yet you're still in denial. Tsk Tsk." Her dark eyes narrow, and I marvel at the shininess of her hair and skin. It's borderline slimy. Yuck.

She laughs meanly and saunters to the mirror next to me, crowding my space. I don't move, and she huffs, trying to throw her elbow out. "You think that means anything? I have something you don't have, dahling, and that's time. Malcolm and I have been in each other's lives for years. I've been down this road with him before, and he always comes back. Always. Do you think you're the first one he's been with other than me? There've been hundreds, dahling. Hundreds of other women, who he fucks and leaves. The only difference is they are smart enough to use birth control. You didn't." She pulls out a tube of Chanteuse red lipstick and swipes more on, simpering at me. I feel a churn in my stomach; could be anger, could be violence.

"So you're saying that Malcolm had to find other women to sleep with, and you were pitiful enough to take him back? Damn, Rach. Maybe you should take some lessons or something." She gives me a black look, and I notice that for all of her beauty, she is ugly on the inside. I still can't believe Malcolm was going to marry her. Fucking yikes.

"Or it could be he needed to find out that only I've got what he needs. He stayed with me, didn't he? And he'll be back as soon as he gets bored with your overfilled breasts and trashy past. Maybe we'll even sue for custody of your little bastard—who knows?"

No. She. Fucking. Didn't.

I step closer to her, barely refraining from whooping her ass. "If you ever mention my son again, if you even think about him, I will rip every hair from your bony head. Do you understand? I'll wipe the floor with your face." The door behind us opens, and Valentina comes stumbling out, drawing to a complete halt as she stares at Rachel in disgust. "What the fuck are you doing here?"

"Oh, you're still in the country? I thought perhaps Penelope's hatred of you would have sent you off to some poor dirt village in the middle of nowhere, where you could work out your mommy issues." Valentina takes a deep breath and a step. "Do you really want to continue your fight with my family, Rachel? We've been nice up until now, but I know Malcolm's patience is wearing thin."

Rachel laughs, her head thrown back, bone-white teeth glistening. "And just what do you think could you do to me? My family name alone will shield me from anything. We are inviolate honey. Not like this piece of filth that is polluting the Clare DNA. This whole thing is an abomination."

I growl, my fists balling up. *Don't punch her, Rory. Don't do it.* "You are living proof that genetics don't mean shit. Even the 'best' families can produce a throwback." She stares at me, that stupid, pitying look on her face.

"So funny you should bring up genetics. Because I didn't know that cheating was hereditary." I freeze and blink hard, taking another step.

"Yes, I know all about your father and his tacky little affair. It would be a real shame if that story got out. Think about how it would make you look breaking up a marriage just like he did." Valentina makes a noise, and I feel a coldness sweep over me.

Okay, you know how in the movies someone sees red and then goes absolutely HAM on the villain? People, I am seeing red. I slowly toe off my heels, taking away four inches of height but giving me much-needed balance.

"Hold this, Val." I hand her my clutch and think back to the last time I was in a fight- eleventh grade. Sarah Maverick—my nemesis since kindergarten—made a slick comment about my mama, and before her mouth even closed, I leaped on her back, yanking her hair and biting. She screamed herself hoarse, and it took three people to pull me off, but it was worth it. She never came at me again, nor did anyone else. I could take Rachel with my eyes closed. Rachel's eyes flicker in slight alarm, and I bend my knees to jump when a strong arm wraps around my waist, pulling me against a hard chest.

"Not here, baby. Don't let her goad you into ruining your night," Malcolm's breath is hot in my ear, and I feel the haze of my WWE debut fading. My breath is coming out in rugged pants, and I shake away my anger, realizing how much crazy I was about to unleash. I turn my face into his shirt, my body trembling from the comedown.

"You best get your ass out of here. I don't know how much longer he can hold her back. Or how long before I want to get my own licks in." Saige's voice rings from behind me. "I've also asked security to escort you out. Don't worry about Pierre—I told him you were indisposed." I peek at my best friend, who has also taken her shoes off and is holding one out like a weapon. I snort my laughter, as does Malcolm, who buries his face in my hair, chuckling.

"And if you even think about releasing that story about Rory's parents, I will tell everyone we know about how you used to buy your papers from the nerds at Yale. I bet the alumni board would love to hear that." Valentina hisses at her, arms crossed in solidarity. Rachel looks at all of us, bright red spots popping up on her cheeks.

"This isn't over." She yanks on the door, colliding with Hendrix, who is just outside. "Hendrix," she nods regally.

"Bitch," he salutes, and Rachel growls, stamping off, meeting the black-clad security guards, who discreetly follow her to the front door. Saige slips her shoes back on and pulls me away from Malcolm, fluffing my hair as Eve, who came out of nowhere, pats my cheeks with a cool cloth. It takes them one minute to get me back together, and Malcolm squats down, helping me put my heels back on.

"What story was she talking about?" Malcolm asks, kissing me lightly and herding everyone out the door.

"My parents," I tell him, stopping and gritting my teeth. I will not cry. Malcolm stops and bends down to look at my face. "About your dad?" I nod, and his jaw clenches. "She won't dare. Rix, it might be time to pull the pin." I look at Rix, who has a devilish smile on his face. He also has no shirt on, distracting me and Saige, who is drooling like Bernoulli when he sees cheese.

"All you have to do is say 'when.'" Hendrix takes Saige's fist and pulls it through his elbow. She's so messed up between wanting to demolish Rachel and wanting to lick Rix's chest that, for once, she doesn't object.

"Let's talk about it tomorrow. Ace, you good?" I looked up at him, all my anger leaving me drained. He was right. This is my night, and I refuse to let that...gremlin ruin all my hard work. She'd already tried to take this away from me, and I refuse to let her get any more. If Malcolm and Rix have a plan, I want in on it. Fuck that chick.

"I'm good. Saigey, let's go find The Moaner. I want that contract."

❦ 41 ❦

NO MORE GOODBYES

I watch Rory pace around the house, muttering to herself, stopping to sketch something on her iPad every few feet. She's been like this for days, ever since the Discovery opening party and the brief meeting with The Moaner. She'd shaken off the bathroom fight with Rachel and turned on the charm. It only took the Pierre guy one minute to fall under her spell, which annoyed me to no end, but I took it for her. He held her hand the whole time he spoke to her, and Rix had to hold me back from ripping his arm off.

"Magnifique dame, votre talent n'est éclipsé que par votre beauté." *Gorgeous lady, your talent is only eclipsed by your beauty.* "I understand that you are interested in our upcoming project. Tell me your thoughts." She grinned at him, tossing her head and spouting off historical facts and design ideas. He listened closely, nodding his head a few times, and when she finished, he gave her a short bow. "Impressive, ma belle. Our leaders have an open video call soon; I will send the information along with ma dulce, Saige. They will go over the next steps and, of course, will look for feedback from other partners. I am happy to tell them your designs are fresh and intuitive, though they will see the accolades themselves. Please have her look for my email." The information came the following Monday, with two hundred different firms attending.

Chanteuse had strict demands and guidelines and was very clear they would ruthlessly cut any prospective designer if they didn't meet a single deadline. This didn't phase my girl at all; so far, eighty firms had already been eliminated. Saige told me privately that Clare Design was still in the running but that Rory didn't want to tell me. I knew they would be, my father's reputation and experience being what it was.

"She doesn't want your loyalty to your father to be affected by your relationship with her. She already feels bad about the estrangement." I nodded, knowing that Rory needed to know that nothing in life was more important than her and Roman. I'd been taking things slow, easing my way into her heart, though I wanted to bulldoze my way in. But knowing her stubborn ass, if I went too fast, she'd scamper back to her apartment like it was a bunker. As it was, I heard her telling Boone that she needed boxes for packing, and he gave her some bullshit excuse. He gave me a dirty look when he reported it, which was unnecessary. There was no way I would let the two of them go anywhere. I'm even willing to put up with her puppy, who, at eight months, was a huge furry monster that still didn't like me. Right now, he is following me around the house, slinking behind planters and doors as if anyone could miss his bug-bushy tail. God forbid I'm holding Roman because Bernoulli just glares at me, not moving more than one foot away. If I try to leave the room, he growls, though it's for nothing because I know he can be bribed with cheese and peanut butter.

"How long have you been standing there?" I smile at her confused look and brush my knuckles down her smooth cheek. "I've been following you for about twenty minutes." She bites her lip and holds up the stylus. "I'm sorry. I get in the zone and forget my surroundings. Did you need something?"

Yeah, your clit on my face. "No, I just like watching you. Your ass when you walk is like a beacon." Her face turns pink, and she fumbles with some imaginary buttons on the iPad. "Oh."

"You shouldn't be embarrassed by that, Rory. I think I've made what I want from you plain. I've had my hand in your pussy enough times." The pink turns bright red, and I love that I have that effect on her. "In fact, it's been too long since I've tasted you," I tell her, pulling the iPad out of her non-resisting hands and backing her into the room.

"I don't think we've been in the lobby together. Let's check it off of the list."

"Malcolm, umm," she starts ending on a moan, as I yank up her t-shirt and pinch her hard, pink nipple. I look over her head and spot a custom oversized chaise that my designer insisted I needed, which at the time I hated, but now I am convinced it's the chaise from heaven. I throw the iPad down on a chair and fist her shirt, guiding her until the backs of her legs touch the chaise.

"Bend," I tell her, and I push her over, holding her back until she is lying down. "Off." I yank her shirt over my head, smirking at the front, which says, "Mom of Future Yankees Player." I groan at the sight of her bra—a sheer silver mesh that frames her breasts beautifully. My dick throbs, letting me know that he is at his limit— he wants in.

"You drive me crazy, Rory. No one else has ever made me feel like this. Just you." I pull down her jeans, zeroing in on her matching panties and the wet spot that is calling to me. "Jesus, look at you. Fuck you are so goddamn sexy." I throw her jeans over my shoulder and lean down, latching on to that wet spot, her essence a balm to a starving man. Her back arches as I suck and bite down on her lips, nibbling and tonguing her until the wetness is seeping. "I need to add these to my collection." I had a whole handful of her panties at this point, shouting down her complaints of mismatched sets. I offered to start taking her bras, too, but the glare she gave me let go of that idea.

"Stop. Taking. My. Underwear." She rasps, and I grin against her mound, pinching it.

"Never." I slip my fingers into the sides, slowly pulling them down, my mouth watering at how they clung to her wet lips. I slide them down her legs, tucking them into my pocket, before leaning down and unclasping her bra. "I like the front ones." I throw that over my shoulder, too, taking a moment to feast on her naked form. "You're a fucking fantasy." I lift her legs and bend them at the knee, spreading them wide. I stare at the visible throbbing, my hands shaking as I unzip my pants. "Rory, once I get inside of you again, you're mine. All the way. No more running." I push my pants down, and her eyes go wide at my lack of boxers. My dick is rock-hard and pointed at its favorite destination. I reach behind my neck and pull off my shirt, stroking my dick, the head leaking smooth desire. I kneel between her legs and alternately watch her face and the creeping flush of an orgasm on her pussy.

"You're close already, baby? I've barely touched you." I grab one leg behind her knee, stretching her out, groaning at the sight of her opening.

"You got me all worked up...plus you're naked. What did you expect?" She pants while reaching up to tug on my hair. I rub my head n her clit, my pre-cum helping me glide back and forth. Her hold on my hair tightens, her little sounds drive me crazy, breaking down my control. "Hold on, baby." I take her other leg and drape it over my arm as I slowly ease inside of her. "Fuck." She felt like the silkiest satin, felt like home and love, felt like mine.

Cave, here we come.

I pull out and thrust back in quickly, waiting a moment before repeating the motion, picking up my pace as her moans turn into screams. I slam my mouth over hers, swallowing the sounds while doing my best not to come. Her walls are trembling, the slickness getting thicker. "Rory, I need you to come. What do you need?" My voice is harsh, the huskiness echoing throughout the room.

"Harder, Malcolm. Please." Her back arches, mouth open as she begs me. My chest feels one hundred feet wide—all I want in my grasp.

"You ask so pretty, baby. Like this?" I pump harder, no longer keeping up the sweet. I grind down on her clit with every thrust, and her mouth stretches on a wail, and I feel the pulses pulling on my dick, the buildup vanishing as my dick stiffens.

"Gah! Fuckkkkkk!" My body moves frantically, each spurt pushing my soul into hers. A final shiver, and I collapse on her, chuckling at the grunt she lets out at my weight. "Am I too heavy?"

"Yes, but no. Shift a little to the left." I do as she asks, and she takes a breath, wrapping her arms around me and squeezing. My eyes unexpectedly sting, remembering how she did this the first time we were together, the rush of emotions choking me; the knowledge that this tether, this connection doesn't have to end on a distant goodbye. I return her hug, kissing all the skin I can reach. Rory is silent, and I rear back to look at her face, surprised to see her already staring at me, her silvery eyes glassy. "What's wrong?" She better not say she regrets anything because I am not opposed to fucking her into submission.

"I'm just thinking about Boston...," she sniffs. "That goodbye was hard." She squeezes me tighter as if I was going to run away. It would take a crowbar to separate us, and that is fucking perfect for me. She has no idea how much I grieved for her and wished for her just minutes after leaving her that morning. The day she walked into my office, glowing in that green dress with my son tucked so safely, was when my heart started beating again.

"Let's make a pact, hmmmm. We will never use the word 'goodbye' to each other. We can say, 'See you later,' 'Until next time,' or something like that. But not goodbye."

She's silent for a moment, unconsciously twisting my hair around her fingers, scratching at my scalp, and then starting over again. I'm about to start purring like a cat. "I think I like that idea."

"Excellent, now you have a choice. We can do this again," I thrust my already hard again dick deeper into her heat, "before we get interrupted again," I shift until I hit a spot that makes her gasp. "Or I can let you get back to your pacing while I watch your ass in those pants." I rub that spot again, and she moans softly. "I like option one."

"Malcolm?" She breathes out, meeting my strokes while digging her nails into my back.

"Yeah, baby?" I can already feel the zip of release running down my spine.

"I still want my undies back."

42

I'M JUST ALONG FOR
THE RIDE

Valentina: Have they come up for air, yet?

Montgomery: Who?

Valentina: Mal and Rory, fool

Mongomery: I don't know who that is

Saige: Lucky. I almost caught them in the office. Ew

The Package Matches The Ego: I need details

Cameron: Rix, so help me…

The Package Matches The Ego: Who me?

Valentina: You are disgusting LMAO

Montgomery: It's genetic, you know

Valentina: EWWWWWWWW

Malcolm: Can you just leave us alone?

Rory: How do I get off this chat

Cameron: Well, look who managed to make
an appearance

Cameron: And I can confirm it is genetic 😉

Valentina: MY EYES

"Really, Saige?" I call out to her, hearing her snicker.

"Learn to lock the door when your man comes to visit, Ro," she calls out, still cackling. I scowl at the empty doorway, muttering to myself. It's not my fault she doesn't know how to knock. I wasn't expecting him to show up on the day we moved back into the office, but he did, with a giant bouquet that matched the fresh ones in my room. I kept my excitement hidden, but it was all for nothing because when he kissed me for luck, that turned into a whole other game, and we wound up on the couch when Miss Barge In caught us.

Plus, Malcolm is not my man.

"Are we back to that again?" Saige breezes in, iPad in hand, and the preliminary plans for the Grant-Alloy project. I admire her burnt orange silk blouse, cream flowy pants, and coffee-colored heels. Her deep, creamy skin is glowy, and I eye her suspiciously. "Why do you look so rested?"

"Facial, girl. I invited you to go, but you were too busy being loved up. And stop changing the subject. Are we back to the whole "he's not my man" bullshit?" She goes to my drafting table, unrolling the plans while giving me the stink eye.

"He's not." She makes some horrible noise, a combo cough-snort thing while plopping a hand on her hip and glaring at me. I try to return the look but fail miserably.

"Rory, give it up. You guys have a baby. You live together. All of NYC has pictures of you two booed up: at the opening party, at the park with Roman, even at the hotdog stand," she ticks everything off with a pointed nail, and I mess with some papers to distract myself.

After the Discovery success, pictures of Malcolm and I were everywhere. The paps did their job and reported every single detail included in our press release and then some. The most popular picture (which Malcolm printed and framed) is when a reporter asked me how Roman was. I had a giant smile on my face, and the flashing bulbs got a really good shot of my boobs in that sheer dress. I wanted to crawl into a hole and scream, but Valentina assured me that having a flattering photo circulated was ten times better than a bad one—it fed their appetite and helped calm things down. Malcolm took Roman I on a long walk in Central Park a few days later. We tried to stay incognito with baseball hats and baggy sweats, but it wasn't us who was recognized—it was Roman. He was sitting up and screeching at everyone, and that's all it took. Luckily, everyone was mostly respectful, and the two guards Malcolm had following us took care of everyone who wasn't. And even though I didn't see them, the paparazzi photos appeared the next day.

"But there are circumstances behind all of that. It's not like we chose any of it." I can feel heat spots popping up on my face.

"So you didn't choose to hook up after meeting at the bar?" I growl and shrug.

"And instead of just hiding Roman away, you didn't choose to let him know about his son? Did he kidnap you into his apartment? You tripped and fell on his tongue? His penis?"

"Saige!"

"Don't 'Saige' me. All of those things were choices. Every single one. What are you afraid of? That man loves you to death—you can see it plain as day on his face." She pokes me in the arm and yanks gently on my braid. I sigh and drop onto the couch, burying my face into the cushions.

"My dad loved my mom too, Saige. Everyone used to talk about them. He used to go out of his way to make sure he told her every chance he got. That didn't stop him from stepping out with Mandy, though. My mom never recovered from it. If I let Malcolm take up that kind of space in my heart...I don't want to feel that kind of pain. Not to mention the humiliation. "The homewrecker's home gets wrecked." I'd have to pack up Roman and enter witness protection."

After I made Malcolm disappear because I would unleash the Kraken on his ass.

"Rory, you were a kid, so maybe things always looked rosy to you, but there is no perfect marriage. Your dad made a mistake, but that doesn't mean Malcolm will. I can tell you, with everything I have, that he loves you on a level you may not be prepared for but desperately need. I bet he always has. And I know you feel the same. You can try that "parents with privileges" shit with everyone else but me. I still have the receipts from all the boxes of tissues I had to buy when you were crying your eyes out over him. "Saige, why would my first one-night stand in years affect me like this?" Remember that? We got drunk and tried to find him a billion times. Now you get what you want, and you're trying to push it away. Make it make sense, Ro."

I grunt and push myself up, blowing some escaped strands out of my face. "I know it sounds crazy."

"Yeah, it does. I can't believe he is putting up with it, but then again, he would yank the moon out of the sky for you. He already quit his job, cut off his parents, and gave up his privacy for you. I can totally see where your worries are coming from."

She sarcastically tacks on the last part, stomping over to answer the phone. "Miller-Jones Architecture, this is Saige." I tune her out and stare at the preliminary sketches I sent to Nick Grant this morning. We are far from breaking ground, but I didn't want him to think I was pushing him to the back of the line because of the Chanteuse competition. Every time a new round of firms gets eliminated, it's all over the news, even in Chicago. Nick's wife has been awesome about cheering me on, so I know he's aware. I hear Saige say goodbye in French and look up. "Who was that?" Her eyes are lit up with excitement, and she starts jumping in those heels.

"That was Pierre. Chanteuse just announced the list of the final five finalists, and WE ARE ON IT!" I scream and join her in the jumping, both of us saying unintelligible things and hugging. Saige has tears on her face, and my eyes won't stop leaking.

"Is everything alright?" I grin at Bart, the security guard that Tam assigned to

Be with me during the day. He drives me to work and is stationed by the elevator just in case a reporter sneaks past the shared reception downstairs. We've only been back a week, and already, two suckers have been caught. My landlord apologized and switched the receptionist to a beefy guy who loves the Yankees and cleans his nails with a pocketknife.

"Bart, we made the final five!" His face lights up, and he gives us a high five. "Congrats, Mrs. C!"

Wait.

He leaves the office texting as he goes, and only a few minutes later, my cell phone rings. "Ace."

"Malcolm, we made the final five!" He chuckles, that deep voice sending shivers up my arms.

"I know, Bart just texted me. I'm so fucking proud of you, Rory. I knew you could do it." I'm smiling so hard, and I can feel my cheeks crack.

"I still have four more people to beat, but the fact that I made it this far...I mean, I'm shocked." Saige is holding her tablet over her head and pointing at something. "Hold on a sec. I'm going to put you on speaker." I push the speaker button and take the tablet from Saige.

"Okay, the Chanteuse email says there is a dinner in two weeks with mandatory attendance. Blah, blah, blah, plus one..."

"I'll be your plus one. Keep going." Saige snickers at his tone, and I roll my eyes. "Ohhhhh, it's at the Hotel Rose Èlegant. I've always wanted to go there. Let's see....oh." I pause at the bottom, where all of the finalists are listed. Fuck.

"What is it, baby?"

I wince and take a breath. "Well, ummmmm, your dad made the final five too. So, we'll have to see him at the dinner." This has disaster written all over it.

"Don't you worry about that. Percy is a lot of things, but he is always civil. He won't try anything when such a prestigious contract is on the line. And if he says one thing out of pocket, I'll handle him." Ouch.

"Malcolm..."

"No, baby. My father made his choice, and I made mine. You and Roman are the best thing that ever happened to me. He should have been happy for and supported me, but he chose my mother's vinegar instead. They will have to live with the consequences. I was willing to give up my happiness for my mother's health, willing to be miserable forever, but they couldn't consider my feelings for one minute when it came to my son and his mother. Sorry, not sorry."

"Damn," Saige whispers, eyes wide.

"Now we are going to celebrate. I'll get the text chain going. Saige, you are invited, too. Seven O'clock? I'll text you the place."

"Ummmm, okay."

"Saige, make sure she gets out on time. I can already tell she is anxious to get to work." I suck my teeth, and they both laugh. "You got it. I'll drag her out by her hair if I have to."

"Just be gentle. That's my hair to pull. Ace... you're a fucking rock star." He hangs up, and Saige laughs at my red face.

"Yeah, that sounds like a man looking for another woman. Sure."

43

IT ALL COMES DOWN TO
THIS...KINDA

"I feel like we just did this, yeah?" Rix says, a lazy smile on his face. For once, he doesn't have on some ridiculous outfit or a hairstyle like the queen from Star Wars. I didn't expect him to show up and wait with me, but when he heard that everyone else was coming over, he showed up, too. Boone laughed himself to death when he opened the door, and Hendrix was standing there in plain sweatpants, a t-shirt, and fancy sneakers on his feet. His hair was in a simple ponytail, and the first thing I could think to blurt out was, "Are you sick?" He rolled his eyes and asked Boone (who was still laughing) for a martini.

"You mean waiting for the girls? I have a feeling that I'll be doing this for the rest of my life. The four of them are joined at the hip. They've even got a private group chat, and when I asked Rory what she was giggling about, she clammed up like a mob witness. I can only imagine what kind of trouble they will get into— I might need to share your retainer for Wicker." I came home from a meeting looking forward to seeing Rory and was informed by Julian that the 'get-ready' activities had already started, and I was welcome to hang out with him and Roman since they would be busy for hours. I took a few calls and then sprawled out on the floor with my son, who finally got the hang of crawling and is now on a mission to put everything he can find in his mouth. His partner in crime, Bernoulli, is doing the most by dropping toys and kibbles everywhere, and I can hear Boone's horrified shouts all over the house. I got dressed about an hour ago, donning a custom Chanteuse suit I had made last year. It's a dark navy, with a subtle purple stripe that seems more of Hendrix's speed than mine.

Rix seems amused but pensive. "I called the hotel manager and ensured they knew you and Rory would be treated like royalty. If you need anything, call him. I texted you his direct number." When Rory told me that the finalist dinner was at the *Rose Èlegant,* the US's only recognized seven-star hotel, I deliberately didn't tell her that Hendrix owned it. I doubt even my parents know, as he bought it through one of the LLC — Le Laurier Company— subsidiaries. Rix wanted to roll out the red carpet for us, but I know it's essential for Rory to be treated like everyone else. He agreed, but only if I let him tell the manager that his brother and his partner were in the building. He also threatened that any photos leaked by the staff would be cause for immediate termination with no references.

"You have a plan if Percy and Penelope start some shit?"

I snort and rub my face, smooth for the first time in weeks. "Not really. I'll play it by ear. Hopefully, they won't try anything, but given it's been a few months, they probably have pent-up stuff to release." He grunts and polishes off his drink, and we start discussing the Yankees off-season and whether they will ever get out of the first round of the playoffs again. I took Rory to the last game of the series, and she was so pissed at the loss that she asked me if I could buy the team so she could run it. Of course, she forgot there were people around, and the next day, the gossip pages were rife with rumors that I was going to buy the Yankees for Rory. She got a kick out of that one and laughed until I had to kiss her to shut her up.

"Agreed. If I know our Mother, she has something up her sleeve. Be on the lookout." He finishes up his drink, staring at the floor. His phone beeps, and he whips it out, grimacing at the message.

"Everything alright?" I ask him, slowly realizing that he's not quite himself. He looks up and gives me a crooked grin, a ghost of his typical bravado. "Yeah. Got something I'm working on that is giving me a hard time. I'll get it sorted eventually." I hear the excited chatter of the girls coming and give him one last look before turning my attention to the doorway where Rory appears, an exasperated look on her face. I give her a slow once-over, feeling my blood heating up and a tightening in my pants. Rix lets out a long whistle, and she gives him a cheeky grin.

"If you weren't the love of my brother's life, I would steal you away and hide you on one of my islands. A tux? I like it."

I like too. She's shirtless underneath the fitted black tuxedo jacket, and though it's tasteful, there is no mistaking the generous cleavage she's displaying. There are no pants, just those shapely legs covered in sheer black stockings and ridiculously high red heels. Her glorious hair is in a loose bun, simple makeup except for the red lipstick swipe. She looks chic but professional, sexy, yet approachable. Her jewelry is a statement, the diamonds I bought and her single strand of Cavensih pearls. Damn. You'd think I would be used to her outrageous beauty, but nope. She knocks me down in sweats or like this— dressed to kill.

"I figured since Chatneuse is a fashion brand, She'd be able to get away with something a little more daring," Valentina says, flopping down on the couch next to Hendrix. She leans on him before frowning and giving him a once over. "Are you sick?" I snort and hold out my hand for Rory's. She laces her fingers through mine, and I gently kiss her. "I already can't wait until we get home," I whisper against her mouth, feeling her lips stretch into a smile.

"Told you the long-last lipstick was the right choice. He can't keep his lips off of her." Saige plops on the other side of Rix, who immediately wraps an arm around her. She sighs in annoyance but says nothing.

"Hater." Rory mouths to her while pulling me along.

"Don't forget that we are all meeting here in the morning for a download. Saige and I are spending the night. We'll make sure to wear earplugs, just in case." Val gives me a grin and I glower at her.

"Valentina..." Saige snickers, and Val's grin gets bigger. I sigh and signal to Boone to have the car ready.

"I think we found her in an alley somewhere." Rory laughs, and I hug her close. "Let's do this girl."

THE *ROSE ÈLEGANT* TAKES UP ALMOST ONE CITY BLOCK, THE FRENCH Baroque style highlights the gleaming white stones. The flags of visiting dignitaries and VIPs fly from golden posts, the most prominent of which is the French flag. Tam pulls smartly up to the hedge-lined valet line, giving the attendant our names. He checks his tablet before waving us to another driveway, where we wait for our doors to be opened.

"How are you feeling, baby? Nervous?"

She gives me a wide, saucy grin. "Nope. I live for this type of stuff. I've never been afraid of competition, even at this level. My mom used to say I was born trying to win. It's why I love baseball so much. Just a six-month-long chess match." Our doors are opened, and a trim, handsome man hands Rory out, bowing slightly. "Miss Miller-Jones? Mr. Clare? I am Mikel. I am happy to escort you to your dinner with the Chanteuse group. Please follow me."

We walk through the luxurious lobby, heads turning as we go. It's clear that many of the guests know who we are, and I've never been prouder in my life as Rory keeps her head high with a secret smile. We follow Mikel into one of the exclusive restaurants and through an archway of roses, straight into a private room at the back of the space. He stops and bows again, gesturing us inside. I pull Rory's arm through my elbow and feel her take a deep, excited breath. Hendrix told me the room was recently painted the same light pink and gold as the Chantuese logo, with silk hangings and sprays of rare Damascus roses in large vases. There are already quite a few people here, and we walk forward when Pierre spots us, hurrying over.

"Madame Miller-Jones, Rory, so good to see you. My heart was happy to see your name on the list of finalists, though I should have been expecting it. Your ideas have been a topic of conversation." He bows to both of us, a small smile on his face. "Please come and meet my superiors." I spot my parents at the edge of a group, giving my father a polite nod when he sees me. My mother also nods, though her expression isn't as frosty as I expected. Her eyes flicker to her right before returning to mine, and my stomach tightens when I see Rachel clinging to a man's arm, gesturing wildly with his hands. "You have got to be kidding me," I growl, and Rory snarls. "She's like a bad fucking penny."

Pierre waits politely at the edge of the group until he catches the eye of an elegant, white-haired woman dripping in emeralds. She glides forward, and Pierre whispers in her ears while she slowly looks us over. Her eyes light up, and she walks closer, holding her hand out.

"Madame Miller-Jones? I am Élyna Chantuese. I have been looking forward to meeting you. We dined at your latest project last night —*comme c'est unique!* The owners were kind enough to give us a demonstration of the refresh system—it is already the talk of the industry. I feel a Michelin star coming." Her heavily accented French is charming, and Rory's grin is starry.

"It's a pleasure, Madam Chanteuse. Thank you for the compliment. Please meet Malcolm Clare." I step forward and give Élyna a brief bow and kiss on each cheek. Her face turns a little pink, and she smiles.

"Of course, I know who he is—*Le plus bel homme de New York*. I'm stunned to see that pictures don't do you justice. What a striking couple you are. The suit is *magnifique* on you, Monsieur Clare. Are you sure you wouldn't like to give up your business and model? I fear you would dominate the runway." I laugh out loud at her cheekiness and bow again. "Thank you, Madame Chanteuse, but I like being in an office a little too much."

"That is not a Chantuese dress," a deep voice says, and Élyna smiles and pulls the handsome silver-haired man to her side. I recognize him as Lucas Chanteuse, Élyna's older brother and the company's controlling owner. He eyes Rory, whose smile edges toward mischievous.

"Nope, sure isn't. I don't like being a follower, don't you agree? It's so unoriginal." She peers around the room, where almost every other guest, including my parents, is in a Chanteuse design. Her eyes twinkle, and the austere man's face breaks into a wide smile.

"*Bravo, madamoiselle!* You have spirit as well as talent. Please come meet the other finalists, though I believe you are acquainted with a few, no?" His eyes twinkle back at her, and she laughs, shaking a finger. "I hope I'm not sitting next to you at dinner. You'll get me in trouble."

He laughs louder and takes her by the hand, leading her to the larger group.

"Ah, but that's the fun of it, no? Come, let me introduce you to your in-laws—I find all this fascinating." Rory snorts, which makes him chuckle again. "You ain't the only one."

Lucas' laughter touches every wall, and Élyna and I follow.

Let the games begin.

44

EPILOGUE

By the way....

The Yankees won the World Series the next year. Suck it.

HENDRIX

Y ou're probably wondering what I am doing on the terrace when all the celebrating is happening downstairs, right? Well, every great mastermind is allowed to gloat in private.

What am I talking about? Well, let's chat.

I've always worried about Malcolm. When we were younger, I had to stand by and watch as our parents snared him in their iron web of tradition and control, just slightly too absent to do anything about it, to guide him down a different path. I tried to talk him out of his tactic obedience, but he dug his heels in, informing me that our mother already had one bad boy to worry about—she didn't need another. Plus, with Valentina and Montgomery coming behind him, he wanted to set a better example. He's always been good. Good. Good. Good.

Whatever.

Even so, I kept an eye on him. When I was in Canada or away at school, I hired a few people to keep tabs on him and make sure that he was happy and thriving. I keep an eye on all my siblings, especially Val, who was determined to forge her own path despite the privilege she was born into. Her security reports almost give me heart attacks as she would traipse deeper and deeper into economically depressed areas, always searching for ways to help, for ways to uplift. At one point, her team was twenty people deep, though I only let her see two. Malcolm may have been physically safer but never emotionally—his parents saw to that.

Don't ever let someone tell you being rich isn't fucking awesome, by the way.

I knew when good old Penelope and Percy sat him down and told him he would be engaged to that gold-plated harpy, I knew when he met Nick Grant in college, knew about all the women he slept with, knew when Percy was about to turn Clare Inc over to him—I knew it all. I never interfered, letting him make his own decisions and tell me about his life and frustrations. And when he had finally had enough and ran off to Europe, I sat in my office and applauded. Mother called me, angry and demanding, and I nodded and made sympathetic noises while reading the reports of my brother's whereabouts, cheering on his rebellion. When he landed in Boston, I immediately called Summerlin, one of Percy's old college friends, and asked him to check in, hoping he could encourage even more bad behavior. Summ, who hated how our parents treated us, was more than happy to oblige.

I shouldn't have worried.

His tail told me all about the gorgeous redhead Malcolm left with, and I directed them to dig into who she was. I knew all about the new Mrs. Clare long before anyone else did. It was plain to see that although Malcolm was pining for her, even when he attempted to go along with that prison sentence, I mean wedding. I put a detail on her, and let me tell you, when they reported that she was pregnant, I almost ran and told my mother so that I could see her head explode. Instead, I ramped up her protection and spied on her until she started looking for a nanny. I had Wicker purchase the placement agency and ensured they sent over the worst possible candidates until I could offer up my guy, Julian.

Yes, Julian works for me.

My aunt, Sinella (you'll meet her later), who always loves to be in on any scheme, suggested a puppy, which worked out perfectly. It gave Bea an in from day one and a way for Julian to let me see Roman without suspicion. I let things play out, convinced Malcolm would break free of his chain and claim his family. But when he didn't, I casually remarked to Cameron, planting a seed that we needed more help, and, well, you know what happened from there. And now here we are, my baby brother finally happy, married to that incomparable woman, and if I'm not mistaken, another baby is on the way.

"Um, Rix?" I turn to Montgomery, who looks like he is about to come out of his skin. "What's up?"

"Uhhhhh, hell is breaking loose. Valentina just announced her engagement to Julian. Mom and Dad are freaking out, and Malcolm keeps laughing. Cameron doesn't know what to do, either." I take a long sip of the excellent French champagne and hand the bottle to Monty, who takes a swig.

"Julian can handle it, Monty. Trust me."

"How can you be sure? I don't want Val to go through what Malcolm and Rory did. The family just got back together." His brows furrow and he has an awkward face. I smile and pat him on the shoulder. I want to tell him that Julian Akira (real name Davoren), the oldest son of the Baron of Killkilleen, a billionaire in his own right who joined MI-5 straight out of uni in an act of rebellion, can handle our parents. His own family despaired over his defection, though I know he made amends recently when he had fallen in love with my baby sister. Bea had recognized him immediately, and I had to admit all of my surveillance after her (polite) demands.

But that's a story for another time.

"Did I tell you I met someone?" Monty's eyes bug out of his head, and a smile splits his face.

"Wait, like met met? Or like hooked up met?" He jiggles in his tuxedo, ready to go and snitch to the family. But he's distracted like I expected.

"Nah, no hook-up. She won't touch me with a ten-foot pole. I just need a little more time with her. No woman can resist all of this." I wave a hand down my body, ignoring my brother's eye-roll and scrunched-up face. "What? You doubt me?" I point at my chest and give him exaggerated eyebrows. He paints his face blank and looks at me up and down like he's contemplating.

"You're not as good-looking as Malcolm, but you have potential." I put down my glass and leap at him, ignoring his yelps and getting him in a headlock, like I've done all of our lives. He cracks up, and I take my time messing up his hair and finishing with a wet Willie, which has him squealing and yelling. I let him go as he continues to hop around with disgust.

"You ass! Do you know how many germs you just stuck in my ear? Not to mention, God knows where your mouth has been!" I chuckle and lean on the railing. "It hasn't been anywhere. I told you I met someone." He stops his dramatics and stares at me with my same wide hazel eyes.

"Wait. You mean you've been...celibate?" His face is a contorted mess of faux-horror and hopefulness. I nod, and he gasps, this time for real.

"Oh. My. God. Are you serious? Hollleee shit! Does Malcolm know? Does Val?" His hands windmill, and any minute, he'll levitate in excitement. "I've gotta find Cameron!" He hurries off and flings the door open, stopping abruptly in the doorway.

"Wait. Who is she?"

I smile.

THANK YOU!

Hi Friend!

Thank you so much for spending your precious time reading Malcolm and Rory's story. Rest assured you will be seeing them again soon.

Not ready to let the Clare family go? Scan the QR code below to download a FREE special epilogue featuring Hendrix.

Curious about Nick and Kenna? There is a sneak peek around here, too. For the whole Power Series scan below.

Never miss a release— Newsletter sign-up. Be the first to hear about free content, special reveals, sales, and more. You can also access extras on my website. Join the Blake Squad today!

SNEAK PEEK—MOST RECKLESS

Every year, *Persuasion Park Magazine* publishes its "Most In The City" List of New York's most (and least) eligible bachelors. Untamable, unapologetic, and unforgettable, these are the men riding for the most brutal fall of them all...

Heir to two fortunes.
Pleasure seeker
Bad Boy

Rix Le Laurier is everything you don't (do) want a man to be: brooding, bored, too handsome for his own good, sexy without trying, and almost hysterically allergic to commitment. So where do I meet him? A sex club. Figures, right?
Things go wrong in a big way, really fast, and I have to rely on him for my very life. Does this stop him from trying to seduce me? Nope.
Do I resist? Of course, I do. Any other man would give up. But not Rix Le Laurier. He just tries harder and harder.
Until I finally give in. FML.

(Buckle up, this one will make you laugh *and* cry.)

SNEAK PEEK—THE POSSESSION SERIES: 'HIS TO BELONG TO'

Hi—You can start here if you want to meet Ayden and Cassidy... Warning: heartbreak ahead.

Before

The Surrey-Mark Hotel is famous for three things.

One- the opulent appointments of its guest rooms and private clubs. Situated in a hidden nook in the heart of Knightsbridge, the Nash-inspired architecture highlights the ultra-luxe decor, marked by pristine antiques, lush textiles, and warm lighting. Each of its fifty-five suites is filled daily with fresh flowers (personally chosen by each guest), beds made with the highest thread count available, and stocked with the rarest wine and spirits. The top three floors are a combination of privately owned lofts and leased apartments occupied by everything from a tech billionaire to a Middle-Eastern prince.

The second, is the Surrey's stringent promise of absolute discretion. Employees are put through rigorous background checks, social media monitoring, and several non-disclosure agreements. So important is this vow of prudence, that some workers don't even tell their families where they work. Guests can be assured that all of their deeds (good and bad) will be studiously ignored, making the hotel a favorite of visiting diplomats and the Hollywood elite.

Lastly is the 'Campus'—a clubby bar with high-backed leather booths and a selective clientele. Billion-dollar deals and noble marriages have been arranged inside of its walls; it's not unusual to hear plans for ending wars or the next electric car being spoken of in hushed tones. It's not a place for the newbie: the Steward closely guards the entrance to the Campus- a position gained only by heredity or decree. In the two-hundred and thirty-five-year history of the hotel, only four families: The Soames, The Westons, The Mayerlys, and the Thackers have held that role- a source of pride and distinction. The current Steward- A Soames/Thacker offspring- is a veritable lion with his entree cocktail- simultaneously rejecting and granting admittance with a ruthless relish.

So you can understand my utter confusion when I overhear the absolute bullshit coming from the two knobs sitting behind me. I'm in the process of nursing my fifty-year scotch and debating on taking home the hot little blonde who's been eye-fucking me the last hour, but I keep getting sidetracked by their nonsense. I've been halfway listening to these two idiots blathering about this and that for the past hour- and I'm tempted to have the Steward kick them straight to the street. I managed to block out most of what they were saying until I unwittingly tuned back in.

"It's her. I would know those lips anywhere," Arsehole Number One says excitedly. He has a flat American accent, along with a sickening tendency to form foamy spitballs at the corner of his mouth. The first time I turned around, he had two large ones sponging his lips together.

"No way, dude. She's supposed to be what-five-ten or eleven? She's a supermodel for chrissakes. This chick is nowhere near that tall," Arsehole Number Two replies. "Plus, what would she be doing here? Chicks like that are like on the Riviera or Ibiza—not in an old ass hotel in London."

Alright, first, he mispronounced Ibiza (as most Americans do), and second, did he call the Surrey-Mark an 'old-ass hotel'? I glance/glare over my shoulder again, but they are both oblivious. Their attention is focused squarely on a booth to the left of all of us. I crane my neck to see who they are talking about, but all I see is the very top of a dark head of hair.

"I'm telling you she is the most beautiful woman I have ever seen. I'm about to go over there and ask for her autograph," Spitty is practically bouncing off of his stool. His top-shelf whiskey sloshing all over the tabletop, and the spitballs have returned. I can feel my top lip curling involuntarily as I take in his ill-fitting suit and sweat-stuck hair. The two fingers that are clutching his rock glass are stubbed with dirty fingernails, and ink stains his palm. His partner is no better with a shiny bald head and smarmy smirk glued to his face.

"You're drunk, bro. That ain't Melina M, and that chick is nowhere near as hot. Hey, maybe she's an escort? I read an article about how hookers in Europe post up in tony places like this and look for rich men. That whole nerdy thing she has going on is probably just a front. Listen, how much cash do you have on you?" He pulls a pitiful stack of notes mixed with American dollars, and his friend does the same. They whisper loudly, predicting what kind of service their money can buy, while the object of their focus remains blissfully ignorant to the hell about to be unleashed upon her.

I take the last sip of my scotch and sigh deeply. There's no way I can let this poor girl be subject to these two twats. I throw a few fifty-pound notes down and slide out of my chair. I know Melina M person-ally— she runs in the same fast circles that I do. There's no way she would be caught dead in *Campus*. It's too quiet, too cerebral for her. She prefers the flashy lights and stormy scenery in Chelsea, *Mahiki* in Mayfair, or Notting Hill. Areshole Number Two is partially correct, at least.

I slip past them to the right and make my way in a full circle, passing acquaintances and the hot blonde who I'm still taking with me. I give her a quick wink and a nod, and she squeals something to her friend. I'll remember to have her repeat that sound when I'm stroking into her later.

Not-Melina's booth is curved into a corner, almost facing the wall. As I round the curved seat, I see that her tousled dark head is bent over a laptop and that she is simultaneously typing and making notes onto a ratty pad of paper. She's all dressed in black and utterly unaware of the fact that someone is standing in front of her. I clear my throat loudly and wait.

Nothing.

I clear it again and knock lightly on the table.

Still nothing.

I lean over and see that she has headphones in her ears and can faintly hear the steady beat of a dance track. Her fingers are flying over the keyboard, and she whips a calculator out of nowhere, punching in numbers at a record pace. An accountant, perhaps? A student? I move closer to get a look at the writing on the pad, jostling the table a bit, and her head shoots up in surprise. Her eyes lock onto mine, and her mouth forms a soft "O" in shock.

Fuck me standing. She's gorgeous.

I can see where the resemblance to Melina is causing spasms in the bloke at the bar. Melina is famous for her abundant pout and brilliant blue eyes. I can't tell the exact color behind her thick glasses, but her pillowy and wide lips are the stuff of dreams. Her skin is like heavy cream, and even with the dim light, I can see a flush creep up her cheeks. Her thick dark hair is full of curls and bumps, spilling in wild abandon around her shoulders. I know I'm staring like a fool, and I mentally shake myself out of my inspection. I glance up and see the Twin Terrors about to make their way to her table.

"I don't have time to explain, but trust me, just follow my lead," I hurry and slide in close to her, draping my arm around her shoulders. She fits perfectly under my arm, and I feel her stiffen. Leaning in, I place my lips close to her lobe. The scent of her- heady vanilla mixed with fresh lavender tickles my nose. "There are two men who are headed this way- and trust me; you do not want to face them alone." Her breath quickens, and she nods once. I keep my face buried in her fragrant hair as she quickly flips over her papers and shuts her laptop. She turns her body toward mine slightly and curls into me.

"Excuse me, are you Melina M?" Arsehole One asks without preamble. His friend is standing slightly behind him, that smarmy expression creasing his mouth. His eyes flit over us and lock onto me.

He takes in my tailored suit and zeroes in on my Rolex Daytona watch. His mouth opens slightly, and he takes a little step back. Smart man.

The vision in my arms turns her head slightly and gives the duo a hard look. "Excuse me?" Her voice is a bit raspy but sweet. The biggest surprise- she's American.

"I said, are you Melina M? Ya know, the model. Are you her?" Spitty's voice is grating and loud, and sure enough, a round spector of saliva is growing at the corner of his mouth. I can see her eyes zoom in on it, and feel her spine stiffen in disgust.

"No. I'm not." She turns back into my chest with a huff, but the two won't leave.

"Are you sure? I mean, you look just like her," the fool rambles while whipping out an outdated cell phone with a cracked screen, "See?" He shoves the phone close to her face, and I feel a growl crawl up my throat. The blurry picture is one of Melina—and yes, the resemblance is uncanny, but this sod is pissing me off with his rudeness. He's pushing himself into what I consider her personal space, and any minute he's going to be touching her. Fuck this.

"She said no, mate. I suggest you leave before I have you removed, or I will do it myself." I grit out the last bit and lift my hand in a slight gesture. I see the Steward quickly take in the scene and lift his antique phone. After a few words, he nods at me, and I turn my eyes back to the soon-to-be-departed. "That wasn't a request. She's not who you think she is. Now kindly leave." I lock eyes with his friend, and my threat is clear—I'm not one to be messed with. My eyes flit over his shoulder, and I watch as two hulking yet discreet security post themselves at the entrance. All I need to do is lift an eyebrow, and they will be tossed onto the street.

"C'mon Sid. It's not her like I said." Arsehole Two pulls at his friend's arm and whispers something low. Spitty sniffs nastily and shoves his phone back into his pocket. "Nah, you're not her. My bad." His wet lip curls up, and they turn to amble drunkenly toward the exit. The two guards follow them at a distance while I once again meet eyes with the Steward. With a quirk of my mouth, I ensure they will never be allowed back.

"Thank you."

The angel in my arms has pulled back from my tight embrace, peering up at me through her glasses. A thick strand of her hair has fallen over her cheek, and I unconsciously tuck it behind her ear. I take in her unbelievable features from a smooth forehead, down her slim, straight nose locking onto that mouth. Her lips are upturned with a dark pink color, a slight indent in the middle of the lower one. They look like cotton candy and wet dreams. I can already picture them wrapped around my cock, and it twitches hard with the mental image.

"Are you ok?"

Her rough little voice is puzzled as I shake myself and realize that I've not only been twirling her hair around my finger, but I've also been staring at her from a very short distance. I probably look like a complete lunatic.

"I'm fine, love. How are you? They didn't frighten you too much, did they?" I find that I don't like the idea of her being upset. At all.

She snorts, rather undaintily, and waves a slim hand. Her baggy black jumper slides around, and I see a tattoo of something on the inside of her wrist. "Nope. Guys like that are a dime a dozen back home. Just your normal dudebros. How did you know they were going to come over here?" Her glasses slide a bit down her nose, and she shoves them back up.

"I was sitting at the bar and overheard them. Do you often get mistaken for Melina?" I can't believe that this is the first time. Though we are seated, I can tell that my new friend isn't very tall compared to Melina's stature, but that face... The resemblance is unreal.

She shakes her head, and her glasses slide down again. I reach out and slide them up myself. Her breath catches, and she clears her throat. "I don't even know who that is, so no."

"She's a model—a rather famous one. We have mutual friends, so I can assure you that yes, you do look alike. I'm amazed that this is the first time someone has mistaken you."

Her mouth is slightly open, and her eyes widen. "A model? Me?" A giggle bursts from her lips, and I watch as twin deep dimples pop out of her cheeks. Sweet fuck. This woman is lethal. She needs to put those away before she hurts someone.

"I can barely walk across a room without tripping, let alone down a catwalk. Agh! I'm only five foot two. How can I be a model?" Her laughter is infectious, and I find myself chuckling along. "Well, you are outrageously beautiful. It's not that hard to imagine." I reach out and gently trace one of her dimples with my pinkie. Her smile widens, and her blush is delicious. "Bifid zygomaticus," she blurts out, and I blink. "What?"

"Um, bifid zygomaticus. Dimples. A non-dominant genetic trait." She points at her face; I laugh quietly. "I see. Well, I rather fancy your bifid...things. They only make you more gorgeous."

"I don't know about all of that, but thank you." Her head dips, and she fiddles with the frame of her glasses. Talking about her looks makes her nervous. Interesting. I find that once you start complimenting a woman, she either preens or pretends modesty while transparently seeking more praise. But this quirky little bundle of beauty is genuinely embarrassed. I lift her chin with two of my fingers and meet her gaze. I wish the lighting was better so that I tell the exact color of her eyes; I want to see if they change with desire and pleasure. And I want to be the one to cause it.

"You don't have to thank me for stating the obvious, love." Her lips part and I can feel the little puff of her breath against my mouth. My tongue makes a brief appearance in response, and her breathing quickens. I slide the hand that is propping up her chin down her silky throat and around to the back of her neck. Her thick hair curls around my fingers and I tilt her head intending to devour her.

That is until a rather irate throat-clearing interrupts us.

We jump apart guiltily, both realizing how entwined we had been, and rather publicly. Campus is not the type of place for this level of intimacy, and I'm shocked at my behavior. I just met this woman, and I'm already trying to caveman stomp my way into her knickers.

"Hullo?" The throat clearing belongs to the blonde in the red dress that I had marked for the evening. Up close, she is more on the hard-looking side, but she would have made a suitable throwaway. Her arms are crossed her thin chest, and she is glaring at the woman sitting next to me. Any minute now, she is going to say something that I absolutely do not want her to say, so I head her off.

"Leave your direction with the Steward, sweetheart." She perks up, the anger draining away immediately. I have no doubt she knows who I am, and all she wants is reassurance that she will get her turn. "Go on now."

She bobs in some odd semblance of a curtsy and clatters off to the Stewards station. I can see her gesturing excitedly, while his genetically placid expression never changes. I turn back to the beauty in my arms, who is frowning at me. Fuck.

"Did you need to leave with her? I hope I'm not causing any problems for you?" She begins to nervously pack her computer and that ratty notebook, her face splotchy with what I can only deem as embarrassed anger. Her movements are jerky, and I can see that she is about to bolt. There is no fucking way I am letting her go anywhere.

"I don't know her at all," I tell her calmly. "I didn't buy her a drink; I didn't pay for her meal—I know nothing about her. She mistakenly thought that I was going to approach her, so I did what I thought was necessary to make her leave without causing a scene. Now, are you ready to leave?" I gesture to the coat she now has draped over her arm, and an ancient leather bag slung over her back.

She stares at me, her eyes darting over my face searching for honesty. I never lie to women, ever. I prefer my dalliances brief, true, but I am always brutal with my upfrontness—I find that it lessens the sting when I move on to the next flower. Too, my mum always says that women can sniff out a lie faster than a bloodhound.

"You mean ready to leave with you?" She puts it right out there, so I see no reason to put up any pretense. "Yes."

She blinks at my response, and I can see the wheels turning. "I... don't ...why?" She can't be serious? I was about one minute away from stripping her down in front of everyone in this place.

"Why? Because we need privacy for what I want to do to you." More honesty.

Her pupils dilate, and she gulps. "We just met like fifteen minutes ago."

"True. But I knew in the first minute that I wanted you. And if we hadn't just been interrupted, I'm quite sure everyone in here would have known it as well."

I slide out of the booth and hold my hand out to her. "Come." She stares at my hand, teeth nibbling violently on her bottom lip. She moves to stand without taking my offer, and I move closer. I tug her lip out from her teeth and ghost a kiss over the tortured mound.

"Come, love. Let's go."

I brush another kiss over her cheekbone, eyelid, and forehead. Her breath catches while she nods once. Slipping the surprisingly heavy leather bag from her shoulder, I drape it over my own while lacing her fingers with mine. We pass the Steward, who discreetly avoids eye contact and slip through a small hallway to a private elevator. I use my left hand and press a keycard against the rosewood panel. The doors slide open, and I board while pulling her behind me. "You live here?"

"Sometimes." I touch the keycard to another console, and it lights up gently with the letter "P." I peek at her from the corner of my eye and see that she is staring at the floor- her bottom lip retaking punishment. I reach over with my free hand and slowly stroke the side of her face. Her head snaps up, and her light-colored eyes focus on mine. We stare at each other in silence, a tight rope of desire-and something else I can't name- tying us together. I barely hear the chime of the lift reaching our floor as the door opens to the spacious flat that I keep here. I flick a switch in the foyer, and the ample open space floods with light. Leading her like a small child, I drop her case onto the antique settee and turn toward her. She is standing still, arms still clutching her overcoat, body language screaming that she wants to run. Her precious face is turned away, eyes taking in the luxurious appointments before finally settling on me. Walking toward her slowly, I unbutton my jacket and reach up to remove her eyeglasses. I place them on the small table next to me and tug the coat off of her arm. Cupping her face in my hands, I tilt her head back and get a first look at her eyes. They are an unimaginable blue-green, the color morphing the longer I stare. She is truly a magnificent specimen, and the lust mixed with innocence shining from her warms me rapidly.

"I don't normally do this," she blurts out. "I mean I don't meet men, and then just leave with them. Like never." Her fresh breath dances across my lips, and I can't wait any longer. Pulling her toward me, I nip first her top, then bottom lip, before slipping my tongue in between. Her plump mouth molds under mine and I twist and plunder inside of it, my hands tightening on her cheeks and pushing into her thick black hair. We kiss for long minutes before I pull back and answer her.

"You didn't need to tell me that, love. I already knew." Despite her heartbreaking beauty, there was a sincere naivete about her-she seemed so oblivious to her appeal, yet strong enough not to care when confronted with it. So different than the viciously self-aware women I usually fuck. I dive back into her mouth, licking and salving as she responds sensuously, soft groans humming in her throat. I can't control my hands as they stroke her throat and slowly travel down her sides, sliding under the oversized black jumper and land on her satiny skin.

Her waist dips in deeply, and I tease the curve with light circles before moving up to the full flesh of her breasts. I rest my fingers just below her nipples and continue my assault on her mouth. Our tongues are twisting and dancing, with me biting on her lips before pulling away to nip at her throat. Her head drops back, pushing my hands a little further onto her breasts, and I can feel the hard nubs nudging my palms in need. I want to pull and suck on them, taste them, and roll them between my teeth, but I wait.

I stop my feast on her neck and swing down to swoop her into my arms. She buries her head in my throat, her warm breath sending chills down my body. I carry her to the bedroom, kicking the door open, and dropping her beside the large bed. She watches me—a heartbreaking combination of want with shyness. I step back and slowly unbutton my shirt, never taking my eyes from hers. It drops to the floor before I slid my belt out of my pant loops and undo them, letting them join my shirt on the floor. Her eyes widen and fasten onto my cock, which is straining hard toward her, its head already protruding from the waistband of my boxers.

"Come here, love." A brief hesitation, and then she takes two steps forward into my arms. I push her jumper up and off before she can protest and drink in her gleaming skin and the lushness of her breasts. They are decidedly more substantial than I expected, and I immediately cup them, running my thumbs hard over her nipples and pinching gently. Her bra is sheer and I quickly unclasp it before continuing my torture. Her body is trembling and her head is buried against my shoulder, her short breaths and whimpers driving me onward. I dip my head a capture a begging nipple between my teeth lashing it gently with my tongue.

My hands slip down the back of her pants and grab her ripe arse and squeeze. Christ, it's thick and firm, and I want nothing more than to sink my teeth into it. Releasing her nipple, I unzip her pants and slide them down, following them onto my knees. I lift one foot, and then the other removing them and tossing them behind me. Her legs are slim and healthy, and I run my hands up her calves and kiss her thighs before I settle on the deep shadow hidden by her modest underwear. I place a kiss on the top of her mound before I slip a finger into the side and stroke the back of it lightly across her clit. The warm wetness makes a growl jump out of my throat, met with an answering moan from her. I pull her knickers down, kissing my way across her stomach before standing and nudging her backward onto the bed. She's swaying slightly, and I ease her down, her hair spreading like a thick black cloud.

"You're so fucking beautiful." I stroke myself leisurely while cataloging her unreal perfection. Her body is a wonderland of curves and valleys with flawless skin, dusky brown nipples, and delicate lines. The dampness leaking from my cock smooths my way and I lean forward and slip two fingers into her mouth, letting her taste my desire. Her tongue swirls around them suggestively and I smile. "Later."

Impatiently shoving my boxers down, I kneel in front of her and push her legs up until her knees touch her chest. Without hesitation, I dive forward and fasten my lips to her clit, sucking hard. Her back bows, and a scream erupts from her mouth as I ruthlessly devour her, her legs shaking uncontrollably. Her head is thrashing on the pillow, and I can feel her body tightening. Her clit is throbbing in my mouth, and I lick all around it, her candied taste sliding down my throat. I pull off and hold her hips firmly. "Let go, baby." Sucking once again, she detonates, raspy moans meeting the pulses from her body. I lap up her wetness and alternate licks with deep kisses as she pants, muttering something under her breath. Before she can recover, I slide a finger into her wetness, the tight walls of her pussy grabbing me greedily. She cries out as I add another finger, pumping slowly while kissing her still sensitive clit. I blow on it gently, keeping up my motions, before twisting my fingers slightly, searching for that small patch that will push her once again over the edge. I find it and stroke it softly.

"Good God, what are you doing?" Her slim fingers tangle into my hair as I smile devilishly and keep up my attack. "I...oh...fuck!" Her body convulses again, and her whimpers turn into a small yell. She falls back, breathing hard, head lolling to the side. I slide my fingers out, sucking on them lavishly. Her legs give out, and she is sprawled out like a starfish. I climb over her and brace my arms on either side of her head. Her eyes are tightly closed; luscious lips parted slightly. One eye opens and peeks at me before shutting quickly. I chuckle and run one hand down her face.

"Are you ready for me?"

Both eyes pop open and she grimaces. "I think you broke me."

I laugh harder. "Well, let me put you back together." I reach over to the small side table and grab a condom. Sitting back on my heels, I slide it on, watching her face and licking my lips. "Hold on to the headboard." Her eyes widen, but she obeys. I grab the back of her left knee and drape her leg over my arm. I push forward until it's straight up and then catch my considerable length. I urge the head until its notched at her entrance, the slickness guiding my way. I lean forward and slide my tongue into her mouth as I slide my way inside of her. My cock pulses in need, my breath halting as I fight for control. I want to pound into her, but I know I won't last if I do. I rock back and forth until I'm entirely inside of her and slowly press hard against her clit.

"Fuck. You're huge." She's panting again, her arms straining upward. Her pupils are fully dilated and her whole body is painted with a rosy flush. Her nipples point straight up and I suck one into my mouth before letting it go with a pop.

"Yup. I am." She rolls her eyes before releasing a breathy chuckle. I pull out and then surge forward hard, repeating the motion over and over, forgetting my earlier quest for control. Her pussy is tight as a fist, clasping and unclasping me, wetness spilling out of her and coating her thighs. The sheets are damp with our shared sweat as I rut harder and harder her cries getting louder. "That's it, baby. Give me another." She begs me incoherently - to never stop, to go harder, to make her come. I rub my thumb rapidly over her clit and she goes off. A burning sizzle gathers at the base of my body and zig-zags up my spine— I grip her arse so hard I know I will leave marks. I come violently, I swear my heart stutters as I stroke into her until the hot spurts stop. I collapse on top of her, her arms wrapping around me limply, hearts beating on top of the other. We both try to get our lungs back, and she makes a funny choking noise, letting me know that I'm too heavy. I roll off and onto my back, staring at the dark ceiling. "I think you broke me this time."

She lets out a sugary giggle, and I smile back. I swing out of bed to dispose of the condom. Like the gentleman I am, I wet a washcloth with warm water, and head back to the bed. She has turned onto her stomach, a pillow on top of her head. "Can you breath under there?" She muffles something to me and shrugs. I nudge her open and wipe inside of her thighs. She squeaks a little and tries to close her legs. I smack her cheek and continue my cleaning. I reach under a bit and brush her abused nub, another squeak slash moan coming from under the pillow. I raise a brow that she can't see and repeat the motion. She moans again and I toss the washcloth and replace it with my fingers. "You can't possibly be ready to go already, are you love?'" I stroke her slowly and insistently, moving in and taking a hard bite of that arse. She yelps, but her hips move in time to my movements. "There she is. I love how soft you are. Your pussy is so wet and beautiful. Do you know how beautiful you are? Every bit of you," I purr to her until I feel the waves of an orgasm flow through her- this one soft and easy. "Good?" I know it was, of course.

Her slim arm shoots out from under the pillow and gives me a thumbs up. I laugh hard as a twinge of something crawls across my chest. I rub it absently and settle in the bed next to her. Drawing the thick blanket over her, I drape a leg over the back of her thighs and maneuver over. Her skin beckons me, and I stroke her back quietly. "Take a nap, love. I'll wake you when I'm ready for more." An indignant noise floats up, and I slap her arse cheek again. I smile in the dark and let sleep overtake me.

The persistent sound of the house phone pulls me out of my deep slumber. I woke her up twice last night, taking her ferociously both times. I think I set a record for giving a woman orgasms, and I want to beat my chest like a Neanderthal. The phone is still ringing, and I rub my face and head, muscles sore and tight. A little bit of sunlight breaks through the thick drapes, and I turn my head. The space next to me is empty, but I can see that the bathroom door is closed. I swing my legs over and walk to the sitting room. I notice that her eyeglasses are missing and don't think anything of it until I see that her handbag is also gone.

"Love? Are you alright?" I walk back into the bedroom and tap on the bathroom door.

"Love?" I twist the door handle, and it opens easily to a dark room. The light comes on as I enter and see the sterile space is undisturbed. I stand there confused and walk back into the bedroom, slipping my pants on. I look around the whole area and see that all traces of her are gone— I'm having a hard time computing what I am seeing. Because *I know* that what I am thinking is impossible, surely she didn't ...leave?

The phone rings again, and I snatch it up. "Yes?"

"My lord, you asked for an eight am wake-up. It's eight oh two." The polite and deferential voice grates on my growing nerves, but I contain it. "Thank you. Could you send up a pot of coffee and then someone from Security?" I will send out the entire army if that's what it takes.

"At once, my lord. Is something amiss?" The voice is now politely worried.

"You could say that." I hang up and prop my hands on my hips.

I can't believe she's gone.

And I can't fucking believe I didn't get her name.

His To Belong To: Book 1 of The Possession Series

SNEAK PEEK— IMPELLED, THE POWER SERIES

(This is Nick and Kenna's story, The OG couple.)

I was supposed to be spending the night here and wanted nothing more than to escape to my room, pull off this tramp towel I was wearing, and bury my head in a pillow. I could hear the last of the guests leaving and just wanted to go to bed. I nodded politely at a couple who'd I met a few times and made my way around. If I used the back stairs, maybe no one would see me, and I could avoid having to deal with you-know-who.

The cleaning crew was getting ready to start their late-night work, and I managed to make it to the narrow staircase that the servants used to get to the top levels. I took off my heels and put my foot on the first step.

"Where are you going?" I heard that deep, deep voice say behind me.

You have got to be fucking kidding me.

"Not that it's any of your damn business, but I am going to bed." I didn't even turn around. I took another step.

"Here? Don't you have your own place to sleep? Does my aunt

know that you are planning on staying here?" Suspicion tinted his words.

"Yes she knows, I have a room here. What's it to you?" I still didn't turn around. I took another two steps.

"What's it to me? It's my family, that's what it is. I don't know you or what your agenda is. Somehow, you have managed to convince my aunt and uncle that you belong here, belong with us. Maybe they are fooled by that innocent act that you put on, but I'm not," his voice hardened with every word.

Anger vibrated up my arms and made my shoulders shake. I turned my head just enough that I could see his silhouette but not his full face.

"You just managed to call your whole family gullible idiots and me some snake in the grass while painting yourself the savior of the fucking universe. Congratulations. You did that with what, twenty words? That's a talent for sure," I sneered.

He grabbed my arm and spun me around. I almost lost my footing and had to brace myself against him to stop from falling. I still had my shoes in one hand, so the other gripped his chest tightly for balance. We were face to face by only inches, and I could smell not only the liquor he'd drank but the muskier scent of his expensive cologne.

"What do you want from us? Money? Connections? A fucking husband?"

I push him and retreat up a few more steps. "What do I want? I want you to go back to that hole you slithered out of. I want to make the last four years disappear so that MY family didn't spend all that time hurt because of YOU. I want you to go straight to hell, where you belong."

I punctuated each word with a jab of my heels, and for a coup de grâce, I threw the first shoe and then the other shoe at him. I don't even wait to see if they hit home; I just run up the stairs straight to my room and slam the door.

Come tomorrow I'm going to have a stern talk with Felice about her cousin. There is no way I can be around him for any length of time without trying to recreate a Friday the 13th movie.

To start The Power Series and fall in love with #NickandKenna, click here.

ABOUT THE AUTHOR

JM Blake has a few thoughts about life:

-Wine and coffee are a must, daily
-I talk through every movie and TV show-
you have to get used to it if you want to be my friend
-Cats beat dogs, hands down
-Nerds run the world
-Nothing beats a good sex scene
-Chocolate is the food of the gods
-"The Talisman" is history's most perfect book

Chat me up:

Instagram: @authorjmblake
Twitter: @authorjmblake
BookBub: JM_Blake
Verve Romance: JM Blake
GoodReads: JM Blake
Website: www.authorjmblake.com
Facebook: @jmblakewriter
TikTok: http://bit.ly/3nKYNvh